COLD CO

Christopher watched as Juli̶e̶ ̶̶r̶e̶a̶c̶h̶e̶d̶ for the tea. The blanket escaped her grasp and slipped down, allowing him to see that her dress was soaking wet on the top as well as the bottom. It clung to her body, revealing her full breasts and a waist which was again the width of a handspan.

"You are shivering," Christopher said, his voice almost accusing. "If you continue to wear that dress you'll take cold. Come here, and I'll unbutton you."

Juliet's eyes widened enormously, and she did not move. Undressing before him was unthinkable, but as she shifted nervously, her wet dress pressed against her raising goose bumps, bringing on yet another uncontrollable shiver.

That brought Christopher to her side. "This is not, I think, the time for maidenly modesty," he observed as he undid the first button. . . .

Emma Lange is a graduate of the University of California at Berkeley, where she studied European history. She and her husband live in the Midwest and pursue, as they are able, interests in traveling and in sailing.

Emma Lange

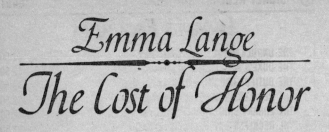

The Cost of Honor

A SIGNET BOOK

NEW AMERICAN LIBRARY

NAL BOOKS ARE AVAILABLE AT QUANTITY DISCOUNTS WHEN
USED TO PROMOTE PRODUCTS OR SERVICES. FOR INFORMATION
PLEASE WRITE TO PREMIUM MARKETING DIVISION. NEW
AMERICAN LIBRARY. 1633 BROADWAY. NEW YORK. NEW
YORK 10019.

SIGNET TRADEMARK REG. U.S. PAT. OFF. AND FOREIGN COUNTRIES
REGISTERED TRADEMARK—MARCA REGISTRADA
HECHO EN CHICAGO. U.S.A.

SIGNET, SIGNET CLASSIC, MENTOR, ONYX, PLUME, MERIDIAN
and NAL BOOKS are published by NAL PENGUIN INC.,
1633 Broadway, New York, New York 10019

First Printing, February 1988

1 2 3 4 5 6 7 8 9

PRINTED IN THE UNITED STATES OF AMERICA

1

"**L**ud, but I never should have let you drag me to the wilds, Jack! We're like to be trapped here all our lives." The speaker, immediately recognizable as a young dandy from London, scowled as he slammed down a glass which was empty for the time being of the Cock and Bull's surprisingly palatable claret.

"I dish not drag you anywhere, Alfred Morely," protested his companion, his slightly slurred words revealing that he had spent some time matching his friend drink for drink. "It was your eagerness to escape your creditors which made you tag along with me."

With a sheepish grin Alfred lifted his glass in salute and admitted the truth of Jack's analysis. "You saved me with this timely visit home. I'm so deep in dun territory my father's threatening to withhold my allowance. He's been damned nasty about the whole thing. Doesn't understand how a fellow can't seem pinched, if he's to cut any dash at all. And no matter what my mother says, I'm not getting myself leg-shackled to some pasty-faced heiress."

"Leg-shackled!" Jack exclaimed with horror. "But you are only three-and-twenty!"

Alfred nodded morosely as he filled his glass and added a touch to Jack's.

"Not that I wouldn't like a different sort of wench right now," Jack grumbled half to himself. "There's not even a serving girl here to give us some sport."

Alfred smiled slyly. "I may have remedied that, old

boy. I told Crawford to find me someone young and comely, if he had to drug her to get her to my bed."

"Good Lord, Alfie!" Jack sloshed some of the contents of his wineglass onto the floor. "Surely you never said such a thing to that man!"

"Did!" laughed Alfred. "Should've seen his face. Only nodded. Gad, I think he might do it."

"He'll do anything for you. Never seen such an eager-to-please fellow. Only hope he knows you were joshing him."

"Scarcely was," Alfred muttered as he helped himself to more wine. "I've not seen a young, desirable-looking wench since I've been down here."

The actual amount of time Jack and Alfred had been at the Cock and Bull was only three days, but to young men accustomed to the distractions of London it seemed a very long time indeed. A recent spate of exceedingly heavy rains had made the roads impassable, forcing them to take shelter at this small rustic inn near the village of St. Mary-on-Medway, a full day's drive from Jack's home. The only bright spot in the situation other than the fine claret they had been drinking in quantity was that, having been among the first to be marooned, they had been able to secure for themselves separate rooms as well as the inn's only private sitting room.

As the two young men were opening yet another bottle of the sustaining claret, a knock sounded at the door, followed closely by the innkeeper, who bowed in a tall, broad-shouldered figure. Jack, aware he'd paid handsomely for the private room, opened his mouth to protest the intrusion, when his bleary eyes registered the quality of the stranger's greatcoat and rain-spattered boots. From what were undeniably a pair of Hoby's finest, Jack's eyes, widening in sudden recognition, traveled to the stranger's face. The golden-haired, coolly assured stranger, with features so perfectly cut he had been likened to Apollo, was none other than Christopher St. Charles, Earl of Hartford. Kit to his friends, he was Lord Hartford to Jack and

Alfred, who had prior to this only glimpsed him from across the room at White's.

"I say, my lord, we are honored," gushed Jack. He rose unsteadily to his feet, and emboldened by the wine he'd drunk, stretched the truth a little. "I dare-say you don't recall it, b-b-but we were presented to you at White's. I'm Jack Whitcomb and this is my friend Morely."

Alfred looked a little dazed at being suddenly confronted by such a nonpareil but managed a creditable bow.

"Gentlemen." Hartford nodded briefly. "I'm afraid you may regret my arrival, for our host here"—he indicated the innkeeper, a small, nervous man who was smiling obsequiously at all the grand gentlemen gathered in his modest inn—"has informed me there are no rooms available for the night. I am hoping to prevail upon one of you to allow me to share yours."

As the earl's light blue eyes studied them both, Jack could think of nothing but how a waggish friend had told him once that Hartford's eyes were so piercing it was likely they could cut stone.

It was Alfred who had the presence of mind to realize he'd not be able to sleep a wink with a man like the earl lying next to him. "Nonsense!" he cried a little too loudly. "You shall take my room. Jack and I shall be the ones to share."

The earl bowed slightly. "My thanks, gentlemen," he drawled.

Then, both to repay the young pups for their kindness and, it must be admitted, to drink off his irritation at being held up by the weather, Hartford ordered the innkeeper to bring several more bottles of the claret.

That irritation was considerable, as he had been lured down to Kent in the first place under false pretenses. An old friend, Ned Boscum, had written to say he had a hunter he thought might interest the earl. The hunter was a beauty, strong, alert, and possessed of a smooth canter, but it had taken Christopher less than an hour to realize the real object Ned had invited him to look over was his daughter, not his horse.

The earl smiled grimly to himself. Most likely he'd insulted Ned by leaving so hastily. He'd endured one night, out of consideration for his own horse, and then had braved the muddy roads to escape.

"Did you really land a blow to Gentleman Jim's jaw, sir?" Jack, far gone enough to reveal the un-*ton*-ish admiration he and most of his fellows had for Hartford, recalled Christopher from his musings.

The earl eyed the younger man's slightly unfocused but nonetheless enthusiastic expression coolly. He had been subjected to too much toadying in his life not to have developed an unfortunately cynical view of his fellowman. However, perhaps because he decided Jack's admiration would demand little from him, or perhaps because he recalled that he owed the two boys something, Christopher admitted he had landed the blow. And then with an engaging grin which made both Jack and Alfred smile back, though they were not aware they did so, Christopher added lightly that it was only fair to tell them that before the match ended Jim had returned the favor.

The wine was of good enough quality that the earl did not begrudge answering when the boys questioned him about another legendary feat, this one with a chaise-and-four on the Bath road. After accepting their toast to his remarkable time, he even listened to their tale of woe about being stranded in St. Mary-on-Medway with good grace. All in all, Hartford's forbearance made it several bottles of claret later before he decided he had indulged his benefactors—and himself—sufficiently and bid them adieu.

Once in his room, he undressed quickly, thinking as he did so that it was a piece of luck he had left his valet, Harkins, in London. The fastidious man's reaction to his boots would have been no less than apoplexy, and Christopher was most certainly not in a frame of mind to listen to Harkins' irritable grumblings.

Crossing to his bed, he twisted his mouth in an ironic smile. It was not such a piece of luck that he had left Leslie behind. The voluptuous widow would have served excellently as a way to pass the time until the weather changed. But he had dexterously avoided her half-serious suggestion that he bring her. Had he not, he'd have been announcing Leslie's promotion from his mistress to his countess, and that he was not prepared to do. Neither Leslie nor any women he had met had given him sufficient reason to overcome his determination never to marry.

As he bent to blow out the candle beside his bed, Christopher's eyes narrowed suddenly. There was someone in his bed—a feminine someone, if the light-colored wavy hair streaming across the pillow and the curve of her hip under the sheet were any guide.

That she was a doxy of Morely's whom the young fool had been too foxed to remember, the earl assumed at once. Certain he and Morely would not share the same tastes in women, Christopher reached for her, impatient to have her out of his bed.

At that moment the girl turned over, half-opening her eyes.

Though young, just the age he had imagined a boy like Morely would prefer, Christopher saw she was not unattractive. To be fair, she had a surprisingly sweet, delicate beauty. It was seldom one saw a serving girl with a heart-shaped face, sculptured, well-defined cheekbones, and such a soft mouth. Christopher's eyebrow lifted slightly as his gaze settled at last on her unblinking eyes. They were very large, and though it was difficult to see in the dim light, he thought they looked a smoky gray color. The long, feathery lashes surrounding them, he had no trouble seeing. As his gaze roamed to that part of her anatomy revealed by the loose sheet, Christopher conceded that young Alfred was not nearly so lacking in taste as he had thought.

His regard returned to her face, and just as he thought that no matter how fetching she was, she was still too young and inexperienced for his tastes, a slow, sleepy, decidedly pleased smile spread across her features. Though it was not nearly so knowing as most of the come-hither smiles he was accustomed to receiving, the young doxy's smile was related to them, and, as had been the case with a good many of the other smiles, Christopher St. Charles found he had no interest in resisting it.

"Sweeting, you are a surprise." He grinned down at her.

The young woman watched captivated as the golden-haired man's face was lit with a boyish warmth. At the flash of white teeth in his sun-darkened face and the irresistible sparkle in his crystal blue eyes, her smile widened.

"I see you don't care that I'm not Morely," Christopher said, slipping into the bed.

A slight frown gathered on the young woman's brow, dimming her smile, but the earl with practiced ease smoothed her wrinkles away with a long, heady kiss. "You may be younger than I'm accustomed to, but I think we'll contrive," he whispered softly into her ear.

Hartford's experienced hands caressed the young woman's surprisingly soft and supple body, eliciting a long, languorous sigh. When she shuddered and pressed against him, her young body yielding its sweetness up to him, Christopher felt an unexpected response. True, she was not very experienced, but her ardor made up for it. Unexpectedly he found he enjoyed the game of teaching her what he desired.

It was only when he moved to consummate their union that Christopher realized the extent of the girl's inexperience. To his surprise, he found she was still a virgin.

"Do you mean to sell this?" he asked her huskily, unable to refrain from nuzzling her ear.

The girl said nothing, but her body arched against his, speaking a language as old as mankind. It was the only answer Christopher needed. With consummate skill he accepted the unspoken invitation and made her a woman.

2

"**O**h!"

The Earl of Hartford's eyes snapped open at the sound of a strange voice.

A pair of enormous charcoal-gray eyes were staring wide-eyed at him from the opposite side of the bed. Groggily his mind struggled to place them, and then, just as he recalled the young girl he had pleasured himself with, she startled him by bolting from the bed, taking the quilt to wrap around her.

Slow to throw off the effects of the substantial quantity of claret he had consumed the night before, Christopher's mind could only consider one surprise at a time. The first to be digested, as he watched her retreat, was her hair. Like his, it was blond, but of such a different hue it was almost another color. Strikingly long, it flowed over her breasts to her waist, gleaming like silver in the sunlight.

Her hair, however, did not hold his attention for long. As they had the night before, it was her eyes which drew him. They were, he saw, focused now with undisguised horror upon the dull red stain exposed by the disarranged bedclothes.

"Who are you?" she whispered, her great eyes flying up to meet his.

Absorbed with the strangeness of her behavior, it took Christopher several moments to realize that the girl's speech was as proper as his own. He sat up, the better to look at her with suddenly narrowed eyes, and his reply when it came was cool.

"It's a little late for that look, don't you think? You had the opportunity last night to change your mind." He was about to tell her to take the ample change to be found on the table beside his breeches and go, when the sound of raised voices in the courtyard distracted him.

"You must have seen something, man! She brought your wife our cook's tisane, and no one has seen her since. She can't have vanished into thin air."

At the sound of the voice the girl let out a strangled cry. "Father!" she gasped, running to the window, the long quilt trailing behind her. Whatever she saw in the courtyard sent her leaping backward away from the glass as if it might burn her.

Grimly aware he was not likely to get any more sleep this morning, Christopher rose to retrieve his breeches from the chair where he had laid them. There was a shuttered expression on his face as he digested the fact that the speech of the man the girl had called father was that of a gentleman. The girl, it seemed, was no actress.

"That is your father?" he asked in clipped tones as he walked up behind her.

To his annoyance, the girl jumped.

"Who are you?" he demanded sharply—too sharply, it seemed, for the gray eyes, fastened on him now, widened with alarm.

"She had tea with Cook . . ." The innkeeper's placating tones drifted through the window before Christopher could force a reply.

"I . . . I must go," the girl cried frantically.

"No doubt you'll need your clothes," was the earl's sardonic reply, and he gestured to a little pile of clothes on the couch.

Immediately the girl rushed to retrieve them, then fled to the screen which stood at the opposite end of the room. When she had disappeared from sight, Kit, too, attended to the task of completing his toilette.

When he had put on his shirt and boots and liberally doused his face with cold water, he turned back to find the girl peering out the window again, one hand be-

8

hind her, holding her unbuttoned blouse together. Her clothes, he noted, were plain, patched, and muddied.

"May I help?"

The girl jerked around, irritating him again. Nor did she do him the courtesy of replying. Instead, she leaned back, for he was much taller than she, and her eyes traveled slowly down his dressed form, taking in his fine lawn shirt, the exquisite fit of his buckskin riding breeches, and, finally, the perfection of his boots, however mud-stained, with a look which could only be described as dumbfounded. Whether it was more unsettling to be regarded so closely, or to have the resulting reaction be so far from flattering, Hartford was not certain, but he was certain he was growing extremely impatient with this puzzling slip of a girl.

"I take it, then, you wish to parade around half-clothed?"

His caustic words brought a deep flush to her pale cheeks, but slowly, as if she were loath to do it, she turned her back to him.

"This is in my way," he fairly snapped, throwing a portion of the long, heavy curtain of her hair over her shoulder.

He saw a quick blush stain her cheek, but the girl lifted the rest of her hair out of his way, holding it while he expertly fastened each of the small buttons of her blouse.

When he had finished, Christopher did not release her. Quite the opposite, he took her by the shoulders and turned her around to face him, his blue eyes narrowed upon her. "I want your name, girl." His tone was quiet, even soft, but there was no mistaking the steel in it.

The girl blinked lashes which he noted absently were indeed as thick and silky as they had appeared to be the night before. Her delicate face lifted to his, and he saw her unwavering eyes were dark with distress. When she did not answer, his hold tightened and he shook her.

"Now," Christopher growled.

There was no denying the intensity of his demand.

9

The girl's lashes veiling her eyes, she whispered. "I am Juliet Barre."

"And why is your father in the courtyard of this inn inquiring in what can only be termed a desperate voice as to your whereabouts? Had he no idea of your assignation with Morely?"

"I had no assignation with anyone!" was Juliet Barre's anguished response.

"Then why the devil were you in Morely's bed?" Christopher exploded, feeling as if he had walked into a madhouse.

Juliet's answer did nothing to improve matters, for she only answered faintly, "I don't know."

"And I suppose you don't know why you stayed there when I got in?" Christopher retorted angrily.

Juliet's vivid features turned an ashen hue. "I . . . I don't remember," she said, but her eyes fell from his and two spots of color appeared on her high, rounded cheeks.

Christopher stood regarding the girl, aware that she did in fact remember something, and aware, if the tight clenching of her hands were any indication, that something distressed her greatly.

Grasping her slender hands in his own much larger ones had the effect of bringing her regard flying back to his. "I am not overfond of mysteries," he began crisply, "and I should very much like to get to the bottom of this one. Now, you say you don't know why you were in this bed, nor do you remember much of what occurred after I got into it. I can assure you, however, you were there and that you were a willing partner after I joined you. I am not in the habit of forcing virgins."

Juliet blushed fiercely, but Christopher continued remorselessly. "There is no point in looking away, we have gone quite beyond that, my dear. When I let go your hands, you are going to sit on that couch there and explain why you came to the Cock and Bull and then never left."

Once again the Earl of Hartford's voice held the steely note of command which had wrung compliance from people with a great deal more polish than young Juliet Barre. Still, Juliet did hesitate a moment, her large eyes flicking toward the door. But when the earl took her arm in a firm grip, she was obliged to recognize the extent of his determination. She did not try to pull away as he led her to the room's only chair, and waited while he seated himself only a few feet from her upon the bed.

Christopher cocked his head at the silent girl, his eyebrow lifting. "Well?" he demanded impatiently.

Juliet glanced at him briefly. Then, lacing her slender fingers tightly together, she began a faltering explanation in her quiet, educated voice. "The innkeeper's wife, Mrs. Smithby, has the grippe, and our cook has a special tea which can relieve it. Yesterday, just before dinner, I brought Mrs. Smithby the herbs for the tea."

St. Charles examined the girl as he listened, his mouth tightening at what he saw. Though her skin was more golden than was fashionable, it was exceptionally fine-grained. No servant he knew of would have skin so soft and clear.

"A man, a servant, I think," Juliet Barre continued, frowning slightly, "accosted me in the hallway. He asked if I should care to earn something for . . . for going to his master."

She dropped her head slightly, letting her silvery hair slide forward to act as a curtain, and though he could not see her expression, Christopher did see her shoulders lift as if she had had to take a deep breath. He resisted a fleeting impulse to reach out to her. It was imperative he understand what had happened, and he thought it likely that if he touched her, she would cry.

Her resources gathered after her pause, she continued in a relatively level voice, "I ignored him and went on to the kitchen, where I brewed the tea for Mrs. Smithby. I have come on the same errand before, and Appleby, the cook, always has tea and a treat for me. When I sent Mrs. Smithby's tea up to her by a maid, I sat down to drink mine, but the man who had accosted me came in. He told us there was a fracas going on in the courtyard, and said we'd better come to help him, as he could not find Mr. Smithby. I went along with Appleby to see what I could do, but by the time we arrived, there was no one in the courtyard. I returned to the kitchen, finished my tea and cakes, and left. I remember getting as far as the pond on the path behind the stables, and then . . . I'm not certain what happened. I got very sleepy, and I think I sat down to rest, but in truth I don't quite remember."

"Damn!" It was softly spoken, but the Earl of Hartford put a wealth of feeling into the word. He was remembering young Morely's speaking of his valet last night. An eager-to-please, bang-up fellow, he'd called him. There had even been some drunken boasting about having him fetch a girl whether she was willing or not. It had been late in the evening, and Christopher had not been paying much attention, though he was thinking now that he should have.

"Miss Barre," he began slowly, and Juliet looked at him with eyes whose slate color reflected both fear and confusion, "I cannot say for certain what occurred here, but I begin to fear we are both the victims of a bizarre set of coincidences. I'll discover the truth of exactly what happened later. It's unlikely the supporting cast in our little drama will be leaving today. The rains seems to have stopped, but the roads will take some time longer to dry. The particulars can wait until I have returned you to your family."

The earl's perfectly reasonable scheme elicited a surprising response, for Juliet sprang from the couch at once, shaking her head so violently her long hair twisted around her shoulders. "Oh, no, sir. There's no need for that. I don't want you to take me. I can find my own way home. I only want to leave as soon as possible."

"Don't be a fool." Hartford dismissed her protests with an exasperated wave of his hand. "What will you say to your family? That you fell asleep beside a pond in the pouring rain and did not awaken until this morning? It might serve if they believed in pixies, but I doubt we could be so fortunate. No, my girl, I am afraid you and I will be doing a good deal more than going home together."

"What . . . what do you mean?" Juliet spoke to the earl's back, for he had risen from the couch and was crossing the room to his coat with long determined strides.

"What do I mean?" he replied, his voice as mocking as hers had been anxious. "What I mean, Miss Barre, is that unless I very much miss my guess, I am honor-bound to marry you."

As a proposal of marriage, the earl's left a great deal to be desired, and Juliet might well have been forgiven her reaction to it. Her hand flew to her gaping mouth as her eyes widened with shock. "No!" she gasped with as much denial as if he had suggested she must go to live with the aborigines in the Americas.

Something flickered briefly in his eyes, then was gone, leaving them quite cold. "Yes," he replied inflexibly, the steel having returned once more to his voice. "But I forgot you do not even know who your future husband is. Forgive me, my dear, I am not usually so remiss. We seem to have gone about the business of courtship in the most unconventional way. I am Christopher St. Charles, Earl of Hartford, at your service, ma'am."

If the earl had thought to impress Juliet Barre with mention of his title, he succeeded, though not perhaps to the end he had expected. As he announced his full name, Juliet's face drained of all color, so alarming him that he stepped forward to catch her lest she faint. She did not, though she did remain staring at him with such dismay that Hartford was moved to say, "You needn't look so pulled at the prospect of being my countess, Miss Barre. I assure you it will be a marriage in name only. I shall go my way, and God knows you may go yours."

3

They got home somehow—Juliet never afterward recalled exactly how—and when the door of the vicarage opened, her mother, father, and the five of her brothers and sisters still at home tumbled out all at once to fall upon her. Juliet returned their embraces, but she did not feel the same doing it as she normally would have done. In the past, though she had more taken it for granted than actually realized it, her family's warm welcome would have made her feel safe and secure. Today it did not, and the contrast was so striking that she felt almost a stranger among them.

After assuring themselves that she was indeed alive, her mother and father turned anxious eyes to the tall, elegantly turned-out man who had escorted her into the vicarage. When the earl identified himself, even Mr. Barre, who truly believed that all God's creatures were created equal in God's eyes, was overcome.

It was left to the earl to take charge of the chaotic scene. In his cool voice he inquired if the vicar had a room where they could be private. There, in the same tone, he concisely explained Juliet's disappearance to her astounded parents.

As Juliet listened for a second time to a proposal of marriage from the earl, she did not find that repeating his effort in any way improved his performance.

"Dressed as poorly as your daughter was, the valet not unnaturally took her for a serving girl. Unfortunately, because I did not hear her speak, but only . . . ah, saw her, I assumed the same. Though I cannot accept fault for the situation, I realize that having been the instrument of your daughter's ruin, I must, in honor, offer for her."

To Juliet's utter dismay, her parents did not even look to her to ask what she wished to do, but instead turned to discuss their decision between themselves. The idea of marrying the cool, arrogant stranger who eyed her parents with such a knowing gleam in his eye prompted Juliet to try to take matters into her own hands. "Please, Mama, Papa! The earl has done me a great honor, but I beg you do not accept his . . . offer. There is no need. It was all a mistake!"

"My dear"—her father shook his gray head—"there is no other way." And then, without more ado he told the earl how grateful he and Mrs. Barre were that he was a man of such honor.

Her fists clenched tightly, Juliet listened as Lord Hartford informed her parents that he would return in a week's time with a special license. To Juliet he only said, "Until then, Miss Barre," before he was gone.

Throughout that week, Juliet alternately protested, pleaded, and argued. "He is a stranger, Mama," she cried, her gray eyes dark. "Please! He is an earl. I know nothing of the nobility. I won't know how to go on at all!" And:

"Oh, please, Papa, do not force me to wed him. He does not care for me!"

It was all to no avail, as she had feared it would be. From the moment he had told her his name, one so lofty that even she had heard of it, Juliet realized his wishes, whatever they were, would prevail over hers.

Certainly Mrs. Barre, a dreamy romantic who had never lost her girlish conviction that everything would always turn out for the best, did not protest greatly against the strange twist of fate which would ally her daughter with a wealthy member of the highest nobility.

"My dear," she sighed. "There is no question of crying off. And what does the earl's being a stranger have to say to anything? He is such a man! Quite the most breathtaking one I have ever seen!"

"Mama!" Juliet cried, scandalized by such a shallow argument.

"Looks are no hindrance," Mrs. Barre responded blandly. "After all, you shall be married for quite some time, God willing.

"And, Juliet, if only you will think what you are about, your manners are pretty enough for anyone. It is only that sometimes you give no thought to your appearance, and you must, you know, for one's appearance is considered extremely important in society.

"At least there is no need for you to worry about keeping a household. You are the one who does our accounts as it is, and I have taught you to handle servants. The earl's household will be a great deal larger, of course, but the same principles will apply.

"Oh, my dear, it is fortunate that you are the most beautiful of our daughters!"

Juliet blinked at the non sequitur, for she had always considered her older sister Rosalind with her brown hair and dark brown eyes as the family beauty.

"You will a diamond of the first water when you are dressed in the right fashions!"

Juliet sighed then, realizing her mother had, as was her inclination, confused reality with her dreams. Juliet knew that no matter what she wore, she would never be a diamond.

It was left to her sympathetic but more astute father to point out the most compelling reason for the imminent union. Sitting down beside her, he had brought her head down to his shoulder and smoothed her unruly hair back from her face as he had used to do when she was upset as a child.

"Jule, my love, I'd give you anything to have kept this thing from happening to you," he told her quietly. "But now that it has, it's best to put our regrets behind us. There is the possibility of a child to be considered. I am certain you would not want your child, through no fault of its own, to be an outcast.

"I am not pretending the earl won't be difficult. He is higher in the instep than anyone you've ever known, but I don't believe he will be as impossible as you do.

16

He's behaved most honorably in this matter, after all. I think you've only to appeal to his better nature, my dear."

At that Juliet raised her gray eyes from their deep study of the pattern of the tattered rug on the floor, and Mr. Barre, misinterpreting that look, smiled. "The earl is immensely wealthy, you know. No, don't stir, as if wealth were an unimportant consideration. Think, my dear, what you can do with it. Ros was right when she said you needed a chaperone, not because you might misbehave, but because you were likely to give away your pelisse if you thought someone else had a greater need of it. With Hartford's riches you'll be able to do a great deal for those in need."

Of them all, the only argument which succeeded with Juliet was the reminder that she might be with child. There was a boy in the village who was scorned by adults and children alike because he had no father, and his plight had often roused her sympathies.

The other arguments and assurances Juliet dismissed. Her mother had ever been fanciful, seeing everything just as she wanted it to be, while her father, though more pragmatic, was excessively charitable about people, invariably believing them capable of more than they themselves knew. Never mind that he was often right, Juliet thought that in this particular case his assessment of the earl's character was absurdly optimistic.

When it came time for her to walk down the aisle, at the end of that week, Juliet had to hold tightly to her brother Robbie's arm. If she were to loosen her grip, she knew her trembling legs would not support her.

Far ahead, waiting before her father, was the earl. Though Juliet had tried her best to keep this moment from happening, now that it was here she could not seem to tear her eyes away from him. A single shaft of light from one of the little Norman church's windows glanced off his golden head, making its color more brilliant than ever. His dark coat and pants only amplified the effect, and Juliet was forcibly reminded how she had, that fateful night, thought him a god.

Beside him was his best man, introduced later as Lord Tony Halsey. There was no one else present on the earl's side of the church, Juliet knew without looking. The earl had sent word the night before through his valet that his mother would not be present. She had a twisted ankle. A likely excuse, Juliet had remarked, though her mother had scolded her.

The earl did not smile when she reached him. Aware of that fact and of the indissoluble nature of the ceremony, Juliet scarcely heard her father's voice or even her own as she faintly spoke her vows. It was only Hartford's firm voice she heard clearly.

A wedding feast followed the ceremony, but Juliet retained little impression of it beyond mounds of food she could not eat, and wine that made her dizzy. All too soon, she was in the earl's carriage, regretting the absence of Lord Halsey. Though she had paid him only scant attention, she had remarked that her husband's friend had sympathetic eyes. Her husband's crystalline gaze, in contrast, was so shuttered that Juliet found it impossible to think of anything to say to him.

At last she could bear the taut silence stretching between them no longer. Understandably curious about his family, she cleared her throat and asked whom she could expect to meet at his mother's home.

He turned slowly to her, his look heavy-lidded and inscrutable. "Only Mother. My sister, Serena, is with her husband in Vienna."

Juliet stared. It seemed that was all he was going to say to her. Though she did not know it, her eyes were very wide, clearly revealing her sentiments about his terse reply.

After eyeing her steadily a moment, Christopher evidently judged her outrage justifiable, for he turned to face her more directly and added, "My father died some years ago. There is an uncle in Leicester, but he and Mother have never maintained close relations."

When he did not look away, Juliet asked about the place where his mother lived, and was rewarded with

18

the information that the estate was named Longacres, was in Surrey, and was not the family's principal seat. Longacres had been purchased for Lady Eunice by the earl's father when she had complained that Hartford Hall in Lincolnshire was too rustic and too far away from London for her tastes.

There was a distinctly mocking note in her husband's tone as he told her this, which Juliet noted and put aside to be thought about at a later time. For now she was too relieved that he had answered her at such length to think of much else.

Her expressive eyes, when she turned again to look out her window, were as light as her spirits. That is to say they were not as light as they might have been, but were considerably lighter than when she had first entered the carriage.

Her husband, noting the change, was not displeased. It had been mean-spirited to take his frustrations out on her, he knew. It was not her fault that he who had sworn to avoid the trap of marriage, because he well knew how unpleasant a wife could be— the dowager countess had taught him that, if nothing else—should have had to offer for her, a chit who had nothing to recommend her but her rather too innocent beauty.

His feelings were beside the point. He could not simply have left her to bear the burden of his carelessness—and it *was* that, for he had known she was a virgin—alone. He was not such a cad.

Looking at his new wife, it occurred to Christopher to wonder what she expected of their marriage. She seemed so young she'd likely never thought of marriage, or if she had, it was of some Prince Charming who would come to cater to her every whim.

Christopher smiled grimly to himself. If that were her expectation, she was in for a surprise. He might have been fool enough to marry her for the sake of his honor, but he was not fool enough to pay with the rest of his life for that honor. It was he, not she, who would hold the upper hand in their marriage.

He looked at her again, observing the softness of her skin, the delicacy of her profile, and the unusual color of her hair. With a little polish, something to wear other than that gray bombazine dress, and her hair trimmed, she might do nicely enough in the end.

But she would have to mature. She would need time to learn her role as his countess and how to go on in his circles. When she had done that, he would see how he found her.

Not that he would ever let her get too great a hold on him. His mouth twisting in a bitter grimace, he recalled when he had first realized his father's red-rimmed eyes and shaking hands were caused by continual drinking. He'd been young, seven or eight perhaps, when he'd heard two maids discussing it. Almost before they'd said it, he'd known that drinking was his father's way of escaping his mother. The sixth earl had not been able to stand up to his countess's constant shrilled demands and so had retreated behind a bottle.

Being a child, Christopher had blamed love for his father's weakness. Why else had he not risked Lady Eunice's ire, and done as he pleased, at least once? As an adult Christopher knew the answer was not so simple, but he remained wary of that emotion nonetheless. Whatever the truth of his parents' relations, love seemed a threat to his highly valued independence.

Therefore, he would treat his wife nicely enough as long as she did not try his patience, but he would always keep someone like Leslie around. A mistress would serve to remind him how many possibilities there were in life, he told himself, his mouth curving in a decided smile.

Juliet's own thoughts were not nearly so assured as the earl's, and they reached a point near panic while she waited with him for their supper in the inn where they had stopped for the night. Warming her hands at the fire, her back to Christopher, Juliet could not seem to slow the beating of her heart.

It was her wedding night, but her marriage was so outside the usual, she had no certain understanding of what her husband intended, nor, and this was perhaps even more upsetting, did she feel any certainty about what she wanted to occur.

Though her memories were more like dreams than distinct recollections, she did retain a vivid memory of how he had smiled at her that night. Even the recollection could make her pulses leap.

Surreptitiously Juliet touched her hand to her lips. More hazily, but powerfully nonetheless, Juliet's memories included an impression of what had occurred after the candle had been blown out. Her lips had felt on fire. . . .

Juliet shivered. The elegant flesh-and-blood nobleman behind her seemed an entirely different man from the one in her dreams. As handsome, perhaps, but whereas the other man had entranced her, this man alternately unnerved and infuriated her.

Their supper was brought then, mercifully interrupting Juliet's agonizing, but she found she had little appetite and only picked at her plate. Keeping her eyes downcast, she avoided her husband's gaze, until, peeking through her lashes, she realized his fork was still. Without thought, she lifted her large eyes anxiously to his. He was regarding her with a faint, cool smile.

"You needn't look so alarmed, my dear. You are quite safe from me, you know. I have little interest in bedding an unwilling innocent."

Juliet's cheeks flamed. However had he known that she little wanted the intimacies of marriage! At least for now, she could not help but add, her eyes flicking to his firm, well-molded mouth.

The charged silence between them lasted only seconds. Luckily for Juliet's composure it was shattered by the innkeeper entering with the earl's brandy.

"You may show my wife to her room," Christopher directed him at once. "Please see that she is awakened at nine o'clock."

"Yes, my lord." The man bowed. If he thought it odd that the earl should be married to so young a lass dressed in clothes no better than those own daughter might wear, he said nothing. Nor did he lift a brow over the tension any fool could have sensed crackling between his lordship and the sweet-looking girl. They were Quality and everyone knew Quality acted differently.

Juliet rose gracefully from her seat and followed the innkeeper's broad back. Never again looking at Christopher, she was nonetheless utterly and completely aware of his gaze as it followed her from the room.

4

"We are almost there. If you look through the trees, you'll see the house." The sound of Christopher's voice awakened Juliet from a half-sleep she had, lulled by the rhythm of the excellently sprung carriage, fallen into. As soon as she caught sight of the palatial house in which her husband's mother, Lady Eunice, lived, however, all lingering wisps of dullness lifted.

Even from a distance, it looked enormous, but when after several moments the carriage swept free of the trees and drew up before the imposing Palladian building, Juliet had to consciously keep herself from gasping. Its polished stone gleaming in the sunlight, it looked a palace for a king.

Horseshoe-shaped steps led to a massive door which opened as Christopher took her arm. A man with drooping eyes and a drooping mouth bowed gravely to the earl, and after Christopher presented him as Quinton to her, he favored Juliet with a lugubrious welcome.

Ponderously Quinton led them up a sweeping staircase, down one hall, then down another and then another. Juliet tried to concentrate on the echo her footsteps made on the marble floors. Anything to distract herself from the incredible luxury displayed on all sides. Alabaster columns supported ceilings decorated with sumptuous murals, while the walls were hung with Gobelins tapestries and enormous, impressive paintings. Her father had said the earl was wealthy, but this house attested to wealth greater than Juliet had ever imagined. Absurdly her mother's reassurance that the St. Charles household would be essentially the same as the vicarage at St. Mary-on-Medway, only larger, popped into Juliet's mind. She struggled to restrain a nervous giggle just as Quinton came to a halt at last.

Opening the doors before him, he announced in a ringing voice, "The Earl and Countess of Hartford."

Christopher's grip lifted Juliet forward, reminding her that it was her name that had just been called.

"Mother, may I present my wife, Juliet?" she heard Christopher say as she made her curtsy to the stiff figure toward whom they had marched.

"Pray be seated," said an icy voice. Rising, Juliet was about to give her thanks when she had, at last, the opportunity to look at the earl's mother closely.

What Juliet saw froze her smile. The small eyes of pale blue which were assessing her were the coldest eyes she had ever thought to see. There could no longer be any doubt what this member of the earl's family thought of his marrying the daughter of St. Mary-on-Medway's not-very-prosperous vicar.

"You look well, Mother. Your ankle must be paining you less," Christopher remarked after he'd shown Juliet to a chair.

"I am as well as can be expected," was the tight reply.

Juliet's spine stiffened at the thinly veiled scorn in Lady Eunice's voice. Her reception was worse than she had feared it would be, but the unfairness of it raised her hackles. She certainly had not asked to be here.

Glancing toward Christopher, Juliet saw that Lady Eunice had in no way discomposed him. He had taken a seat opposite Juliet, and with his long legs stretched out comfortably before him, he looked the picture of relaxation. His reply to his mother's charged response was a brief smile and a cool "How nice for you." After an infinitesimal pause he drawled with extravagant innocence, "I'm sure I've never seen you looking so fit."

It was a deliberate gibe, Juliet realized. The earl and his mother, it seemed, were not on the best of terms. Looking once again at the dowager countess, it occurred to Juliet that she would not be an easy person to have as one's mother.

Even seated, Lady Eunice was an imposing figure, holding her stately figure upright with so rigid a control that her spine was not allowed to come within inches of the chair's back. A determined chin and sharp nose made her profile a powerful one. It put Juliet in mind of a bird of prey, but she'd have been the first to admit she was not as unbiased as she could have been. She was not being the least unfair, however, when she decided that the earl had gotten his looks from his father. Lady Eunice's features would command attention and perhaps respect, but they would not command praise.

"I have not heard yet from Serena, though I doubt she will be able to come home on such short notice." Juliet marveled that so innocent a statement could sound so like an accusation, and then Lady Eunice was adding, "I have not made any arrangements for entertaining. I was not certain . . ."

As her voice trailed away, Lady Eunice's wintry eyes settled upon Juliet. There was no sign of warmth in that look. Far from it, Lady Eunice's nostrils actually flared as she surveyed Juliet's hair, for one or two long, silvery strands had come loose from their pins during the carriage ride. The dowager countess's unfinished thought could not have been made plainer. She had not been certain Juliet, a mere vicar's daughter, would be presentable, and none of her doubts had been allayed.

"We shan't need entertainments, Mother. We're only here for a brief stay," Christopher drawled smoothly, ignoring his mother's meaning. "I'm afraid a good deal of my time must be taken up with Smathers, anyway. I noticed on the way in that he's not attended to that dam as I asked him to do."

Lady Eunice hesitated, clearly struggling with the question of how to behave. At last, her lips pursing, she consented to her son's change of subject. Turning her shoulder so that she would not be reminded of her daughter-in-law, she began to enumerate rapidly a list of things the hapless Smathers, whom Juliet took to be the earl's estate manager, should be reminded to do.

Dinner was no warmer than the first audience, as Juliet characterized her introduction to Lady Eunice. Indeed, Lady Eunice had gone to the trouble of strategically placing a large silver epergne between her and Juliet, an arrangement which suited Juliet perfectly.

For the most part the meal passed in silence, the only sound being the footsteps of the servants as they moved solicitiously about the table. What little conversation there was passed exclusively between Lady Eunice and her son, allowing Juliet to observe again how little her husband seemed to care for his mother. Christopher never crossed the boundary dividing coolness from insolence, but he came very close.

When Lady Eunice announced to him that she would not—for the first time in years, she added significantly—be going to town for the Season, Christopher did not ask why. Juliet was certain his mother had intended that he should, but instead he drawled negligently, "Suit yourself, Mother. You generally do."

Even from behind the silver epergne Juliet could see that Lady Eunice bristled angrily, but she also noted it was the dowager countess who first dropped her eyes. As, Juliet allowed, she would have done if she'd been subjected to the unflinching mockery in Christopher's eyes.

The atmosphere was so strained, Juliet was delighted to see the lemon pudding make its entrance. Her heart sank, however, when, having finished his portion, Christopher announced he would join the ladies in the drawing room for his brandy.

He was, she knew, being chivalrous, and Juliet appreciated the gesture. She was, however, too drained to endure another hour or two with Lady Eunice, no matter how many buffers there were between them. Catching his eye, she made no effort to hide the plea in hers. "Please suit yourself, my lord, and Lady Eunice, of course," Juliet said quietly. "However, I am feeling quite fatigued from our journey and beg you will excuse me."

For a tense moment Juliet thought Christopher might deny her bid for freedom, but then he inclined his head. "As you will, my dear," he said. "I imagine it *has* been a trying day." There was the faintest of smiles lifting the corner of his mouth as he allowed that the meeting with his mother could not have been easy, and Juliet, as she hurried away, hugged that moment of comradeship to her.

In her room, however, the pleasure that wry smile had brought her faded, for the first sight to greet her reminded her what a sham her marriage really was. The nightgown the maid had laid out for her was the one her mother had packed for her wedding night and was as different from Juliet's usual nightgowns as apples from oranges. The others were made of cotton, heavier for winter and lighter for summer, but this one was not. This one was all silk and lace and was made of a great deal less material than her other gowns had been.

While she was still eyeing the innocent piece of clothing with a rather forlorn expression, the maid assigned her entered the room. Sending a quick apology to her father for her vanity, Juliet allowed the girl to help her into the gown. As the cool silk slid over her with a swishing sound, Juliet shivered, but not for anything in the world would she have taken it off. She could not bring herself to proclaim to the maid and through her perhaps even to Lady Eunice just how equivocal her position as countess actually was.

When the maid had gone, Juliet wrapped a shawl about her for warmth and sat down before the fire to contemplate both her husband and her marriage.

At times in the day and a half since the ceremony it had seemed to her that he did not even like her. Grimacing, she recalled how mocking he had seemed the night before when he'd dismissed her as an unwilling innocent. Yet, tonight, when Lady Eunice's hostility had quite frazzled her nerves, he'd understood.

Sighing, Juliet allowed that a good deal of her problem was that her husband was so very, very attractive. Had he been a toadish sort of person, she'd have been able to dismiss his feelings toward her as easily as she did Lady Eunice's. But he was not a toad at all.

Whatever his looks and whatever his feelings for her might be, Juliet admitted to herself after a while, there was precious little she could do to make him feel more favorably toward her. She knew too little of men. If she had listened more to her older sister Ros, she might have known better what to do. Rosalind had always been the one interested in males. As early as eight she'd had an ardent admirer, and last October, at the age of nineteen, after turning down three prior proposals, she had married a young barrister from Portsmouth.

Unfortunately Juliet had always had too many other interests to give Ros's breathy confidences much attention. She was more likely to be off tending a wounded bird, or playing chess with her father, or reading anything her father gave her to read than tittering with Ros over Jeremy Godwin's brown eyes. Even agonizing over what she would wear to church was beyond her.

Of course it was not as if she had no experience at all with the opposite sex. She had been taken to visit her aunt in Maidstone, which, though small, was larger than St. Mary-on-Medway. Her cousin Mary had taught her how to dance, and at the four assemblies she had attended, she'd not lacked for partners. Indeed several young men had even come back to ask her to stand up with them a second time. But Ros had been right when she had grumbled crossly that Juliet, for all her success, still had no idea how to turn a boy up sweet. It had surprised Juliet as much as anyone that she'd been sought after. She had merely enjoyed herself hugely, and everything had somehow flowed from that.

Gazing at the fire, Juliet gave a mental shrug. It was useless to regret what was, and besides, she doubted that even Ros would have known how to deal with a man like Christopher St. Charles.

Getting up, Juliet decided that at least she would not sleep in the cold, unfamiliar nightdress intended for a bride. Instead she would wear her old familiar flannel. With it wrapped about her, she would remind herself how foolish she would be to hope for more from her husband than she was ever likely to attain.

Instead she would recall how provoking his arrogance could be. If she did not, she admitted ruefully, she might find him too attractive to resist. And if she knew nothing else, Juliet knew by now that the Earl of Hartford was the sort of man who could eat her heart for lunch and forget he had done so by dinner.

5

When Juliet awoke the next morning, the familiar sound of a bird singing outside her window made her smile. The new world around her suddenly seeming less strange, she rose to meet it with renewed spirits.

In the front hall Quinton bowed slowly to her, bidding her good morning in the same weighty tone he might have used to ask after a deceased relative, and proceeded at a stately pace to escort her to the breakfast room.

Christopher was there before her, and Juliet knew so little of his world she did not know to be surprised that he should be up early. Nor did she know enough to be prepared for how he would look when dressed informally in a pair of tight-fitting buckskin breeches and a cambric shirt open loosely at the neck. Slowly she let out her breath, thinking his hair carefully combed could never have the appeal it did now with one lock curling onto his forehead.

"Ah, Juliet. You're an early riser, I see," he remarked, catching sight of her by the door. He did not smile, but his tone was pleasant enough, and Juliet, when she bade him good morning, tried for the same effect.

"Bring Lady Juliet a rasher of bacon, eggs, and some toast, Harrison," Christopher addressed the footman as Juliet went to take her seat.

"But I never eat so much at breakfast!" she protested at once, a little annoyed to have the matter taken out of her hands so summarily.

"Eat what you like," her husband said, shrugging. "I assumed after what you ate last night, or rather didn't eat, you'd be ravenous today."

That he had paid any attention at all the night before to what she'd eaten so surprised her that Juliet only said, "Ah," in a vague way and turned her attention to the coffee she'd been brought.

"Juliet . . ." Christopher recalled her attention to him. "I am about to do the unforgivable as your host and leave you to your own devices for most of the day. I must see the estate manager at once. Certain matters have been left unattended far too long."

The realization that Christopher's departure would leave her alone with Lady Eunice caused Juliet's eyes to express the dismay she felt.

"Mother stays in her rooms until after luncheon," Christopher said, his mouth turning down wryly. That he could read her so accurately made Juliet flush, but she did not try to deny she was pleased with his report. "You'll be free until tea, which is served at four o'clock. I expect you to be there and not to make some excuse to run off as you did last night."

A light pink rose in Juliet's cheeks, but she replied distinctly, "I did not think my company would be much missed."

"I will allow the situation is not easy," Christopher acknowledged, his brow lifting briefly. "But nothing can come of running from difficulties. You are my wife and countess now and have certain obligations to fulfill. Besides," he continued, his expression undeniably grim, "it is best to deal with Mother by looking her squarely in the eye. It's not beyond your capabilities, I think," he told her consideringly.

What he based his judgment on, Juliet could not imagine. The mere thought of Lady Eunice made her quake. Still, the look in his light blue eyes was appreciative, and Juliet found she did not want to contradict him.

He left soon after, telling her to speak to Quinton if

31

she needed anything. Which she promptly did, for she decided that what she most wanted to do was escape from the house. It reminded her too strongly of her mother-in-law.

A scant hour later Juliet was dressed in an old mended dress, a pair of scuffed boots, her sister's handed-down shawl, and a straw bonnet that had seen considerable wear. In one hand she held a copy of Milton's *Paradise Lost* and in the other she carried a basket, for though Quinton had seemed taken aback by her request for a picnic lunch, he had not denied her. There were, it seemed, some compensations to being a countess.

Passing through the formal gardens with their clipped hedges and carefully places statues, Juliet made for the woods situated just beyond a small artificial lake. The path she found led to a lovely meadow with a stream flowing through it. The blues and yellows of spring flowers dotted its bank, and the roots of an old tree provided a relatively dry place to sit.

Juliet picked a few of the flowers to fashion into a chain, which she braided into her hair. It was something she had done when she'd gone fishing with her brother Robbie, and it brought him strongly to mind. Deliberately Juliet turned her thoughts away from home. If she continued in that vein, she realized, she might soon be in tears. Instead, she would investigate the contents of the basket the cook had prepared. She had to laugh, albeit wryly, when she discovered two apples, an entire cold roasted chicken, a large wedge of cheese, a loaf of bread, and a cherry tart inside. It seemed Christopher was not alone in thinking she needed nourishment.

Having eaten very little for days, Juliet made a sizable dent in her feast and washed it down with a bottle of the local cider, which had also been included. With her hunger appeased, Juliet took off her bonnet and leaned against the tree, Milton in hand. As always, she enjoyed the poetry, but the warmth of the sun proved too enticing. After a time she laid the book down and tipped up her face to the sun, allowing its warmth to soothe her. Gently, slowly, with the sound of the flowing stream in her ear, she let the heavy burdens of the past week slip from her shoulders and fell fast asleep.

When she awoke it took her a long, confused moment to realize where she was, but only an instant to know she was quite late. From the sun's position in the sky, she guessed that the hour must be very near to four. Hastily Juliet gathered her things and hurried back.

Approaching the edge of the woods, she was startled to hear voices coming from the direction of a stone bench she'd noticed earlier. Positioned to look at the lake and beyond it to the house, the bench was screened from the woods by a row of clipped hedges.

"I cannot believe he is really married, Hal!" It was a high-pitched, querulous young lady's voice. Intrigued, Juliet stopped to listen.

"Meg told you so, Celeste, and her sister is one of the downstairs maids at Longacres," replied a young man. "I do wish you'd not decided to investigate. Kit was not overjoyed to see us. Damn, but he can look deuced cool when he wants!"

"But I have to know whom he's married! He was supposed to marry me!"

"I told you not to get your hopes up, sister mine. You're too young. Kit's always preferred his women . . . ah, mature." The young man's reply was breezy, too breezy for his sister.

"Oh, you know-it-all!" she scoffed angrily. "You know as well as I that Kit can't marry one of those women. They're for his bed, not his drawing room."

Juliet nearly gasped aloud at such plain speaking, but the young man only laughed.

"Besides," continued the girl, "Lady Eunice wanted me for his countess. She and Mother have always intended it."

"Perhaps that was the rub. It's no secret how Kit and Lady Eunice are forever at odds. But if you don't wish to ask him to solve the mystery himself, you'd best hush. He's coming now."

"Juliet's in the woods," Juliet heard Christopher say. It was the first time she had realized how deep his voice was. There was no question he was a man in comparison with the boy, Hal, who had just been speaking. "We can go in after her, she can't have gone far."

"But my boots will get all muddy!" protested Celeste.

"Wait here, then," Christopher drawled. Juliet could easily imagine the accompanying shrug.

Not wanting to be caught at that particular spot, Juliet hurried away, her thoughts chasing each other in her mind. First and foremost was a concern with Christopher's reaction now that she was late. He'd not be happy, she thought.

And then there was the girl, Celeste, whom Lady Eunice had wanted for her son. Grimacing briefly, Juliet acknowledged that she was more interested in Christopher's attitude toward the girl. Had he, too, wanted her for his wife?

Juliet met the little group just outside the woods. One moment she was alone in the shadows, and then she was face-to-face with Christopher, the sunlight clearly illuminating his expression.

In the moment before he turned to present her to the others, Juliet saw his jaw tighten as his eyes raked her appearance. She'd not given a thought to it until now, but all at once she was aware that her hair, still adorned with wildflowers, was in a girlish braid, that her bonnet was in her hands, and that her cheeks were stinging where the sun had touched them. When Christopher's stony glance lingered ever so briefly on her muddy hem and hopelessly worn boots, she could feel her cheeks heat even more.

"We've guests, Juliet," she heard Christopher saying, his voice giving no hint of his feelings.

During the introductions to Celeste and Hal Darnsby, neighbors whose estate bordered Longacres on the south, Juliet became, if it were possible, even more acutely aware how wanting her appearance was.

Celeste Darnsby was not a raving beauty, but she was, due in part to her impeccable appearance, charmingly pretty. Meticulously coiffed chestnut curls peeped cunningly from beneath her ruched bonnet and contrasted most pleasingly with her milky-white complexion. She carried a frilled lavender parasol which matched exactly her fashionable jaconet muslin walking dress, while her dainty kid half-boots looked as if they'd never been worn before.

Perhaps her brown eyes left something to be desired, but that was only because they were narrowed upon Juliet with an incredulous glare. In the split second when their eyes met, Juliet only just prevented herself drawing back from the venom plainly visible in those eyes. Celeste, it seemed, would not easily excuse her for taking Christopher, and Juliet did not think it would soothe the other girl to learn Juliet's coup had been entirely unwitting.

Knowing she would never forgive herself if she did not, Juliet kept her chin up and nodded as loftily as she knew how. Her hand gripping her basket handle tightly, Juliet turned to greet Celeste's brother, Hal.

It took her a moment to realize that in contrast to his sister, Hal was smiling, and that his broad smile was reflected in his brown eyes. Perhaps a year or two older than Celeste, Juliet judged him to be about one-and-twenty.

"I say, Lady Juliet, you have taken us by surprise. But what a pleasant surprise! What extraordinary hair you have!"

Juliet was embarrassed to have attention called to her inelegant hairstyle, but she decided upon close inspection of the young man's expression that he was being sincere. As if to confirm her estimation, he added in almost bemused tones, "You look rather like a princess in a fairy tale, it's so long. And such an unusual color, too. Almost silver!"

"You are very gallant, Mr. Darnsby." Juliet smiled. "I am afraid you have caught me at rather a disadvantage."

Like several young men before him, Hal Darnsby found that Juliet's eyes, when she smiled, could shine with the most entrancing lights. Tearing his gaze from her sparkling gray eyes, he looked once more at her hair, gleaming like silver in the sun, and thought it quite the most exotic, and therefore, because he was a young man eager for the unusual, quite the most captivating sight he had ever seen.

"Oh, tush!" he rushed to reassure her. "You needn't stand on ceremony with Celeste and me. Here, let me take your basket and your book. By Jove!" he exclaimed. "You were reading Milton. Deuced heavy stuff, Milton. I never quite finished him at school."

Celeste, who was accustomed to being the center of attention, gave a loud sniff and turned the subject. "I declare I am beginning to feel the cold in this ground through my boots. Won't you escort me to the house, Kit?"

The girl's high-pitched voice grated on Juliet's nerves, as did the engaging smile she turned upon Christopher.

He, on cue, bowed languidly and held out his arm for her to take, leaving Juliet to follow behind with Hal. From her position Juliet was able to watch Celeste turn her pretty face up to Christopher to ask with a coquettish pout, "I never knew you to be bookish, Kit. Do you think a young lady must be a reader?"

Juliet bit her lips as Christopher smiled lazily down at Celeste, and though the girl tittered in the silliest way, Juliet found she could not blame her. There was a quality about Christopher's smile which would set any woman to fluttering absurdly.

"I believe," he drawled lightly, "that a young lady should look as lovely and as charming as possible, my dear. What she does after that is her own business."

Celeste's pleased laughter trilled happily, and no wonder, thought Juliet, her throat tightening. There was no question who did, and who did not, look as charming and lovely as possible.

"And have you known Kit long, Lady Juliet?"

Juliet, her attention lamentably elsewhere, was struck dumb by Hal's innocent query. Luckily Christopher, proving to her surprise that he was not quite so absorbed with Celeste as she had thought, came to her

36

rescue. "She's known me long enough to say 'I do,' Hal," he turned to say in an amused drawl.

They had just reached the house, where Quinton, having opened the door, was standing aside for Celeste. Juliet was about to follow when Christopher, his eyes having come to rest on her, added in the same light tone, "I no sooner saw her than I knew I would have her. Isn't that right, Juliet?"

If he had meant to wound her with a reference to the sordid circumstances under which they had met, he succeeded admirably. As the color first rushed into her cheeks and then as quickly receded, leaving her pale as a ghost, Juliet's widened eyes locked with her husband's.

No matter how long she lived, Juliet knew she would never forget how mockingly he regarded her in that brief instant before she recovered her wits and fled into the house.

Outwardly Juliet look composed, if still pale, but there was a lump in her throat which prevented her saying much the rest of the afternoon. Her silence did not greatly matter, for Celeste was full of chatter about her coming Season in London, and Hal was equally excited about the commission in the army his father had just bought for him.

Juliet was past caring what was said; she only waited for the moment she could escape to her room to lick her wounds. When the Darnsbys left at last, she thought herr chance had come, but to her dismay, Christopher was at the door before her.

"I should like to see you in my study," he said in such a way that Juliet did not demur.

As they walked in silence, she darted quick, wide eyed glances at his unyielding expression.

"You may stop looking like some frightened fawn, I don't intend to bite you," he snapped when the study door clicked shut behind him. "Sit down," he added before stalking to the window to stare out, his back to her.

Juliet, looking at his elegantly clad back, tried to calm herself, but it was not easy. She had had little experience in her life with real anger. The last time had been when she was ten and had brought a wounded garden snake into the house, nearly frightening her mother to death. Mrs. Barre had dealt her a sharp slap and then, appalled, had begged her pardon.

When he did at last address her, Christopher's words were altogether different from what Juliet had expected. "I apologize for my comment in front of Hal," he told her stiffly. "No matter how provoked I was with you, I never should have said such a thing."

Juliet searched his face. He did not seem contrite, but he did seem uncomfortable. He reminded her of a sudden of her elder brother Ronald when he had been made to apologize for insulting one of her friends. It was her father who had compelled Ronald's penitence, and though she did not know what motivated Christopher, she could see he did not like his situation any more than Ronald had.

"I am sorry I embarrassed you, my lord," Juliet replied, trying to address what she thought might be the real cause of the problem. "I always wear old clothes when I go walking in the woods."

Perhaps she'd have done better to act angry, not contrite, for he only exploded at her accommodating tone. "Good God, girl!" he exclaimed, his eyes snapping impatiently. "You seem reasonably intelligent. After all, you took Milton along on your frolic in the woods. Look about you. You have enough money at your disposal to buy a dozen dresses for every one you ruin. Heaven knows, after the trouble dressing as a servant girl has caused you, it seems you'd be slow to do it again. You looked a mannerless Gypsy this afternoon." Shaking his head, his crystal eyes looking as cold as ice, he went on, "When you have only one appointment in a day's time, I expect you to be able to keep it and to be dressed properly when you do. Do not try my patience again, Juliet. I know too well the toll of having a troublesome wife. It was the reason my father died an early death. You may not be a harpy like mother, but there is more than one way to be troublesome, and I will tolerate none of them."

Juliet's nails made painful dents in her palms, but she said nothing. Being honest had done little good, and she knew no other course.

For a long, tense moment they stared at one another: Juliet with her chin up but her eyes dark with distress, facing Christopher with his tensed jaw and unyielding ice-blue eyes. Finally it was Christopher who broke the impasse.

"As we seem to have nothing more to say to each other, you may as well go.

"There is one more thing," he said, forcing her to look around when she got to the door. "I've decided to leave for London tomorrow. Have your things ready by nine o'clock."

Juliet nodded and slipped out the door. In the refuge of her room, she stared out over Longacres' terranced lawns and wondered with a sigh if her husband was so short-tempered with everyone or only with the wife he did not want but had insisted upon having.

6

"Lord Halsey to see you, my lord."

Leaning back in his chair, the earl smiled knowingly at his friend. "You've come around quickly enough after getting back, Tony. Was the fishing so good in Scotland?"

Tony Halsey ignored the look as he settled his large frame comfortably in a chair. "The fishing was passable," he allowed. "But it is not the fishing, nor is it, as you think, my inveterate curiosity which has brought me so precipitately to your door. I have come now, else I could not come at all. Mother has sent word that Father is very ill, perhaps . . . well, I am going to Hampshire posthaste."

"I am sorry to hear it, Tony. I know how much you care for him."

Tony accepted the brandy Christopher offered him and heaved a sigh. "It's to be expected at his age, of course, but I find that makes the matter no easier to accept."

A silence fell as Tony studied the amber color of his glass; then, taking a long, sustained swallow, he looked up, a smile easing the strain in his eyes. "But tell me of you, Kit. Distract me a little with what it's like to be leg-shackled."

Kit shrugged and looked out the window as if there might be an answer there. "You know my feelings on marriage in general and wives in particular," he said at last. Looking back at Tony, he added tersely, "I always swore I would never let any woman get her matrimonial hooks in me."

40

Tony cast him a sharp look. "Lady Juliet does not seem the type to possess hooks," he pointed out.

A wry smile broke out on his friend's face. "You're not feeling about my bride as you did about that puppy at Eton, are you? As I recall, you had me fight some bully in order to save it."

"I liked her," Tony admitted, a faint line of color showing on his cheeks. "And I grant I should not like to see your preconceived ideas about marriage keep you from appreciating her. She is quite unspoiled."

"And untutored," Kit added dryly. "You should have seen the Gypsy's clothing she donned to go walking in the woods! She has no idea how to go in society— you've seen her hair and choice of clothes."

Tony took a swallow of brandy. "She has beauty enough," he said when he had savored its taste fully. "You've only to hire a dresser and exert a little patience. She'll come along well enough in the end, I daresay."

"The dresser was a simple matter," Kit retorted. "But patience, as you well know, is not my strongest suit. At times she reminds me of your puppy, and like most young animals, she can be engaging enough at times, but infuriating at most others. Lord, when she appeared looking so unkempt at Mother's, I thought I would shake her till her teeth rattled. Now, don't go looking so morose. I apologized for my loss of temper. You'd have been proud of me. Still, I cannot say I ever fancied being some chit's governess. Damnation, Tony! I married her because it was the honorable thing to do, but I think I can be forgiven chafing a little over the cost of my honor."

Tony, looking slightly surprised because Kit was seldom so forthcoming with his feelings, said at once, "I did not mean to imply you must be a saint, only that you should not be too hard on her. I think it was a very noble thing you did to marry her. Very few men would, you know. They'd have paid off her family, and though you say they were most respectable, I cannot believe the Barres would not have accepted it had you chosen that course."

Kit merely grunted, neither agreeing nor disagreeing with Tony's assessment, nor explaining why he had not chosen such a simple solution to his problem. It was, as Tony had said, the alternative most men of his class would have selected.

Seeing he was not to receive an answer to a question that had piqued his curiosity, Tony went on to point out an asset Kit's bride possessed which he for one thought mightily important. "Lady Juliet may not be in the first stare of fashion, but she does at least seem intelligent."

To Tony's surprise, Kit gave a sudden bark of laughter. "She's intelligent," he allowed. "She was reading Milton at Longacres."

"Milton!"

Kit nodded, still smiling. "Milton. You should have seen Hal's face when he realized what the book was she was carrying. His expression was almost worth having to marry. The first thing she asked to do upon coming to town was to be taken to see the Elgin Marbles. I promise you that Juliet's reaction to them was exactly what any other girl her age would have exhibited upon seeing her completed court dress. She was absolutely in alt."

Kit fell silent, and sipping his brandy, turned to look out the window again. Juliet's pleasure at seeing the Grecian statues had quite amazed him. As had the near-awe she had displayed upon seeing his extensive library. "They are all yours?" she had asked so disbelievingly he had had to smile.

It was lucky she was so taken with his library, for she had, since coming to London, spent a great deal of time there, he admitted. As if to prove to himself he was not the least shackled by his unlooked-for wife, he had been out a great deal. A very great deal, he added with a slight twinge of conscience. He had not taken her with him, of course, she'd no clothes to speak of yet. Nor any idea how to act, he added remorselessly.

But she did not seem so unhappy. Indeed, she seemed quite content among all his leather-bound editions.

Smiling to himself, he recalled how she had looked when he'd taken her by surprise the day before.

Her feet had been curled beneath her, her slippers abandoned on the floor before her. When she caught sight of him, she gave him a rather uncertain smile. He could not blame her for it, the memory of their scene in his study at Longacres coming to him, but neither could he help recalling the smile she'd given Hal when he'd praised her looks. Abruptly Christopher shrugged mentally. If he wanted that sort of smile, he knew, none better, how to get it.

But he had not complimented his wife, though she had been wearing one of her new morning dresses. He had been too taken up with watching her carefully push the book she was reading down between her and the chair so that its cover might not be seen.

Christopher had said nothing, only extended the package he was holding.

More than a little surprised, Juliet had taken it and unwrapped it. "Why, it's a book!" she'd exclaimed joyously, treating him to the full effect of her very charming smile. "But how kind of you, sir! I've not read Miss Austen."

"I thought you might not have been able to get her in St. Mary-on-Medway," Christopher replied, and then in a lazy drawl added, "But I wonder what it is you are reading now?"

Juliet, as he had suspected she would, flushed. She bent her silvery head to look down at the book as if it might tell her what to say, but of course it did not. At last, biting her lip, she faced him squarely to admit she was reading Fielding's *Tom Jones.*

"Ah," Christopher responded, his tone so amused Juliet had reddened further. "And I suppose the good vicar of St. Mary-on-Medway would not be pleased to find you reading Fielding?"

Juliet shook her head. "Papa always said we should feed our minds only the worthiest materials, or we would wind up with worthless minds."

"And how is Leslie taking the news of your marriage?" Tony asked.

Christopher, grinning openly at the memory of how chagrined his wife had looked, had to ask Tony to repeat himself.

"Will Les even see you now?"

"Don't tell me you think I'm losing my touch, Tony," Kit drawled, a teasing gleam in his eyes.

"The devil take you! You know perfectly well what I meant. I thought that when Leslie learned she would never be Countess of Hartford, as she had so devoutly hoped to be, her pique would be greater than the power of your considerable charm."

Kit laughed. "However considerable my charm may be, I admit I took along some emerald baubles to tip the balance in my favor. Leslie's too greedy to withstand such bribery."

"And Juliet? Does she know about Leslie?"

Rolling his eyes to the ceiling as if to ask for patience, Kit shook his head. "No, I have not told Juliet in so many words that I have a mistress. But she knows ours is a marriage in name only. I made that clear from the beginning. She'll not care, Tony, you needn't worry. She didn't want the marriage any more than I did. I confess, though, that it would not matter if she did. I married her, as it was my duty to do, but I'll be bound if I'm going to be shackled by her."

Tony did not know whether to believe that Lady Juliet did not care for her marriage to Kit. If she did not, she'd be the first woman he knew to be so unmoved by his friend. Most women, where Kit was concerned, behaved like moths around a flame. Still, he did not find fault with Kit's attitude. Like Kit, Tony had lived quite some time in London society, where it was accepted that a man would have a mistress. Granted, most mistresses were opera dancers, not striking, wellborn widows, but it made little difference. The principle was the same.

Having married into the nobility, there were many things to which Lady Juliet would have to adjust. Leslie was only one of them. Vividly recalling her wide clear eyes, Tony could only hope Kit's young bride would not be changed too greatly in the process.

7

Juliet winced as a long length of flaxen hair fell to the floor and was quickly joined by another and then another. For the first time in her life her hair was being cut to a fashionable length. She'd trimmed it occasionally, but, having seen how much care Ros's short curls required, she'd always resisted her mother's entreaties to have it cut drastically.

Juliet, carefully avoiding her own reflection in the cheval glass, glanced at the angular woman working so intently on her hair. Miss Trask—or simply Trask, as Juliet called her—was the dresser Christopher had hired for her.

As Juliet recalled the scene when he, the day after their arrival in London, had baldly announced Trask's imminent arrival, a smile flitted briefly across her face.

Having, in the space of four days, been made, without once having her wishes taken into account, to marry, to travel to Surrey, and then to remove to London, Juliet, when she was informed her dresser had been hired without her having the least say in the matter, felt as if her entire life was slipping irretrievably beyond her control. It was not a pleasant feeling at all, and her chin lifted.

"Thank you, my lord," she began in a quiet but still cool voice. "I cannot thank you enough for taking the matter out of my hands. I am certain the task of interviewing candidates for the position was an onerous one."

The earl had the grace to look uncomfortable. "Actually I did not advertise, and so there have been no interviews. Miss Trask comes on the recommendation of a friend whose daughter no longer has need of her." After a pause he grinned ruefully. It was a very engaging expression. "I've been devilish high-handed, haven't I?"

Summoning a great deal of self-control, Juliet did not smile back, but instead said unequivocally and immediately, "Yes, my lord."

Surprisingly, he'd laughed, the transformation his face underwent when he did so causing Juliet's heart to beat considerably faster. "And you are being plain-spoken," he told her, amused. "I am sorry. I should have thought to let you speak with her first, but I'm afraid I've gone too long having things my own way. Will you let her come on trial? She's got impeccable credentials and reams of references. If you don't like her, we can find someone else."

It was true that earlier that same day Christopher had gone to the trouble of showing her around Hartford House himself, but his conciliatory tone still surprised Juliet enough that her brow had lifted before she gave in to the desire to smile and agree to his compromise.

"As you can see, my lady, without all that quite unnecessary weight, your hair curls of itself."

Recalled to the present, Juliet looked once again into the cheval glass. It seemed as if a stranger stared back at her, the fashionable curls Trask had insisted upon were so different. Juliet tipped her head. It felt quite odd not to have her silky hair sliding over her shoulders, but the effect of the new style was not bad, she decided. It was only that she looked so young. Her heart sank a little at the thought. She distinctly remembered Hal Darnsby telling his sister that Christopher preferred mature women.

A faint color rose in Juliet's cheeks. The thought made her recall how he'd caught her reading *Tom Jones* earlier in the week. The teasing way he'd asked her if she were enjoying Tom's altogether amazing escapades had made her cheeks burn and had revealed more certainly than anything else could that he did not regard her as a mature woman.

Nor was she, Juliet acknowledged as she watched Trask thread a ribbon through her hair. There was no use trying to pretend to be other than she was, though she did admit she would like Christopher to be pleased.

Exactly when that change in her own attitude had come, she could not say. Perhaps when he had surprised her by taking her to see the Elgin Marbles after she had said in passing she would like to see them more than any other single thing in London. He'd even brought her a pretty French bonnet with a sporty plume, explaining with a lazy amusement which completely unsettled her that every lady when she went out for her first drive in London should have a new hat.

Not that Christopher had been overly attentive. He certainly had not. He had not been home at all in the evenings, and was even missing some mornings at breakfast. His absence then had given Juliet pause, until she had reminded herself that theirs was not an ordinary marriage. All she could ask of her husband was that he not forget her entirely, and be personable when he did remember her. Those terms he had lived up to, and now she would like to please him by looking her best. Not to entice him, nothing so unlikely as that, but only to repay him, as it were.

"Your dress, my lady."

Juliet frowned a little as she stepped into the dress. She knew the pale green muslin with its rich French work at the hem was the latest thing, for Trask had insisted that was so, but it seemed to her that its fashionable pastel color would only make her own light coloring fade to insignificance. And Juliet did want to look well, for today she was for the first time to meet people in London society.

Celeste Darnsby had sent a note around the day before asking if Juliet wished to accompany her to the park. Christopher had not been home to consult with, but Juliet had decided to accept anyway. Celeste might only want an excuse to linger at Hartford House until the earl came, but at least Juliet would have the opportunity to see Hyde Park at the fashionable hour.

As she greeted Celeste, Juliet knew her misgivings about Trask's choice of color was well-formed. There was no mistaking the relish in Celeste's brown eyes as she scanned Juliet's attire.

Not that much could have threatened the girl, for Celeste looked quite charming in a rose-colored walking dress and stylish leghorn hat. Squaring her shoulders and telling herself the opinion of a girl like Celeste Darnsby could not matter to her, Juliet followed her companion to the Darnsbys' landau, where a maid waited for them.

"And have you been enjoying yourself, Lady Juliet?" Celeste smiled a smile that never quite reached her eyes. "I have been looking for you at all the affairs I've attended. I saw Kit night before last at Lady Coleton's, but I was disappointed not to see you. I suppose you've had your wardrobe to attend to, have you not?"

An elusive memory teased Juliet's mind, and she occupied herself trying to think who it was Celeste reminded her of. The simple game served to stifle her intense desire to ask who Lady Coleton was and whether Christopher had been alone. Still not able to place the memory, Juliet heard Celeste saying, "But now Kit will not have all the fun. He told my father at White's the other night that you would both be coming to my ball next Tuesday."

Their arrival at the park provided enough distraction that Juliet was able to reply with only a nod. It was all she could manage. The idea of attending Celeste's ball was not particularly appealing. Only a few minutes with her, and Juliet was already longing to return to Christopher's library. Of course, that was it! Celeste reminded her of the bookseller in St. Mary-on-Medway. They had the same pointed chins and sharp eyes.

"Oh, look! It is Lord Whiton and Mr. Cordier!" Celeste broke into Juliet's musing as she waved gaily to two young bucks dressed in the latest stare of fashion, with high shirt points and such exaggerated shoulders that Juliet thought they must be padded.

When she was presented, the young men looked at her with obvious interest, but Celeste did not allow their attention to remain on her companion for long. Pretending great excitement over some stray remark of Lord Whiton's, Celeste moved forward just enough that her open parasol completely blocked Juliet from the young men's view.

Not the least put out, for they did not seem especially interesting young men to her, Juliet turned to watch an exceedingly cumbersome carriage lumber in their direction.

Celeste must have seen it as well, for she soon flashed the two young men beside her an arch smile, said she would save dances for them the next evening at Almack's, and efficiently sent them on their way.

With her sweetest smile, which was pretty indeed, Celeste hailed the occupants of the carriage and presented them to Juliet as the Marquess of Hightower and his mother, the marchioness. Juliet knew the title of marquess was a lofty one, and she supposed that fact must account for the exaggerated fluttery greeting Celeste gave the young man, for it was certainly not his looks that had inspired her. His round, smooth face was distinguished only by its utter lack of a chin, and a pair of bulbous eyes.

When both mother and son displayed an avid interest in meeting the Earl of Hartford's wife, Juliet teased herself with the notion that Celeste had invited her to the park in order to impress them. It was fanciful, she knew, but it was undeniably true that the marquess and his mother, though they outranked him, were in awe of Christopher.

"William, for that is what I call the marquess in private," Celeste declared smugly to Juliet when they were once more on their way, "has vast estates. His home, Hightower Castle, is said to be one of the oldest in the country."

"I see," was absolutely all Juliet could think to say, for she truly could not imagine allying herself with such an unattractive man merely because he had an ancient seat. The Marquess of Hightower seemed a poor bargain, when Celeste's quarry had once been Christopher St. Charles.

Just as Juliet was entertaining that uncharitable thought, Celeste, staring down the drive with a horrified expression, gave a loud gasp.

Turning to look, Juliet saw nothing out of the ordinary, though a pair of sleek blacks, their legs prancing in unison, did catch her eye. They pulled a small, dainty carriage painted black and gold, which, though, a trifle gaudy, looked as costly as the horses.

As it crossed the drive in front of them, it came to a halt in the traffic, and quite forgetting Celeste, Juliet looked to see who owned the resplendent rig. The first person she saw was a woman of ripe beauty whose face was turned her way. Her striking black hair gleamed in the sun and was topped by a dashing red hat set at a rakish angle. It sported a white plume which curled by the woman's shell-like ear and ended just beside her eyes, which were, Juliet could see, slanted slightly in the most sultry way. Juliet could not make out the color of the woman's eyes, but she could see that her wide mouth was red, and as Juliet watched, it curved into an alluring smile whose sensual message was unmistakable even to Juliet.

Quickly, as the carriage began to pull out of sight, Juliet looked to see how that inviting smile was received.

The man who had been sitting too far back to see leaned forward slightly as if in response to that smile. His face was turned away from Juliet and toward the beautiful woman, but it did not matter. There was no mistaking that golden head. Christopher wore no hat, and Juliet could see that his hair was ruffled slightly in a most appealing way. Perhaps the breeze had done it, or perhaps the woman's fingers. . . .

Powerless to pull her eyes away, Juliet watched as her husband raised the woman's hand to his lips. It was a common gesture, but the way his mouth lingered on her palm made it seem, to Juliet at least, unbearably intimate.

"Oh dear, Lady Juliet! I never thought we would see Kit and Leslie. They seldom come to the park together. He did buy her the carriage, it is true, but he seldom rides in it. I do hope you are not too upset—"

"Of course not," Juliet interrupted coolly. The only sign that she was not as unmoved as she would like to be was the tight clenching of her hands, but as they lay in her lap, Celeste could not know it.

The bully in St. Mary-on-Medway who picked on children younger than himself might have warned Celeste that despite her sweet smile, Juliet could, if provoked, give better than she got, but he was not present. And so Celeste was not at all prepared when Juliet continued, "Christopher and I have an understanding. You and Lord Hightower will likely have one, too . . . ah, but then again, perhaps you will not. The marquess is not precisely a gentleman the ladies will fight over, is he?"

Celeste's indrawn breath told Juliet she had hit home, as did the maid's hastily concealed smirk, but, begging a hasty pardon from her father, she did not repent. Celeste might not have arranged for Juliet to see Christopher and his mistress, but Juliet had no doubt she had hoped for it. "I should like to return home now, Celeste, if you please," she added in a tone which could not be refused.

On the way back to Hartford House Celeste darted several glances toward Juliet, but Juliet ignored them completely. Her face and manner as composed as if she were alone, she neither spoke to nor looked at her companion. When the carriage steps had been let down for her, she maintained the same attitude and mounted the steps to her home without a backward glance. Had she looked back, she'd have been afforded the pleasant sight of Celeste watching her openmouthed, but Juliet did not look. She had little desire to see the malicious girl ever again.

8

The sight of Christopher in the breakfast room next morning, a wry smile curving his mouth as he read some item in the paper, made Juliet stumble slightly. He'd not come home before she went to bed, and having seen the person with whom he spent his nights, she had not expected him to return at all.

Juliet had tried very hard not to think about the woman Celeste had called Leslie. It had not been an easy task, although she'd not been surprised to learn her husband had a mistress. Ros had told her once that most men of the nobility did, but Ros had not prepared her for how ravishing this one would be.

When she had arrived home from the park, Juliet had found it necessary to take herself in hand and had absolutely forbidden her mind to dwell upon the woman's physical characteristics. It would only serve to make her feel miserable. Instead she bade herself to adopt Celeste's attitude, for, however much she might despise that young lady, Juliet did acknowledge that Celeste was a good deal worldier than she. Leslie, no matter how dashing, was only for Christopher's bedroom, while she, his wife, had her place in his drawing room. It was the accepted way.

That her brave reasoning did not comfort her as much as she wished it might, Juliet was forced to admit as she took in the sight of her husband in a tight-fitting coat of blue surperfine and crisp white cravat tied faultlessly. Unlike the young men she'd met with Celeste, he needed no padding or outlandish styles. His simple elegance suited him perfectly.

Resolutely pushing thoughts of the day before away, Juliet moved into the room, bidding Christopher good morning as she went. He looked up to return the greeting, a smile of welcome in his eyes. Juliet, pleased to see it, began to return the smile, when she realized his friendly expression had turned into one of incredulity.

Quite suddenly she remembered that he had not seen her hair.

"What on earth have you done to your hair?" he asked, confirming her thought.

Juliet did not care for his tone. He was entitled not to care for it, but she thought her curls were not so bad that he had a right to look aghast. As was usual in such circumstances, Juliet's chin lifted. "Trask said short curls were the fashion," she informed him loftily.

Christopher laid down his paper, the look in his blue eyes warning her he would not be placatory. "I do not believe I know of any fashion which decrees a married woman must look like a schoolroom chit."

Juliet flushed hotly at the biting remark. "If the cut of my hair does not suit you, sir, then I suggest you take it up with my dresser, whom, may I remind you, you hired. And now, good day to you. I find I have quite lost my appetite."

Spinning about, Juliet fairly flew from the room. "Juliet!" she heard Christopher call, but she paid no attention except to close the door behind her a little more vehemently. Let that be his answer, she muttered beneath her breath as she raced up the stairs.

Once she was on the window seat in her room, her brave front collapsed somewhat. Balling up her fist, she hit the unoffending seat. How was she to know the style would make her look disastrously young? It was not the sort of thing she knew. If Christopher had wanted a mature woman who knew how to look her best, he should have married that overblown woman who was his mistress.

The spiteful thought brought a faint smile to her face, and after a little she was able to tell herself she was moping shamefully. The answer, she decided as she sent for Trask, was to escape thoughts of Christopher by going out, perhaps on a shopping expedition.

It was revealing of Juliet's character that she never once thought to ring a peal over her dresser's dour head for having suggested she cut her hair so drastically. Trask's assignment had been to turn a country girl into a woman of fashion, and she had done the best she could. The fault lay with Christopher for not informing her of his tastes.

In the beginning Juliet had intended only to buy a present for her mother, but, perhaps thinking to revenge herself on Christopher through his purse, she found that once she'd started, she could not stop. Her mother did get a blue silk shawl, but her father got an original edition of Voltaire, while her younger sisters all got muslin afternoon dresses, and Rob and all her other brothers were ordered coats. Even Ros got something, and a very nice something the silk ball gown was, just the sort of something Ros would adore.

In the carriage on her way home, Juliet conceded with a wry twist of her lips that she had allowed her husband's disparaging remark to send her flying in all directions. The best thing she could say was that her family had benefited from her fit of temper, and then, remembering how her father had said she could use Christopher's wealth to do good, she chuckled aloud. It seemed a clear case of charity beginning at home.

Just then her carriage, which had rounded the corner by Hyde Park and turned into a narrow thoroughfare, came to a halt.

"Likely it's an accident of some sort," muttered Trask crossly.

Juliet leaned out the window and saw that the wheels of an elegant landau had indeed grazed an applecart, overturning it and tumbling its contents into the street. It was the righting of the mess which had halted the flow of the traffic.

Satisfied, Juliet was about to pull her head in, when two figures standing a short distance away in front of a dingy alley caught her eye. As she watched with horrified eyes, one of them, a beefy, rough-looking fellow, raised his large arm and brutally struck his companion, a scrawny, grimy urchin. The child's head snapped backward from the force of the blow, and Juliet saw a trickle of blood, bright red against his dirty face, start to ooze from his mouth.

Apparently unsatisfied with the damage he had already inflicted, the man struck again and then again.

"Stop!" Juliet screamed, leaping down from the carriage.

Perhaps not hearing her, the man hit the boy again.

"Unhand that child!" Juliet demanded as she reached to pull the bleeding, reeling child to safety behind her.

The man, however, though taken aback by Juliet's sudden intrusion into his affairs, saw what she was about and took a tight hold of the urchin's other arm.

"And who the devil be you?" the man growled, turning a pair of mean little black eyes upon Juliet.

A crowd surrounded the three actors in the impromptu drama, its sentiment divided fairly evenly between those who shouted encouragement to "your ladyship" and those who jeeringly admonished the man to stand firm against the "interferin' gentry mort."

"Never mind who I am," Juliet flashed back, eyeing the glowering man angrily. "You are hurting this child, and I demand that you release him."

"Don't let 'er talk to you like that!" yelled several in the crowd.

"This lad's mine, you've no right to tell me what to do with 'im," retorted the man with an insolent sneer.

Juliet turned her attention to the boy. "Is this man your father?"

The boy stared mutely at Juliet, his fearful eyes enormous in his thin face.

"You've no call to ask 'im nothin'," the man shouted, pulling on the boy's arm.

Juliet tightened her hold, and feeling how pitifully thin the child's arm was, turned furious eyes back upon the man. "I'll not release him to a bully like you unless I know you to be his father!" she vowed.

"That's tellin' 'im!" screamed her supporters.

Juliet ignored them and looked back at the boy,

who was still gazing fearfully up at her, the cut on his lip bleeding profusely. "You've no need to go with this fellow if you do not want to, lad," she assured those two frightened eyes. "I shall take care of you, if you like."

"What!" screamed the man, but Juliet never looked up.

"Is this man your father?" she repeated.

This time the child, apparently convinced of Juliet's ability to rescue him, slowly shook his head.

"No," he whispered hoarsely.

"Then you will release him this instant, sir."

"Cor, she's trying to steal the boy!" Juliet heard several people shout.

"He's my livelihood and I ain't lettin' him go," the man snarled at Juliet. His expression was so hateful, Juliet recoiled, but she did not lose hold of the child.

Suddenly Juliet was not so certain what to do, for she was not strong enough to force him to release the boy.

"Make way there! Make way!" With an enormous sense of relief Juliet recognized the booming bass of Christopher's coachman, and watched as, jostling each other for position, the crowd parted for the broad-shouldered man and his two postilions.

Seeing at once that he was outnumbered, the boy's attacker cast a venomous look at Juliet. "Take 'im, then, if you're so fond of 'im," he spat, flinging the boy at Juliet. "You nobs are all the same, thinkin' you can have ever'thin' the way you want it. Maybe some-day you'll find there's a price to pay!"

With that threat, he stalked off into the crowd and was immediately lost from sight. The little urchin sagged against Juliet, too weak from either hunger or his ill treatment or both to stand.

Without hesitation Juliet had the coachman carry the child to the carriage and deposit him on its floor. The man's disgust was ill-disguised as he briefly re-garded the dirty lump with a frown, but Juliet was undeterred. She had seen just the same sort of thing happen in St. Mary-on-Medway. The lower the person

56

was on the social scale, the less likely he was to be generous to those less fortunate than himself.

The phenomenon had not distracted her then, when she had insisted on bringing a penniless soldier into the kitchen for a bite to eat despite Cook's horrified protests, nor did it now. Instead she turned to the coachman with such gratitude shining in her magnificent gray eyes that it made him feel quite bashful, and he even decided that perhaps her ladyship was not so daft as she seemed, leaping to the defense of beggars.

Trask was a more stubborn case. She wrenched the hem of her dress away from the boy's polluting presence, her expression a grimace of horror.

Shrugging, Juliet turned to the boy, who was shivering with fear, and put her hand on his shoulder. She was not at all surprised when he flinched. "You are safe now," she said softly. "No one will hurt you. You will stay with us at Hartford House, I promise."

The boy stared up at her, his expression almost embarrassing her. She certainly did not think she deserved adoration. "We shall find some decent work for you," she added, wanting to be certain he understood the terms upon which she was taking him home. Evidently he did, for though he said nothing, he did nod slightly.

Juliet patted his head, despite Trask's audible gasp, not caring in the least that she had irrevocably ruined her glove. She was far too concerned over whether or not she could persuade Christopher to allow her to honor her promise to the boy to worry over something so trivial. At home she'd always had her father to back her up in a case like this. Here there was only herself, and Christopher was immeasurably more formidable than either Cook or her mother had ever been.

As the carriage went round a corner, the boy huddled more closely against her. His pitiful action brought a determined gleam to Juliet's eyes. She would simply have to bring it off herself, that was all there was to it.

9

Morton, butler to the earl for ten years and before that to the equally high-in-the-instep Duke of Croydon, had a very long thin nose. Juliet had observed that although Morton's mouth and eyes seemed frozen in a single haughty expression, his nose was more revealing.

When she, a poorly-got-up girl of seventeen, had been presented to him as the Countess of Hartford, his mouth had welcomed her impassively, but his nose had first twitched curiously, and then, decision made, had sniffed dismissively. That reaction was as nothing compared to the convulsive quivering with which it greeted the urchin lad who huddled woefully beside her. Indeed so great was Morton's astonishment that even his eyes reacted by bulging.

Luckily the coachman had already suggested a likely niche for the child out of Morton's sway. "Jed Wickam, the head groom, might give the lad a hand," he had said, adding sagely, "Jed's from the country."

Armed with the thought, Juliet nodded coolly to the butler. "This lad will be on the staff, Morton. I should like bathwater taken to my room as well as a suit of livery in his size. And send for Jed Wickam, please."

Juliet Barre St. Charles, when in pursuit of a righteous cause, was not easy to daunt, as Morton found. Despite a severe elevation of his nose, she waited serenely for him to acknowledge her wishes. When he did at last, and not a moment before, she swept the child before her up the stairs to the safety of her room.

A young footman who had watched the interchange confirmed the whole later belowstairs when Morton was not present. "The old man's eyes fair come out of his head at the sight of a dirty beggar in his hall. But her ladyship turned him up neat and tight with a look you'd never have thought to see on her sweet face."

He'd been teased about that last remark, but in the end the others had agreed that Lady Juliet did indeed have a sweet beauty. Still, what the earl would say about this, a beggar no less . . .

When Juliet put the matter to Jed Wickam, he scratched his head and hesitated. But after she described the brutal treatment the boy was accustomed to receiving, he relented, and citing the necessity to practice Christian charity, agreed to find a place for the boy. His only condition was that the earl approve.

That matter settled, Juliet turned her attention to cleaning the boy, who had whispered that his name was Ferdie. With the help of a scullery maid Juliet persuaded him that water would not kill and watched, fascinated, as his hair gradually revealed itself to be a reddish color. The clearer perspective on his badly split lip and ugly purple bruises nearly made her cry aloud, but when he was dressed in the green-and-gold livery of the Hartford servants, she managed to smile encouragement at the shy pride she could detect in his blue eyes. She did not doubt it was the first time he had ever looked so civilized.

Now all she had to do was wait for Christopher, which she did with very uncertain feelings. What his reaction to her part in the escapade would be, she shuddered to think, and what he might order done with Ferdie, she simply could not guess. But dread and uncertainty were not the only emotions she entertained as she waited through the rest of the day and night.

There was something else to consider, and that was a bouquet of violets he'd had sent up to her room. Though there had been no accompanying note, Juliet guessed they were intended to make amends for his remarks about her hair. If so, the gesture was at least partially successful. Juliet knew the Earl of Hartford rarely apologized, and yet he had done so in a particularly nice way in this instance.

None of Juliet's questions were settled for certain that night, as Christopher did not come home before she retired. Nor was there any sign of him at breakfast next morning, and Juliet was put to the task of trying to suppress visions of Leslie. Failing in the effort, she gave up the toast which of a sudden tasted like ash and went instead to the conservatory.

Arranging the flowers was the only duty as mistress of the house which Juliet had assumed. Morton, efficiently capable in every area, never thought of them, and Juliet had gladly taken the chore upon herself. That the butler approved her efforts, she knew, for the only time Morton's nose had twitched appreciatively in her presence was once when he had stopped to admire an arrangement she had just completed.

"What's this gibberish of Morton's about you having brought a street urchin home?"

Christopher's voice echoed sharply around the large open room, startling Juliet so that she broke in two the stem she was holding.

Putting aside the thought that he must be angry indeed, if he had not even taken the time to greet her, Juliet turned. Her hands tightened when she saw him. His coat of bottle green fit him to perfection, emphasizing the lean grace of his body. An emerald pin gleamed in the faultless knot of his cravat, and his breeches looked as if they had been molded to his thighs. Deliberately Juliet unclenched her hands. It was not the time to become distracted by her husband's looks. She would need all her wits about her if she were to satisfactorily explain young Ferdie's presence.

Resolutely facing the cool gleam in his eye, Juliet told him, "I brought the boy here after pulling him from a man who was beating him unmercifully."

"You did what?" Christopher asked too softly for comfort.

Knowing Christopher wanted an immediate answer, and not wishing to anger him further, Juliet described the events that had occurred the day before as collectedly as she was able.

When she finished, Christopher was regarding her with a thunderous frown. "Let me be very clear about this," he said, his eyes flashing. "In the midst of London, on a public thoroughfare, you leapt from your carriage, and taking no servant with you, went to hold a prolonged public debate with a street urchin's roguish master?"

"I know it was most outrageous of me, my lord," Juliet conceded, keeping her eyes upon her husband, though it was an effort. "I did act hastily, but the man was beating him unmercifully. I was afraid that if I did not act quickly enough, he might do the boy permanent injury."

"And you thought you might accomplish his rescue more handily than the postilions attending you, I take it?"

"I confess I did not think of them," Juliet admitted, flushing.

"Of course!" Christopher retorted, his voice clipped with impatience. "That explains everything. Nor did you think, I suppose, of the gossip such idiotic behavior would encourage. It may interest you to know that I was stopped on my way out of White's last evening and asked about the streetside altercation the man had heard my wife was involved in. I wonder, Juliet, how it feels to be notorious before you've even been introduced to society?"

Juliet bit her lip as it occurred to her that not all blows left bruises as visible as Ferdie's. "I have said my action was overhasty," she replied as calmly as she could. "And I sincerely regret that it caused talk. I cannot regret, however, thinking of the child's wellbeing. I could see blood spilling from his mouth even at a distance!"

The earl regarded his wife through narrowed eyes a moment, then said abruptly, "Whatever the circumstances, your precipitate action was foolish in the extreme. And now there is the question of what to do with the boy. We cannot have him here. He'll most likely steal anything he can and make life hellish for the other servants. If you want to keep him out of harm's way, send him to an orphanage."

"Oh no!" Juliet exclaimed. "My lord, you must know the child has been badly battered and will need mothering for quite a while."

It was the wrong choice of words.

In withering tones Christopher inquired. "And who, may I ask, will do the mothering?"

An odd spark lit in Juliet's wide eyes, but when she spoke, she only said evenly, "Wickam has been caring for the boy."

Christopher stared hard at her a moment, but insisted when he spoke that the boy could not remain.

Ignoring that searching look, Juliet, her hands clasped tightly together, did not give up. "Please, my lord," she implored. "You may be angry with me, but the child has done no wrong. If you would only look at him, you would know he has lived a most dreadful life. How can we, who have everything, turn him out to an almost certain death? He doesn't have to work in the house with the other servants, he can work in the stables. Please, at least have a look at him."

"There is no room in the stables, and besides, I doubt he has the slightest notion what to do with a horse."

Juliet shook her head. "One of the stablehands has fallen ill, and Wickam could use the help. I've talked to him, and if you approve, he is willing to teach the boy what he needs to know."

Christopher subjected Juliet to a long, unfathomable look. She did not shrink from the scrutiny, though she remembered suddenly how little he cared for her hair. Quickly she thrust the thought aside.

Her silvery head erect on her slim neck, her eyes dark with her concern, Juliet gazed at her husband, pleading for a worthless urchin as if he were of some importance in the scheme of things.

All at once, uttering an oath, Christopher strode to the bell pull. When Morton entered only an instant later, Christopher bade him bring Ferdie.

Hearing his order, Juliet sank to a seat. Somehow, and she had not the least idea how, she had won through. All she wanted was for Christopher to agree to talk to the boy, for she did not doubt that once he saw Ferdie, he would not be able to refuse him. No one could be so cold as to be unmoved by Ferdie's battered face.

When Morton ushered the pitifully thin child into the room, he hung back at the door as if he were afraid to enter.

Juliet rose at once and went to him, smiling reassuringly. "Ferdie, the earl wants to have a word with you. Don't be afraid, now, he won't hurt you," she said, taking his hand.

Holding tightly to her as she led him across the room, the boy turned his eyes fearfully in the earl's direction.

"What's your name, lad?" Christopher asked when they had reached him.

"Ferdie," the boy whispered. Christopher was not certain if he was so quiet because he was afraid or because his lip was so badly split he could not move it.

"And I understand you want to work at Hartford House?"

When the child did not answer immediately, Juliet intervened. "You must speak up, Ferdie, or the earl will not know how much you wish to stay."

Ferdie nodded then, glancing at Christopher. "Yes, yer lordship," he said.

"And you will do everything you are told?"

The child's head bobbed vigorously.

"Well, then, you may go out to Wickam in the stables. He will tell you what to do."

Ferdie nodded again, and Juliet smiled happily at him. "Go along, now," she bid him, releasing his hand. "Before dinner, though, come to me, Ferdie, I've more salve I'd like to put on your face."

Christopher watched as Ferdie looked shyly at Juliet, his eyes clearly revealing that he thought her some very special order of being, and nodded his understanding of her request.

When the boy had gone, Juliet, her gray eyes shining, looked up at her husband. "Thank you, my lord!" she said. "You'll not regret this."

"I certainly hope not," he responded in tones which indicated he was none too certain she was right. "But if you wish to thank me, Juliet, you may best do so by not again making a public spectacle of yourself. What you did today might be acceptable in your village, but it is not here in town."

"I understand, my lord. I really do. I was foolish in the extreme, I know. I was . . . overcome by Ferdie's predicament. I won't act so hastily again."

"I trust that you will not, as much for considerations of safety as to avoid gossip. It is entirely possible no one in the crowd around you would have lifted a finger to help you had you needed it."

Juliet shivered a little, remembering the voices which had exhorted Ferdie's master. "I do understand," she said, looking earnestly at Christopher. "There were many in the crowd actually in support of that man, though they could plainly see what he'd done to Ferdie."

Christopher nodded, as if satisfied that she did indeed understand the risk she'd run. "Well, if there are no more urchins to be saved, I'll let you return to your flowers," he said, turning to go.

"My lord?" Juliet reached toward Christopher, but let her hand fall before he turned around. "Speaking of flowers, thank you for the violets. They reminded me of the woods at home."

"I'm glad you liked them. I . . ." Uncharacteristically at a loss, Christopher paused to gather his thoughts and then said simply, "I spoke too sharply."

Juliet did not say "You did indeed," though she did think it. Instead she said quietly, "I appreciate the gesture. I like flowers very much."

"I know," her husband told her, a faint smile lifting his mouth. "Morton praises your way with them."

He left Juliet with that bit of surprising news to think on, but though she tried, she could not conjure an image of Morton singing her praises.

10

"You need a touch of this, my lady."

Juliet glanced from the pink paper in Trask's hand to the pier glass and realized that without assistance her cheeks would indeed look exceedingly pale.

For well over a week she had been feeling nauseated. It seemed that the merest whiff of some foods could turn her stomach against her. She knew what her queasy stomach meant. Her mother had had too many children for her not to know. Her monthly cycle, which had always been very regular, was late as well.

"Now, then, my lady, that looks better. You only need your shawl, and you will be ready."

Juliet's stomach muscles clenched but to her relief did not heave. Rising, she accepted the shawl from Trask and then turned to look at herself one last time.

Someone with tight silvery curls, dressed in an elegant ball gown of watered silk, stared back at her. Juliet tried to smile, her lips feeling dry and stiff as she made the effort. The thought of seeing Celeste Darnsby made the prospect of the evening ahead seem even worse.

With the excitement caused by her rescue of Ferdie and his appearance in the house, Juliet had almost forgotten Celeste's ball. It was Christopher who had reminded her.

He found her once again in the library curled up with her book. As she watched him stride into the room, Juliet was struck by the notion that even her husband's walk was arresting. He did not saunter or mince, the two alternate fashions she'd seen the dandies in Bond Street adopt. On the contrary, Christopher's stride was lithe and easy and assured. The earl crossing his domain.

"You did not tell me Celeste had called to take you to the park," he remarked after greeting her and seating himself in the chair across from her. There was more than idle curiosity in his eyes, and Juliet dropped her eyes from that penetrating look.

Spying her empty slippers, she uncurled her legs and placed her feet where they belonged. "I had forgotten it. There's been Ferdie to think of."

Christopher said nothing, and Juliet was forced to look up, having nothing else upon the floor to distract her.

"I wonder why she invited you," he asked, still regarding her closely.

Juliet, who knew very well why but was absolutely determined for reasons of pride that Christopher never know, forced herself to think only of the first part of their ride.

Her shoulders lifted slightly. "Most likely she wanted to show off her admirers. We met several."

There was one more long look, and then he said, "Her father stopped me at White's to say Celeste had been doing the polite and to remind me of her ball."

Christopher paused, grimacing slightly, and Juliet wondered how it could be that such a scowl did nothing to make him appear less handsome. "It will be a fusty affair, but I suppose we must attend. You do not know, of course, but there was talk of a match between Celeste and me. I suppose it is because Longacres marches with her father's land. If we do not make an appearance at her ball, the gossips will say it's because I threw her over. Absurd, of course, but there it is, and I shouldn't like to serve Lord Darnsby such a shabby turn. I've always liked him."

Juliet rather wished Christopher had not chosen to be so altruistic over this particular issue, but she did not think she could object. He might inquire too closely into why she should want to avoid Celeste.

Consequently she said she understood and fought to hide the dismay she felt when he told her it was time she was introduced to society, for people were curious about her.

Knowing his keen eyes would detect her discomposure, Juliet changed the subject entirely. "Allow me to thank you, my lord, for going to see how Ferdie was getting along. He was quite overcome to think the master would do such a thing for him. And your attention has made a difference with the other servants."

"Morton's nose is not so obviously out of joint, you mean?" Christopher asked, making Juliet laugh.

"I think he had hoped of glaring Ferdie away," she told him with a wry grin.

"Well, you must keep in mind that Morton has not quite your degree of compassion. I don't doubt you brought wounded birds home as a child to nurse."

When Juliet said with a great deal of surprise that she had in fact, Christopher's wry half-smile flashed and his eyebrow arched briefly as if to say "Just so." But when he spoke it was to say Ferdie seemed to be coming along well enough. It was not much, but like his visit to the stables, it meant a great deal to Juliet, for it confirmed that he had accepted her waif.

Now, because she had not said she could scarcely bear the sight of Celeste, Juliet had, as she climbed the Darnsby's stairs to reach the receiving line, the opportunity to remark how elegant Celeste looked in a white gauze dress and tiara of diamonds. Christopher greeted her with a kiss on the cheek, which was received with an arch titter, while Juliet only nodded coolly and got in return something that looked suspiciously like a smirk. There was little time to wonder at Celeste's odd expression, however, as Juliet was immediately passed along to her mother and father. Lady Darnsby was quite cool, but Lord Darnsby smiled broadly and told her Hal had spoken very highly of her. When Juliet had been assured Hal was doing very well in the army, Christopher took her arm, and they moved toward the ballroom.

Juliet had to curb a desire to lick her dry lips when the conversation of those close to the door halted as she and Christopher were announced. Their scrutiny turned her cheeks pink, but Christopher, evidently accustomed to such attention, only moved in a leisurely, assured way into the room.

Packed tightly with people, the ballroom was exceedingly warm. Juliet clenched her fist tightly to distract herself from a sudden bout of queasiness, but to no good. When even her palms began to feel clammy, she knew she could not stand much longer.

"I must sit down, please, my lord," she managed to say softly. Christopher, after taking a look at her, escorted her to a chair close to the windows and told her to wait while he fetched her a glass of punch.

Luckily there was a slight draft from the edge of the window to provide her some relief from the heat, and after a few minutes at least some of her queasiness had subsided.

"Lady Juliet?" a masculine voice inquired lightly.

Juliet looked up to see a pair of kind and familiar dark brown eyes looking down at her. It took her a moment, but then she recognized Lord Halsey, the man who had stood up with Christopher at their wedding.

"Lord Halsey, how good to see you," Juliet said, essaying a smile.

"I can't see how you or anyone else would want to see another person in this room. It is beastly crowded and infernally hot. One leads to the other, I suppose. Kit asked me to bring you this," Lord Halsey said, holding out a glass of punch. "He's been detained a moment. I say, do you mind if I sit down? They say hot air rises, and if so, I'd like to make myself as low as possible. Hard to do with my size, but I might as well try."

Lord Halsey's expression was quite baleful as he grumbled about the unpleasant atmosphere in the room. Juliet resolutely ignored any desire to ask why Christopher had been detained and allowed her companion's mutterings to bring a real smile to her eyes.

"There, that's better," he sighed when he had settled himself to his satisfaction. "And you look better too," he added, frankly inspecting Juliet.

"I was very warm," Juliet explained.

" 'Course you were!" he exclaimed, rounding upon her almost belligerently. "Opening the windows is the answer, but our foolish hostess is afraid of London's night airs. We'll all be fainting in our shoes as a result."

Casting Juliet a mischievous glance, Lord Halsey brought out a scented handkerchief and began to wave it languidly to and fro before them.

"Not ruffled by the breeze are you?" he inquired with exaggerated politeness, his large, rather solemn brown eyes twinkling.

Juliet giggled, as she was meant to do, and said that she was not at all ruffled, that in fact the Halsey zephyr felt quite delightful.

It was Lord Halsey's turn to laugh.

"I must beg your pardon for not having come to call upon you, Lady Juliet," he said after a moment. "I hope you will not think that I did not care to. I have been away from town since just after your wedding. My father has fallen ill."

"I am sorry to hear it, Lord Halsey," Juliet exclaimed at once. "I hope he is not very ill."

"I fear he is. The doctor has given us little hope he will live much longer."

"You have all my sympathies, Lord Halsey. A parent's death must be very difficult."

"It is. Not only do I like the old fellow, I fear I am not at all ready to fall into his shoes. I am very likely to make a mess of being an earl."

"You must not refine upon it," Juliet assured him. "We all hold our parents in high esteem and fear we will not be worthy of their example."

Tony's sleepy eyes flashed Juliet a sharp look. To himself he thought: So you are not all pretty eyes. Aloud he spoke more politely: "That is perhaps the most astute thing anyone has said to me this evening, Lady Juliet. It is worth roasting myself in this oven just to know Kit's wife is no silly chit."

"You are teasing me!" Juliet accused with a light laugh, for she was uncertain what to make of Lord Halsey's praise.

"I am not, I assure you," Tony replied. "But I forget that, being unfamiliar with society, you are not likely to know just how many silly chits there are. And silly bucks. Have you been presented to Whiton, by any chance? He looks to be coming our way."

When Juliet looked up, she saw Tony was right. The young dandy she had met so briefly in the park was indeed coming in their direction. He was quite an eyeful, dressed in a lilac coat of superfine and dazzling yellow waistcoat which sported two ruby pins, assorted chains, fobs, and a quizzing glass.

"Looks like a damn jeweler," Tony whispered. "Begging your pardon, of course."

Juliet had no time to reply, though her eyes were dancing as Lord Whiton bowed as low as his starched neckcloth would allow. In a mincing voice he asked if she wished to dance, and though she had little wish to stand up with such a fop, Juliet accepted his invitation. It was a dance, she reasoned, and she had always liked to dance.

She had reckoned without the heat, however. On the floor, it attacked her again. Gritting her teeth, Juliet forced herself through the steps of the country dance, literally willing herself not to faint or otherwise embarrass herself.

At the dance's end, she knew she could not continue without something to drink and asked Lord Whiton if he would be kind enough to get her some punch.

"The refreshment table is just through here, Lady Juliet, if you would care to accompany me?" the young man told her, pointing to the archway behind them, and Juliet agreed at once, thinking it would be cooler there.

The moment she entered the large alcove with its

laden table, Juliet caught sight of a couple standing close together at the far end near the windows where they were out of sight of the ballroom.

Arrested in mid-step, Juliet recognized Christopher and the dark-haired beauty he had been riding with in the park. Christopher's golden head was inclined slightly as he listened to the woman, who was not smiling now. Indeed she seemed angry, for her breast was heaving with emotion.

Involuntarily Juliet noted how daring the woman's décolettage was, and how perfectly her natural endowments swelled above it. Nor was the woman afraid to attract attention there. The opposite, in fact, for she wore a breathtaking emerald necklace which instantly caught the eye.

Juliet saw Christopher's eyes dip to that neckline as he said something with a lazy grin to the woman. The beauty stopped talking immediately. Her expression altering completely, she laughed, a throaty, sensual laugh.

The sound of it seemed to awaken Juliet, sending her headlong from the room with no thought at all for Lord Whiton. She only knew she could not have stood it if they had looked up and seen her watching them.

Without stopping, Juliet made her way around the ballroom. She needed a quiet place to gather her resources, and the only one that came to mind was the ladies' retiring room. As she limply made her way in the direction a footman indicated, the scene she had witnessed replayed itself in her mind. Knowing it was Christopher's suggestive glance at his mistress's bared bosom which made her feel the sickest, Juliet clenched her fist so tightly she hurt her palm and damned herself for a fool.

At her destination there were several ladies repairing the damages an evening of dancing had done to their toilettes. Grateful that she knew none of them, she found a seat removed from their chatter and breathed deeply of the cooler air.

Beginning to feel better, Juliet wondered what she would do. She could not stay where she was all evening, and yet she had little desire to return to the ballroom, not least of all because it was so warm. She had just decided she would wait where she was a little while yet, when the door swung open.

All conversation stopped, and Juliet saw two ladies glance from the newcomer to her with strange expressions. Juliet's stomach, when she looked to see who it was, rolled violently. There, her lush figure outlined in the doorway, was Christopher's mistress.

She was just as beautiful at close range as at a distance. Her black hair, dressed in a mass of luxuriant curls, gleamed richly in the candlelight. Her skin was tinted a perfect rosy pink, and her eyes, slanted as Juliet had noted in the park, were a shade of green almost exactly the same color as her emeralds.

Cold dread settled over Juliet when she realized those bold eyes were sweeping over her derisively.

"Lady Juliet St. Charles?" the woman demanded, stalking toward her.

Juliet nodded, thinking she knew just how a mouse must feel when a large sleek cat sights it.

"I don't believe we've met. I am Leslie Chester-Headley."

There were thousands of polite answers, but Juliet could not think of even one. The malevolent look in Leslie Chester-Headley's green eyes did not allow for much courtesy.

"I see," was all Juliet said.

"If I may say so, Lady Juliet, you don't look very well," the beauty observed contemptuously. "Could it be that those betting on an early heir will be winners? But then, how else could a nameless chit like you have gotten Kit except by using a shabby trick like getting yourself with child?" Smiling triumphantly, she fingered her necklace. "Tell me, Lady Juliet, do you like my emeralds? Your husband gave them to me, you know!"

While Leslie Chester-Headley's insults were still echoing around the intensely still room, a loud, resounding crack startled the listeners. Before she knew what she was doing, before she could think to stop herself,

72

Juliet's hand came up and struck out at the jeering face above her.

Breathless, Juliet stared stunned at the white mark her hand had left, and then watched as the woman's red mouth dropped open in astonishment.

That incredulous look would warm Juliet later, but at the time she wanted only to escape the ugly scene. With surprising strength she pushed Christopher's mistress aside and, keenly aware of the avid interest gleaming in the other ladies' eyes, rushed from the room.

She did not stop to look for Christopher. Not only was another confrontation with his mistress too likely, but also Christopher himself was, for Juliet, too closely associated with the ugly scene she had just left. At the moment, Juliet wanted no reminders at all of the hateful woman.

It seemed an eternity, but in fact it was only a few minutes before her carriage arrived, and Juliet was in it, allowing the night air to cool her cheeks.

Remembering how Christopher could look when he was angry, she pressed a shaky hand to her head. That he would be angry, she knew with certainty. Slapping even the most taunting face was assuredly not accepted behavior for a countess. And to have done so in public . . .

11

When she was alone in her room after dismissing Trask and her overly curious eyes, Juliet sat down before the fire to wait. That Christopher would come, she had no doubt. Her only uncertainty was when, that night or the next day. She thought it quite possible that before he came to deal with her, he would choose to soothe his mistress's outrage. Juliet rather hoped so. Likely his anger would be less heated after a night with her.

But he did not go to Leslie's first. He came home. After only half an hour, onimously soon, Juliet heard a stir in the front hallway. The master had returned.

Juliet arose at once and went to stand with her back to the fire, facing the door. When it was flung open, she felt as braced as she would ever be for her husband's wrath.

It took Christopher only a moment to see her. With a sharp bang he closed the door behind him, his narrowed eyes never leaving her.

"You know, Juliet," he began in a dangerously contained voice when he had stalked across the room to stand so closely before her that she was forced to tilt her head back to see him, "I find it difficult to think how we in polite society entertained ourselves before you arrived. Should it be of interest to you, you may rest assured you are now the talk of the town. Of course people were curious about you before. First, there was your precipitate marriage, and then there were the rumors that you had been involved in a

74

public brawl. But let me assure you, all that was as nothing to this."

Clenching her fists tightly, Juliet just kept herself from flinching. "Is this polite society you speak of the same society which has placed bets on whether or not I am with child?" Juliet asked steadily, her gray eyes holding his caustic gaze.

Christopher's jaw tightened, though whether his anger was directed more at her or those she referred to, Juliet did not know. "There are young pups who will bet on whether or not the next horse to come around a corner will be a black or a roan," he snapped, clarifying the question as to who had roused his anger. "They do not concern us. What does concern us is that you have made a public spectacle of yourself again!"

Juliet's eyes flashed. The unbearably humiliating scene had been caused by his mistress, not by her. "I suppose if you had been called little better than a harlot you would have turned the other cheek, my lord? Forgive me for doubting it!" she cried, too angry now to care how angry she made him.

It was as well she did not care, for his eyes seemed to blaze with his anger as he informed her wrathfully, "We are not discussing the conduct acceptable for a man, we are discussing the conduct appropriate to a countess!"

"I see!" Juliet retorted equally furiously. "And I suppose it is the thing for an earl to dally with his mistress before his wife and indeed all society's eyes? Or for a mistress to flaunt her recently acquired necklace? Why in the name of all decency did you take me there? You must have known it would be an impossible situation!"

Juliet swung away suddenly. Her eyes had filled with tears, and to hide them she gazed unseeing into the fire.

Because she was not looking, she did not see the rigid anger drain from her husband's expression. Indeed he was now feeling something closer to guilt than anger. It was Celeste who'd told him Juliet had caused a scene by slapping Leslie, and her story had thrown

75

him into such a fit of anger, he'd not even stopped to question it. But now, when he did, he knew Juliet was not the sort of person to precipitate such a scene, while Leslie certainly was.

"I did not know Leslie would be attending," he said truthfully. "I would never have taken you had I known."

Had Juliet turned to him then, with her tears plainly shining in her eyes, and asked what was to be done, the course of their interview and perhaps even the next several months might have been very different. But she did not even think to turn to her husband. She still blamed him too much for the dreadful scene she'd endured.

Her back still to him, Juliet muttered angrily that he could have thought to take her away when he had realized Leslie was present. "Instead you fobbed me off on Lord Halsey," she told him.

"That is enough!" Christopher growled. "I did not fob you off on anyone. Tony went to sit with you because he likes you. As to not whisking you away, I thought it would cause less talk if Leslie left, not you. She had agreed to leave when she stopped off at the retiring room."

Remembering the way Christopher had inspected Leslie's bared bosom, Juliet could well guess how he'd persuaded her to leave. The thought made her bite her lip and left her silent.

Looking at his wife's back, which remained stiff although he had condescended so far as to explain his actions, something he'd not done since he was seven years of age, Christopher experienced another burst of anger. She was not being reasonable! He'd done everything he could to right the situation at the Darnsbys'. It was not his fault things had not gone as they should, and he would be damned if he would be made to feel to blame.

It was time he informed her of the decision he'd made coming home. It still seemed a sound one. "You will have to go away, Juliet," he told her, making her jerk around to look at him.

"Away?" she echoed him dumbly.

Christopher steeled himself against his wife's inordinately eloquent eyes. If he did not hold the line with her now, he felt he'd be giving in to her the rest of his life. Besides, it was as much for her sake as for his that she must go.

"Until the talk dies down, it will be best if you go to Hartford Hall. Some might brazen out the gossip, but I don't think you'd enjoy doing that, particularly now."

Particularly now! Her eyes widened, Juliet searched Christopher's expression. He knew she was with child, it was there in his eyes. But what he thought of it, she could not tell.

Agitated, Juliet walked to the window, her thoughts racing. He was right, actually. She would detest having to face people who had thought the worst of her before they'd even met her. And it would be worse now that she was with child just as they'd predicted.

Turning around at last, Juliet found Christoipher was watching her, his eyes half-closed and unreadable. "I should like to go to my home," she told him.

Christopher did not pause long to consider her request. "Lincolnshire is your home now," he reminded her, shaking his head. "Besides, a St. Charles is always born on St. Charles land. It has been so for hundreds of years, and my child will be no exception."

"But it is so far!" Juliet protested.

"You needn't look as if it's the end of the world. It's quite civilized, I assure you."

Juliet's eyes were fixed on Christopher as she tried to fathom the sort of person who would send her to a strange place alone and without friends to have her first child.

Something of her desperation must have communicated itself to him, for he turned abruptly away from her and went to kick angrily at a log on the fire. A shower of sparks cascaded into the room.

It was some time before he spoke again, but when he did his voice had lost its cutting edge. "If you are ever to join society, we must behave somewhat normally. There is enough talk and speculation now. It will seem quite natural that you should go to the Hall for your confinement. If you went to your mother's, your place as my wife would be questioned."

Juliet drew a deep, unsteady breath. She could see it was pointless to argue with him. As her husband there was nothing to prevent him from forcing her to do his bidding. "When?" she asked simply.

"A day should be enough time to pack. You will leave on the day after tomorrow."

Juliet bowed her head, uncomfortably reminding Christopher of a prisoner on the block, but when she looked up a moment later there was nothing submissive in her expression. "Very well, I shall do as you say," she told him coolly. "But I should like Ferdie to come with me, if he is willing. I think his bruises will heal more quickly in the country air." And he'll be a friendly face, she added to herself.

When he had told her he had no objection to her request, Christopher left. Alone with her whirling thoughts, Juliet was able to fasten on only one. Her husband had not said how he felt about their child. It was possible that he had not had time to determine what he thought, but Juliet, not surprisingly, thought it a great deal more likely that he found the idea so unpalatable he could not discuss it.

If that were so, then her departure was for the best, she decided. She would simply have to do her utmost to make a home for herself and her child in Lincolnshire, where they would both be safely removed from Christopher's unreasonable temper.

10

"Never say you are going out in this weather, my lady! Why, I've never heard of such a thing!"

"I shall be very careful, Mrs. S., I promise." Juliet smiled fondly at Hartford Hall's housekeeper. "The babe won't feel the cold, you know, and I shall ask Molly to help me. I do so want to see Ferdie's colt."

Mrs. Stokes clucked unhappily and shook her gray head. "Well, if you must go, you shall need a shawl over that pelisse. You wait right here while I fetch it. That Sally would let you out with so little covering you'd catch your death. . ."

Juliet, whose heavy pelisse was more than adequate to ward off even the severe January chill, smiled to herself as she watched the plump, elderly woman hurry away out of sight. How absurd all her worries about coming to live alone among strangers in Lincolnshire seemed at this remove.

Almost before her carriage had rolled to a halt, Mrs. Stokes had puffed up to take her hand in a warm clasp. "You darling girl," she had exclaimed, peering closely at Juliet's wan face. "You do look peaked after your journey, and I don't doubt you need your bed. Tomorrow'll be good enough for you to meet the staff."

The welcome and the concern had been the same ever since. Unable to have children of her own, Mrs. Stokes took everyone on the estate under her ample wing, and Juliet was only one of her chicks, albeit her most prized. It made no matter that Juliet was her ladyship, Mrs. Stokes had grown up in service to the St. Charles family, and she considered it her duty to cosset, advise, and scold milady as she needed it.

"Now, then, that should be better." Mrs. Stokes nodded, satisfied as Juliet knotted the woolen scarf she had brought.

"You are a great dear to worry so over me," Juliet said, making Mrs. Stokes's round cheeks turn pink. Then as she turned to leave, Juliet added, "By the by, if that was indeed Mr. Briding I saw coming up the drive, please ask Mr. S. to tell him I am not able to receive. It won't be too far from the truth, after all, for I shall be in the stables by then."

Mrs. Stokes found her husband, butler at the Hall for over twenty years, in the vast wood-paneled Elizabethan entry hall. After having relayed the message concerning Mr. Briding, she added, "And is that not like her ladyship to worry whether something is true or not, Mr. Stokes?" Not, as usual, expecting an answer, Mrs. Stokes continued in her knowing way. "She is as good and kind as they come. It's not likely many other tenants had extra rations of meat sent to them as well as wheat and barley just because the winter's been bitter cold. Why, she even sat until the midwife came with that Molly Barker who has no husband to give his name to her babe." Mrs. Stokes shook her head. "She's rare brave, too. Never once complaining, that his lordship hasn't come, and her so near her time. It pains me, he could be so hardhearted. I do wonder what's kept him!"

The countess's lonely arrival had been and still was a topic of intense speculation among the servants. It could only indicate, they all agreed, that her ladyship had fallen out of favor with the earl. And in the beginning, thinking to take their cue from the master, they had, with the exception of Mr. and Mrs. Stokes, been slow to accept Juliet as their mistress. Nor had it helped her case with them that she should be so young.

It was not until late summer that Mr. Stokes, his shrewd old eyes twinkling, had been able to say to his wife, "You ought to see the way Betty and Mary are wearing their arms out with polishing because her ladyship smiled and said she had never seen the tables gleam so."

"She's got the staff eatin' out of her hand," his wife had agreed, beaming with an almost maternal pride. "Her ladyship might only be a slip of a lass, but she's wise as can be about people. She's fair, but firm, Mr. Stokes. Of course, havin' the sweetest smile in Lincolnshire has been no hurt, either."

In the hallway Mr. Stokes turned to look out the window at the leaden skies. "Perhaps it's this icy weather that's keeping his lordship away," he said reassuringly. "I don't doubt he'll be here soon." When his wife had gone out of earshot, he added far less diplomatically, "Leastways he should be, with the lass likely to be in childbed by tonight."

Juliet, holding tightly to Molly Barker's strong arm, was wondering if the ice would prevent her getting to the stable. The going was not easy, especially in her state, but she had little desire to go back. If she did, she would run into Jonathan Briding.

Jonathan and his two sisters, Harriet and Becky, had been her first visitors at the Hall, and over the months Juliet had continued to welcome their lively company. Indeed, she had enjoyed them enough that when Jonathan, who fancied himself an artist, had asked to paint her portrait, she had agreed readily.

And in the beginning the sittings had been enjoyable enough, for Becky and Harriet came to entertain her while their brother worked. As more and more sittings were required, however, Juliet began to fret a little over what she'd agreed to, and that fretting had intensified into something close to alarm when Jonathan in his rather petulant way had decreed his sisters could no longer accompany him. "Their chatter is too, too distracting," he had said.

Juliet had sat twice for the young man since, and could not like it, for his manner toward her had become uncomfortably warm without his sisters present to moderate his behavior. Finally, with her advanced condition as an excuse, she had indefinitely suspended their sessions altogether.

"My lady, you've come!" The piping voice which interrupted her thoughts was Ferdie's. "What a sight the colt is, Lady Juliet! You'll be ever so glad you came to see him. Why, he can't hardly stand up. I never saw anything like it when he was born, his mother had—"

"Hold there, lad, quit pulling so!" Molly called.

"Slow down, Ferdie," Juliet said at the same time, smiling down at the boy. "I am a little too large to be hurried."

Instantly the boy slowed his pace and ducked his head. "Sorry, my lady. He's just that fine!"

Juliet grinned at the child's enthusiasm. Sometimes she had to search to recall the fearful, emaciated, battered boy she had found in London. With the assistance of Mrs. Stokes's vast amounts of food and sympathy Ferdie had changed completely. His face had filled out, losing its pinched look entirely, while his red hair actually had a shine to it now. Quite the best of all, his blue eyes looked out at the world with confidence and excitement.

Ferdie was the only person, other than the coachman and the outriders, who had accompanied Juliet north. Trask had had little inclination to go to Linsolnshire, and Juliet had had even less to take her. Mrs. Stokes's niece, Sally, served as Juliet's personal maid now and was as talkative and bright as Trask had been dour and silent.

"Here he is!" Ferdie pointed proudly to the wobbly-legged colt nuzzling at his dam's belly.

Juliet grinned at the colt's unsteady stance, as did Molly; then, looking at the head groom, O'Malley, Juliet asked, "Is the mother well?"

"Aye, my lady." The dark-haired Irishman nodded. "They're both doin' fine."

O'Malley's green eyes slid to Molly, then quickly looked away, and he moved abruptly to pitchfork a pile of hay into the horse's stall with more force than Juliet thought was strictly necessary. Nor, though Juliet's attention was on the colt, did it escape her that Molly's round cheeks had turned suspiciously pink. Smiling to herself, Juliet thought it likely Molly's baby might have an Irishman's last name soon enough.

"Well! I cannot believe my eyes. You really are here with the ice thick as can be on the walk!"

A broad smile appeared on Juliet's face as she turned to greet the newcomer to the stables. "You are sounding more like Mrs. Stokes every day, Lutetia," she laughed. A strangled sound issued from Molly, who knew, since the arrival of her child, exactly how smothering Mrs. Stokes and her advice could be.

Lutetia Danforth, her small wrinkled face wreathed in a smile, kissed Juliet and ignored Molly's twitching mouth.

"So you've a new colt, Ferdie," she greeted the lad who was sitting on the rail of the stall, oblivious of everything but the wonder before him.

"Aye, my lady." He grinned over his shoulder. "She's a beauty, ain't she?"

Juliet watched the two with a faint smile on her lips. Unless one knew, it would have been hard to tell that the small woman with the unfashionably long pelisse and the rather muddy boots was in fact the Duchesss of Crewe. Lutetia Danforth rarely stood on ceremony.

On the day when they had met, Juliet had been exploring the estate in her dogcart. Spying a riderless horse beside a small stream, she had investigated. To her amazement, when she called, a small wizened woman with sparkling black eyes emerged from the bushes below.

"I'm after these reeds," the apparition announced in an oddly raspy voice. "They're quite rare in these parts. I want them for my garden. You don't mind, do you?"

Juliet had, of course, said no, all the while taking in the woman's old flat bonnet, muddy shoes, and bedraggled long skirt. Her jacket, Juliet noted, actually had a hole at the elbow.

"Lutetia," the woman said when she regained the bank. "Lutetia Danforth," she added, holding out an elegant if grubby hand. "You must be the new countess."

"Yes, I am Juliet St. Charles. Do you live close by?" Juliet inquired.

"At Crewe Cottage," Lutetia Danforth said, waving her hand toward the east. "It's only a few miles away. I'm redoing the stream garden and have had my eye on these plants for an age."

It was then it dawned upon Juliet that the disreputable-looking woman was none other than the Duchess of Crewe, for she knew Crewe Cottage was a house of some twenty rooms situated on an estate owned by the Duke of Crewe. Mrs. Stokes had told her that the duke and duchess lived much of the year in London or on their principal estate in Hampshire, but in the late summer they were accustomed to coming north to play at being rustic in their "cottage."

As she took in the other woman's appearance, a slow, deep smile formed on Juliet's face. Here was a person after her own heart, she thought, and she had been right.

Possessed of a lively mind, the duchess was outrageously outspoken and her forthright manner never failed to either amuse or instruct Juliet, and sometimes both. With the greatest affection, Ronald Danforth, whom Juliet had come to like almost as well, called his wife "the old horn," making Juliet giggle over the aptness of the nickname. Not only did the duchess's voice sound like an old horn, but also her opinions were almost always stated with the unequivocal quality of that instrument.

"Oh!" Juliet said aloud, all thoughts of the past sent flying by the onset of a sudden cramp in her lower back.

"It's your time!" Lutetia crowed excitedly. "Oh, I am glad I came! I was so afraid you wouldn't send for me, you are such a silly chit about imposing."

"So glad I could accommodate you, my dear," Juliet was able to respond in a credibly dry tone as the cramp receded. Slowly she straightened and found that Ferdie, O'Malley, and Molly were looking at her with apprehension evident in their wide eyes.

"O'Malley!" The duchess took charge as Juliet felt the onset of another rippling in her abdomen. "I think it would be best if you carried your mistress to her room. Molly, bustle off and get Mrs. Lyttle sent for, and, Ferdie, you go tell Cook to put on hot water. And please don't look so pulled, child. Your precious Lady Juliet will do just fine."

Twenty hours later Lutetia Danforth was looking at Juliet with a pulled face of her own. The baby was turned the wrong way, according to Mrs. Lyttle, and though Juliet was laboring mightily, it would not come. Finally, after another three grueling hours had passed, Lutetia insisted the midwife try to turn the child.

"But the cord may wrap around and kill the babe," Mrs. Lyttle protested. "I dare not take the chance without his lordship bein' here to agree."

"Don't be a fool!" the duchess blasted her sharply. She frowned at the dark hollows which were Juliet's eyes and the gray quality of her skin. "The girl will die, Lyttle, if you don't do it. I'll take the responsibility. We'll lose 'em both, else."

The procedure was not without pain, and as Mrs. Lyttle wrenched the baby by the shoulder, Juliet screamed.

Mr. Stokes, pacing the hallway outside her door like a nervous father, heard it and paled. Mrs. Stokes collapsed upon a chair moaning out loud.

But then, when things seemed at their worst, Mr. Stokes, who had taken a tight hold of his wife's hand, heard what he had been waiting so anxiously to hear.

"It's a boy!" the duchess cried out, and immediately a lusty wailing filled the air.

13

The duchess's crochet needle seemed to possess a mind of its own as it flashed wickedly in and out of the work in her lap. Certainly she was not paying it the least attention, preferring instead to watch with a fond smile the two people playing chess just across from her.

Her husband's bushy white eyebrows were drawn together as he frowned at the ivory figures on the board before him, while Juliet, his opponent, regarded the board with a countenance which was in contrast serene.

"You've done it, all right." His brown eyes twinkling, the duke shook his head. "You'd think a new mother just coming into the best years of her life would be more accommodating to an old man, but there it is. You younger generation, you're all attack and no diplomacy."

"Saints alive, spare us from Crewe conceding defeat, it is such a tedious sight!" the duchess admonished. "You know very well you enjoy playing Juliet because she is your match, and you had best tell her so, my dear, lest she think you an old bear."

The duke made a mischievous face at Juliet, who giggled conspiratorially, but he did rise and lift her hand to his lips.

"That for you, my dear." He smiled with great affection. "Not only have you given us a darling boy to bounce on our knees, but you have kept your wits about you in the process. It was a memorable match, and I am much obliged."

Juliet squeezed his hand in return, her eyes gleaming fondly. "You are too kind, your grace, you put me to the blush. I know of no more enjoyable way to celebrate my return to the land of the living."

"A premature return, I might point out," grumped the duchess. "Five days' rest after your ordeal is scarcely enough. We are here only because you threatened to invite the Bridings over for dinner, and I believed Jonathan's adoration would be more tiring than Crewe's chess game."

"Lutetia!" Juliet wailed.

"No point denyin' Jonathan has a *tendre* for you." Lutetia's black eyes looked the picture of complacency. "Did he or did he not go all the way to Lincoln for hothouse roses simply because he knew you adored roses?"

The man standing in the open doorway could not hear what was being said among the members of the little group clustered so cozily around the fire, but his eyebrows arched faintly as he took in the charming scene they presented.

As they took the last of their tea, the duchess was saying something outrageous enough to bring a faint line of color to the cheeks of the young woman seated on the rosewood couch. She did not let Lutetia discomfit her too dreadfully, however, for she quickly made some response which was apt enough to cause the others to laugh.

The eyes of the man in the doorway did not leave the young woman. She was not as he'd expected she would be. Her eyes were sparkling as she bantered with Lutetia and subsequently acknowledged some remark of Ronald's, and though paler than when he'd last seen her, her face was alive with her laughter, its warmth enough to enchant even the most critical of beholders.

But it was not only the young woman's mood which surprised him. Her entire manner had changed in a subtle way that he decided after a moment had to do with the new, confident tilt of her head on her slender neck. He watched as she rose to gather up a costly silk

87

shawl and place it round her shoulders. Like the tilt of her head, her movements bespoke a newfound assurance.

Of course, he reminded himself, she was a mother now. The thought made him shift slightly, and turning to say something to Crewe, she caught the blur of his movement.

"My lord!" Juliet gasped. Her astonishment could not have been greater. She actually blinked and looked again.

And then her pulse began to race. It was indeed her husband, looking, though he must just have come from out-of-doors, complete to a turn. There was not a wrinkle in his coat of blue superfine, and his cravat, though casually tied, was faultless. Only his sun-streaked hair was a trifle wind-tossed. A lock of it had fallen onto his brow just above his eyes.

She had almost forgotten how intense their color was. And how powerful they could be when they held one, as they did her now, in a searching gaze.

As Christopher lounged there in the doorway, his eyes seeming to penetrate her mind, Juliet had the fleeting impression that some dangerous, tawny jungle cat threatened the safe haven of her private sitting room.

"Kit!" the duke cried, reminding Juliet there were other people in the room. "Welcome home, lad. You'll be pleased to know you've a deuced handsome son. My congratulations."

"Thank you, Ronald." Christopher's gaze shifted to the duke as he uncoiled his body and came into the room. "You are looking fit," he continued, smiling. "It must be the care your good wife is giving you. Lutetia"—Christopher turned his smile upon the duchess—"I hope I find you in your usual form?" he inquired, saluting her hand lightly with his lips.

Lutetia did not smile. "You do," she said, more than a touch of asperity in her tone. "And I am glad to see London loosed its talons long enough that you could come to see your wife and child. Not that they've missed you overmuch, I daresay. It's just good form."

88

Juliet narrowly missed gasping aloud, but Christopher responded to Lutetia's outrageous welcome with an amused gleam in his eyes. "You have reassured me, Lutetia. Your wit is sharp as always."

The duchess's lips twitched, proving Christopher's smile had not lost all of its power. "Naughty boy!" she scolded, playfully tapping his arm with her needle. "You're too handsome for any woman's good."

Christopher made some answer which Juliet did not hear. Her heart was pounding too heavily. His so very blue eyes were turning back to her now.

"I hope I find you well, Juliet?" he asked, raising her fingers to his lips.

Flustered, because though he had greeted Lutetia thus, she had not expected it, Juliet flushed, but her voice when she spoke was remarkably steady. "I am fine, my lord. And your—"

"Fine!" Lutetia rasped indignantly. "Your wife had a dreadful time delivering your son, Christopher St. Charles, and if she won't tell you so, I will."

"Lutetia!" Juliet's tone was stern. "I concede that I had a difficult delivery, but I am, now, five days later, well over it. You and Mrs. S. must not continue to enact a Cheltenham Tragedy over me, I beg you."

"Cheltenham Tragedy, indeed! We thought we might lose you. And I am going to enlist Kit to look after you. Mrs. Stokes, nay the entire staff, are so much putty in your hands. They'll never be able to stop you when you try to do more than you should. Kit, you will see to her, won't you?" Lutetia turned her snapping black eyes upon Christopher. "This girl's very special to me."

There was an infinitesimal pause while Christopher's gaze flicked from Lutetia to Juliet, and then he bowed toward Lutetia.

"I shall do my best, your grace."

Ronald rose then and stretched his hand toward his wife. "My dear, I believe that it is time we go. My old bones tell me they are ready for their bed."

His expression was bland, but his wife from long experience knew not to argue. "Don't move an inch, my love," she exhorted Juliet as she came to kiss her cheek. "There's no need for you to bestir yourself. I shall look in on you tomorrow."

"I shall be sorely affronted if you do not come to chide me, Lutetia," she said, smiling. "And I hope you will accept a rematch, your grace?"

"Of course, my dear. Honor as well as pleasure is at stake, after all," he assured her with a smile. Then, after bidding Christopher good night, he herded his wife from the room.

When they had gone, an awkward silence fell. As Christopher walked to the fire to nudge a log with his toe, Juliet watched him, still scarcely able to believe it was really he.

Did he not believe in the mails? He'd written to her only twice since she'd left London. Once to tell her the name he wanted for his son, and the other time on estate business. Neither letter had mentioned a trip north.

Juliet squared her shoulders. However unexpected his arrival might be, he was entitled to hospitality. "You must be in need of some refreshment after your journey, my lord. Is Mrs. Stokes seeing to it?"

The sound of her voice brought his golden head around. "Mrs. Stokes consented, after some grumbling, to bring me supper. It would seem she shares Lutetia's opinion that I am a little late in arriving."

But you evidently do not believe so, Juliet thought. Aloud she dismissed the matter indifferently. "They both like to mother me."

"You have fared well, then?"

Juliet inclined her head gracefully. "I hope my reports reflected that?" She had written to him dutifully once a month.

"Hmm," Christopher acknowledged, his eyes not leaving her. "Was the childbirth as difficult as both the Stokeses and Lutetia have taken such care to inform me?"

Juliet had been her own mistress only a while, but it had been long enough for her to resent immediately what she regarded as a patronizing tone. "I cannot remember, my lord," she informed him coolly. "Through some trick of the mind, I find I can remember little of that day. Except for Charles, of course," she added, a quick smile animating her features. "Would you care to see him?"

"He is asleep?"

When Juliet nodded, Christopher shook his head, "Then I shall not risk offending Mrs. Stokes by being late. She said my collation would be ready in a trice."

A silence fell between them then. Juliet wanted to ask how long he would be staying, but knew the question would be unforgivably rude. It was his house, after all.

"Ronald and Lutetia come often?"

Tension had begun to creep into the silence, and Juliet, relieved to have it broken, nodded. "Lutetia does. His grace comes once or twice a week to play chess."

"Does he allow you to win?" Christopher asked in an idle way which tested Juliet's patience.

"No, indeed he does not," she said curtly. "I win on my own merits."

Christopher's brow lifted, his obvious surprise further trying Juliet's forbearance. "Crewe is quite good, as I recall," he remarked.

Juliet looked up swiftly enough to catch a suggestion of laughter lurking in her husband's eyes. It emboldened her to reply crisply, "As am I," with only the faintest of grins.

When Christopher chuckled, his eyes as they remained upon her reflecting a half-smile, Juliet could feel her cheeks color. Uncomfortable with such close scrutiny, she cast about for some way to divert him, and asked how his journey had been, her voice sounding only a little breathless.

Christopher shrugged. "Tedious as always," he said indifferently; and then, his eyes traveling to the table beside her, he asked, "Did Lutetia bring you those roses? She must have been put to a great effort to come by them now."

"No." Juliet's eyes fell to the dozen long-stemmed

red roses gracing the table at her side. "No, the Bridings sent them," she said after a moment, still looking at the roses and not at her husband.

Her gaze averted, Juliet did not see how curiously he eyed the light blush which suffused her cheeks. He began to speak, but a knock at the door interrupted him.

It was Mr. Stokes, and when Christopher had departed with him, Juliet rose to go closer to the fire.

She had imagined Christopher's arrival a thousand times, but of course the reality was little like her fancies. Juliet wrapped her shawl about her more tightly. He had looked at her so intently in that moment when she'd first caught sight of him, she'd felt an almost physical release when he'd turned his attention to Ronald.

She wondered what he had learned, but before she could hazard a guess, her mind had fastened on how cool his tone had been when he'd mentioned Charlie's birth. Perhaps he was only feeling guilty over not having been present, but he could at least have said he was glad to have a son and heir! As it was, Juliet still had no idea how he felt about having a child.

But as always with Christopher, things were not simple. Only a few moments later, when he had teased her about the chess, she'd felt she might drown in his, for once, warm gaze.

"Blast and damn him!" she swore as Robbie had once taught her to do. "He's only come to cut up my peace."

Squeezing her eyes shut, Juliet let herself recall how angry and unforgiving he'd been the last time she'd seen him, though he bore some of the responsibility for her disastrous first outing in society. It was not the only time he'd made her feel a foolish, wayward girl.

She straightened her shoulders. Things were different now. She had birthed a child and successfully run an estate since then. And he was meeting her on ground she had made her own. "I'll let him neither slip under my guard nor browbeat me again," she told herself fiercely. "I shall be as calm and collected as possible, and when he leaves, as he surely will, I shall happily wave farewell."

"My lady?" It was Sally at the door, Charlie in her arms. "I thought I heard voices," she said, looking around the room.

Juliet smiled sheepishly. "Just me, Sally, giving myself a stern talking-to," she said, extending her arms for her son.

"Master Charlie was just awakening, my lady, and I thought to bring him before he started crying for you."

"Thank you, Sally, you're very good to him."

Sally's cheeks were pink as she let herself out of the room, thinking to herself that in truth it was her ladyship who was good to her son. Most noble ladies had wet nurses for their children, but Lady Juliet had only laughed at the idea, saying as she had gone to all the trouble to have him, she was not going to miss loving him.

Juliet lightly stroked the downy golden fuzz on her baby's head. Cooing softly, she thought she had never seen such a beautiful child. Of course—and a rueful smile appeared on her face briefly—he looked the image of his father. He had Christopher's bright gold hair and blue eyes, though they were not yet so piercing. Even his mouth, though tiny, looked to have been formed from the same perfect mold as his father's.

Suddenly little Charles gave a cry and began to nuzzle energetically at Juliet's breast.

"Ah, so having entranced me, you are ready to get down to the really serious business of life, I see." Juliet laughed, shedding her shawl and unbuttoning the front of her specially constructed dress.

She was nearly finished nursing when a knock sounded at the door. "He's not finished yet, Sally," Juliet called softly, not bothering to turn around.

"So he is here."

Juliet jumped at the unexpected sound of Christopher's voice.

"I went to the nursery, but no one was there," he explained as he walked around Juliet's chair to see his son.

Groaning to herself, Juliet looked about for her shawl. Why had she taken the thing off? she wondered frantically. Oh, he had better not say anything disparaging!

"I know it is not the fashionable thing for me to nurse . . ."

Juliet got no further. Christopher was staring, an arrested look on his face, at the child still nuzzling at her breast.

The moment seemed to stretch on forever before his eyes lifted to meet hers and a brilliant smile illuminated his face. "From the looks of it, I'd say Charles Andrew Michael St. Charles doesn't care twopence for fashion. He looks entirely content where he is, and I cannot say I can fault him for it."

When Charlie slurped noisily, Juliet forced herself to look away from her husband. And she needed a reason, for Christopher's smile had quite taken her breath away, and had, she was afraid, left her gazing at him like a fool.

"Are you quite finished, then?" she addressed her son, her fingers feeling clumsy as they fastened her dress under Christopher's gaze. "Perhaps you would like to hold him?" she asked his father.

The Earl of Hartford's gaze became less difficult to hold then, for his smile faded. "I think I'll leave him with you," he said uncertainly, bending down beside her at last for a closer look at this infantile image of himself.

Charlie, delighted by this newest addition to his court, for he was accustomed to adoration, grinned widely and reached out to touch his father's face.

"Hello, old man." Christopher intercepted the little fist with his hand. Charlie's fingers tightened, and he gurgled excitedly.

"He's got a powerful grip." Christopher looked from Juliet to the child in some surprise.

Juliet's mouth lifted. "It's true of all children, actually. Not, of course, that Charlie's not exceptional. If you have an hour or two, even Mr. S. will be glad to enumerate his amazing accomplishments."

"What do you think I had for dinner conversation?" Christopoher inquired wryly.

"Take him a moment, will you, so that I may get up?" Juliet asked, thrusting the child upon his father. If she had thought Christopher looked uncertain a moment ago, he looked positively undone now as his normally capable hands searched unsuccessfully for the proper place to take hold.

Swallowing a grin, Juliet took possession once more, and Charlie laid his head on her shoulder. "He's tired, I'm afraid. He was kept up later than usual."

Christopher frowned. "Is that wise?"

"Oh, I don't think he'll suffer unduly. But it is time he go now. Do you have everything you need?" she asked politely, and when he had said he did, she nodded. "Good. I must ask you to excuse me as well. Despite my protests to the contrary, I find having guests has tired me as much as Lutetia said it would."

When Juliet had gone, Christopher regarded the empty place where she had stood holding his child in such an easy, comfortable way, Mrs. Stokes's lecture during dinner ringing in his ears.

"In the childbed her ladyship was from two o'clock one afternoon to nearly four o'clock the next. She was white as a ghost, my lord, and her eyes nearly black."

Damn! Christopher swore, suddenly angry with Juliet for the unpleasant feeling of guilt which swept him, Abruptly he stalked from the room. He would search out a bottle of brandy and put from his mind the rather too-late-to-do-any-good thought that it would not have hurt him to brave the weather and come to the Hall a week earlier.

14

A gaggle of geese, squawking angrily, scattered away from the earl's roan stallion as it thundered down the drive. Christopher smiled at their antics, for his invigorating ride had put him in the best of spirits. It was one of the pleasures of the country to be able to ride hell for leather in the early morning, and, on this estate at least, to find everything looking to be in exceptionally good order.

Drawing up at the stables, he recognized the ruddy-faced young groom as the urchin Juliet had rescued in London. Still pleased with the world, Christopher surprised the lad by asking, "How are you, Ferdie? Dobbins seems to be treating you well enough."

"But Dobbins is gone, sir," Ferdie answered, ducking his head shyly.

"Oh?"

"Dobbins retired, sir."

Christopher turned in the direction of the deep voice. It belonged to a stranger, an Irishman, judging by his brogue. As the earl took in the man's blue-black hair, green eyes, and broad shoulders, his brow arched sharply.

"I am O'Malley, sir." The Irishman doffed his cap. "Lady Juliet hired me on last summer when the rheumatics made it too hard on Dobbins to go on."

"I see." Christopher inclined his head and went on his way, though not before noting that O'Malley was able to lead his restive mount, Ajax, away with little trouble.

A shuttered expression having replaced his smile, Christopher stalked into the house and ordered Stokes to send Cartwright to his office.

"Mr. Cartwright will not be in today, my lord. Perhaps you would like to speak to her ladyship—"

"I hardly think I need my wife's assistance to learn what Cartwright's been up to," Christopher informed the old man bluntly.

His lordship had already started down the hall before he finished his statement, and Stokes, allowing himself a small smile, saw no point in shouting after him that he was likely to see his wife a good deal sooner than he realized.

Christopher threw open the office door, startling Juliet, who sat pen in hand at the desk.

As startled as she, he barked curtly, "Whatever are you doing here?"

"Good morning, my lord," she thought to say as her eyes flicked over him, lingering for a fraction of a second on his buckskin riding breeches. She had quite forgotten how little his thighs needed padding.

Forcing her wayward thoughts back to her husband's scowl, Juliet curbed the urge to bite her lip. "I am doing some of Mr. Cartwright's work. His wife died, you know, and with eight children to look after, he has been worn to a frazzle. I thought that if I did the books, it would give him some time to gather his resources. I used to do them for my father, you know."

"No, I did not know," Christopher replied in clipped tones. He had come to stand in front of the desk, his fingertips resting lightly on it, his eyes frosty. "How long has this been going on?"

"Awhile," said Juliet, keenly aware of the look in his eye.

"Mrs. Cartwright died in May, I believe."

"I said awhile," replied Juliet, her tone resolutely even.

"You have taken too much upon yourself without consulting me, Juliet. You cannot turn the estate into a charity project. If Cartwright needs an assistant, he is being paid well enough to hire one himself. At the very least, you should have informed me of the change."

She had known this would not be easy, Juliet told herself, commanding herself to patience. Buying the time to compose herself, she absently pushed an errant curl from her cheek with an inky finger. Taking a deep breath, she said with commendable calm, "I did tell you I was assisting Cartwright in one of my letters, actually. What I am doing now is, I allow, perhaps more than merely assisting, but I think you should look at the books before you judge me. I believe I have carried out my task quite competently.

"I certainly did not think of my work as charity. I like to use my mind, you see. And as this is where I am to live, I thought it only wise to use it to learn as much as possible about the estate."

Juliet, vastly pleased with her calm rebuttal of each and every one of her husband's objections, was most surprised to see him extend a clean white linen handkerchief to her. "For the smudge on your cheek," he said impassively.

Christopher's expession might not have indicated what he thought, but Juliet's did. As she rubbed vigorously at her cheek, the small, even tooth nibbling at her lip indicated her chagrin. How unfair that Christopher would not remember how well-spoken she had been, but only that her appearance had been imperfect, she fumed.

Not a little disheartened, she rose and informed him with as much dignity as possible, "I should like to go to Charlie now, but if think you'll need me, I can return in about an hour's time." The truth was, it was Charlie's lunchtime, a fact her full breasts signaled, but she could not bring herself to speak so plainly.

Christopher took back the piece of linen, whose whiteness was now married by a black smudge, and told her reasonably enough that he could wait to ask his questions at luncheon. Before she was out the door, he'd sat down in the chair she'd left warmed.

Charlie fed, Juliet entered the small Jacobin room where she took her meals, and wondered what Christopher would think of it. Having little relish for eating all alone in the large formal dining room, Juliet had had this heretofore unused room opened and aired. The view, through a pair of old mullioned windows, was particularly nice, for it looked directly upon a flower garden and beyond it to one of the lakes that dotted the estate.

"Very nice," he pronounced before he sat down. Juliet smiled, pleased, but soon found her husband had no intention of allowing her housekeeping changes or the delicious roasted squabs they were served to distract him from his inquisition.

In meticulous detail he asked about everything that had been done. Why was a tenant's roof finished in slate and not wood like all the others; why had rye been sown a year early in one of the fields; was the unusually high price gotten for the wool accurate; why had extra rations of food, particularly meat, been sent around to all the tenants; and, finally, was it not an excessive expenditure for medical supplies that had been recorded?

For those decisions which had been Cartwright's, Juliet merely passed along the estate manager's explanations. The slate roof was a result of Ronald Danforth having ordered too much for a project, Juliet told him, adding, "I thought that because slate needs replacing less often than wood, it would be a good idea to take advantage of the bargain price Ronald offered us."

"And how do you justify the increased amount you've spent on medicines and additional food supplies?"

"Sick and underfed tenants are of little use, it seems to me." Juliet held her husband's imperious gaze, quite forgetting the food upon her plate. "Are my figurings satisfactory otherwise, my lord?"

"They are." Christopher nodded. "I cannot quarrel with your ability to do mathematics. I am only concerned about someone with your soft heart holding the purse strings."

Stung, Juliet defended herself immediately. "I may

be compassionate, but I am not a fool. Cartwright approved everything I did."

"It will take me some time to determine if Cartwright acted judiciously or was swayed by your not inconsiderable talent for pleading the case of those less fortunate than yourself." Juliet was not given the time to decide whether Christopher had insulted or complimented her, for he continued, "Now that I am here, I shall relieve you of the burden of managing the estate."

Juliet eyed him a moment, then nodded. She had no doubt he was vastly more capable than she. He had a great deal more experience, and Cartwright had often extolled his abilities. "As long as you are here, I think you are by far the better person to do the work, and I should very much like the time to spend with Charlie."

Juliet turned her attention to her plate, wondering if her husband would notice the "as long as you are here," and if he did, if he would make mention of it. She would dearly love to know his plans.

Christopher did not appease her curiosity, though his next words did give her a better understanding of why he had come in the first place.

"Actually there is something else to keep you busy. I had word from my sister, Serena, that she'll be returning to England for a brief visit in a month's time, and I've invited her to the Hall. It would be an opportune time to have Charlie's christening."

Juliet nearly choked on a bite that suddenly seemed too large for her throat. The months of having everything her own way were certainly coming to an end with a vengeance! As a vivid recollection of Lady Eunice rose in her mind, Juliet wondered bleakly if it was too much to hope that Christopher's sister might be much different from her mother.

Christopher had risen from his place, but Juliet, distracted by her fancies, paid him little mind until she realized he was speaking to her.

"Tell me how you came to hire O'Málley."

"O'Malley?" she asked, scarcely able to recall who O'Malley was.

"Yes, how did you come to choose him as Dobbins' replacement?"

"Oh, O'Malley. Ronald Danforth recommended him. His references, of course, were quite good as well. Is he not satisfactory?"

"He seems quite capable. I only wondered how you found him."

"You might ask Ronald about him, if there is something you wish to know. I hope you won't find fault with him, though."

"Oh?" Christopher asked, coolly eyeing the distinct alarm revealed in her gray eyes.

All at once, taking in the severe expression on Christopher's face, Juliet realized how silly her concerns would sound to him. The thought made her, for some reason, chuckle. "You'll truly think me daft now." She smiled.

It was the first time his wife had ever smiled quite so unselfconsciously at him, and it was a moment before Christopher said evenly, "Try me."

"Would you sit, please? It makes my neck ache to arch back so." When he had rather grudgingly complied, Juliet pushed her plate aside and leaned forward. "Likely as not you won't approve what I've done, but my father always told us to practice Christian charity more than we talked about it, and—"

"Juliet . . ." Christopher frowned. "Get on with it."

Juliet bit her lip. Really it all did seem a little absurd, but she had started, and now she would have to finish. "You see, Molly Barker had a baby, but there was no father."

"Surely you are not implying Molly has anything in common with the Blessed Mother?" Christopher inquired dryly when Juliet hesitated once again.

"Christopher!" She was clearly appalled. "That's nearly blasphemy."

When her husband unexpectedly laughed, Juliet quite forgot her concern with his immortal soul. His face wiped clean of any mockery or arrogance did look appealingly boyish.

"You know very well what I mean," she chided

when he was only smiling. "I kept her on because I did not think it my place to judge her, and she is a very good worker. And more compelling still, O'Malley, I really believe, has an interest in her. Mrs. S. agrees, and we believe that in time he will ask her to marry him."

Christopher St. Charles, if the truth be told, felt a fool as he gazed into his wife's candid eyes. They were sparkling with zest for her plan to legitimize a wayward maid's child, and compelled him to admit, as he recalled the suspicions he had harbored in relation to O'Malley, that perhaps he had been in London's jaded circles too long.

"If they both do their work satisfactorily, I can see no harm in your scheme," he allowed at last, rising to go. At the door he turned back to inquire peremptorily, "I trust your plans for the afternoon include a rest? You are looking paler than you did this morning."

Flustered by his concern, Juliet blinked. "Well, yes," she stuttered. "I had planned to take a nap. Christopher," she called when he was almost out the door, "Charlie wakens from his nap around three o'clock. He's at his best then, if you would care to see him."

"Until then." Christopher nodded and departed.

15

Over the next several days Juliet saw little of Christopher during the day. When he was not occupied with the estate, he went hunting, for game was plentiful and Cook was glad to have the fresh provisions. What wasn't eaten by those at the Hall was to be sent, Christopher informed Juliet with a dry look, to the tenants.

Juliet, for her part, had Charlie and Lutetia, who came to visit almost every day, to busy herself with. The duchess ostensibly came to assure herself Juliet was recovering nicely, but actually, as Juliet laughingly pointed out, she spent most of her time cooing with Charlie, whom she adored.

As, it quickly became apparent, did his father. Nearly every day at three o'clock Christopher came to Juliet's sitting room to play with his son, and coincidentally to have tea with his son's mother. Considering the circumstances of Charlie's conception, Juliet greeted his interest in their son with profound relief and even gratitude. It seemed almost a miracle that Christopher should accept him so.

The first day Christopher was home, Juliet worried about how she might entertain him after dinner during the long stretch of time they would have all to themselves. At the end of their meal, when she was still cudgeling her brain, Christopher asked her if she would be retiring soon.

Accustomed to both Lutetia and Mrs. Stokes trying to mother her, Juliet answered with a tinge of exasperation that she was not yet reduced to going to bed with the sun.

"Then I hope you are in a mood to grant me a game of chess. I haven't played in some time, but I remember being able to hold my own with Ronald."

It was the first time her husband had asked her to do something with him just for the pleasure of doing it. Aware of that fact and of the faint smile playing at the corners of his fine mouth, she felt her heart skip a beat.

There is nothing more to this than the need to while away long country hours, she cautioned herself, as she said she would enjoy a game.

The old ivory board, a relic of King James's time, Christopoher told her, was soon set up in the library, where a warm fire blazed. Christopher granted her the first move, saying lightly, "It's a woman's prerogative."

The empty phrase disconcerted her, for he'd never called her anything but a child before. Immediately she bent her head so she could not see him, and told herself she was being ridiculous.

Unfortunately the standard opening gambit she made only allowed her the opportunity to sit back and observe how the dark brown of her husband's velvet dining jacket contrasted with his blond hair, making it glow like gold in the firelight. She had almost forgotten how handsome he was. His straight nose, square jaw, white teeth, and firm but sensitive mouth were the definition of masculine beauty. Then, when one saw the blue of his eyes, it was as if life were breathed into his perfect face.

The space between them seemed to shrink to nothing, and Juliet became aware how alone they were with no one but the servants and their son in the house. Realizing the direction of her thoughts, she flushed.

"Your move, I believe."

Juliet's thick lashes dropped. Did he know that she had been staring at him, or what she had been thinking? Looking up quickly, she could not tell. His light blue eyes were on her, but they told her nothing.

Finally, forcing her attention back to the board, she

took note of the unusual countermove he had made and realized Christopher had been modest about his abilities. Intrigued, she considered what she should do, and after making her play, waited to see how he would respond. Unconventionally, she saw, for his move was not one she had expected.

Gradually, as she concentrated to keep up with his play, Juliet became less nervously aware of her husband. She might still experience a little frisson of pleasure when she looked up and saw him there—he was too handsome for her to be indifferent—but as she was forced to consider her strategy, she forgot to be overwhelmed by him.

Toward the end of the evening she realized of a sudden that it had been almost an hour since she had worried what he might be thinking of her hair or her dress, and she smiled at how oblivious she had become.

"And well you might smile. That move should trap my bishop."

Juliet looked up, startled.

"Ronald did not play with one eye closed, I am learning."

"I beg your pardon?" At a loss, Juliet frowned.

"I mean Ronald did not let you win. You won on your own merits."

"I told you that before," she said simply.

"So you did," Christopher conceded with a half-smile. "You must forgive my doubts, but I have never played a woman before and was not certain you would know if he had allowed you the victory. Where did you learn?"

Juliet flushed at the unaccustomed praise, but managed to reply normally enough that she had learned from her father and older brother. "My father may have let me win once or twice in the beginning, but Andrew never did."

Juliet looked from the board back to Christopher and chuckled. "Nor have you, my lord. I may have gotten your bishop, but it looks as if you will have my king."

Christopher inclined his golden head. "It would seem

so. Shall we play it out, however? Your defense, I confess, intrigues me."

Juliet's gray eyes lit at that. "My father called it the Colonel Lewis shuffle." When the earl's brow lifted in question, Juliet grinned. "When Colonel Lewis settled in St. Mary-on-Medway upon his retirement from the army, he used to come to visit Father often, but only for very short periods at a time, perhaps fifteen minutes at the longest. When finally Father asked him why, he confessed, sheepishly I might add, that he was avoiding his wife. Father understood at once, as Mrs. Lewis was a very domineering woman who had often said she could not stand to see a man sit idle."

Her eyes sparkling, Juliet watched as Christopher threw back his head and roared with laughter. "How very apt," he remarked, still chuckling.

Colonel Lewis' example notwithstanding, Juliet's king was caught, and she had to concede the match. As she did the next night and the next. She always made a good game of it, however, and as she learned his style of play, Christopher was increasingly hard put to retain his crown.

As their matches became a custom, Juliet found herself looking forward to them for many reasons, not the least of these being the conversations they had. How the inhabitants of St. Mary-on-Medway became such a frequent topic, she was not certain, but Juliet often found herself making Christopoher laugh with some story like that of Colonel Lewis.

Her husband in turn commented on matters to do with the estate and beyond that made wry, astute observations on events of the day. Having never spoken with anyone who knew so much about the workings of the government, or who was personally acquainted with so many of the important figures connected with it, Juliet had dozens of questions for him. To her surprise, he took her curiosity in stride and never used his patronizing tone when he answered.

Only once, when she had peppered him with questions about a speech a member of Parliament had made on the Irish Question, did he call a halt. "That is enough for tonight, Miss Inquiring Mind," he had laughed. "I shall have to go back to Cambridge if I allow you to go on at this rate."

Nor had he been much exaggerating, Christopher mused to himself. His wife had one of the most inquiring minds he'd ever encountered, and after only a little thought was capable of grasping anything he had to tell her.

Much as she was capable of learning how to improve her chess game, he added wryly. He might have won each of their five previous matches, but she had him in trouble now, if she moved her knight correctly.

Sipping his brandy, Christopher let his eyes linger on Juliet's gleaming head. Her hair, he was glad to see, had outgrown those absurd curls. Pulled into a smooth knot at the top of her slender neck, it had a graceful look to it.

Her hair was not all that had changed. Even her features were not quite the same, seeming more finely etched now that they had shed the indistinctness of girlhood.

The same silk shawl she had worn on the night he had come home lent a touch of elegance and color to her appearance. Christopher's eyes moved from the shawl to Juliet's skin at the thought of color. It was still pale, and he frowned slightly at this evidence that she had not fully recovered. The soft freshness of her skin was something he had admired from the first.

"Checkmate!" The glad cry interrupted him, and absurdly, for he had lost to her, Christopher smiled, not even trying to resist those enormous shining eyes.

"That will teach me not to let my attention wander," he said, still smiling.

"And what were you thinking of? Surely not the Irish Question," she was giddy enough to tease him.

Christopher laughed with her and shook his head. "No," he allowed, his eyes on her. "I was thinking how much better you look."

"Oh." Juliet looked away quickly. Her pulse was beating rapidly, and she felt a fool to be taken so off guard. It was a simple statement, referring to her health. But the look in his eyes . . . No! she had imagined that warmth.

"Mr. S.!" Juliet fairly cried out when Mr. Stokes showed the good judgment to choose that moment to bring in the tea cart and thereby rescue her from her self-induced fluster.

Juliet grinned engagingly at the old retainer and pointed to the board. "Come and witness my feat, Mr. S. I have defeated his lordship, though only because he was woolgathering, of course." Emboldened by the butler's presence, she flashed Christopher a saucy smile. "But nonetheless, Lord Christopher has had to yield to me."

"Mayhap I'm not surprised," observed Mr. Stokes with a shrewd gleam in his eyes as he smiled upon the earl and his countess.

Christopher looked up sharply, but the old man only looked at him with bland innocence before he turned away to the tea tray. Juliet, for her part, did not seem to take any notice at all of Stokes's odd response, though she did not try to meet his eyes either.

16

All in all, Juliet was amazed by how well things were going, particularly when she considered where she and Christopher had left off. Granted, Christopher was not acting like a husband. There was no intimacy between them, but he had been entertaining and even pleasant. Would they continue like this, their relations gradually improving until . . .?

Juliet tossed her head. No, she would not put her fancies into words. With Christopher, as she knew better than most, everything, no matter how promising the situation might look, could change in the twinkling of an eye.

"My lady?"

It was a footman come with the mails. Looking at the salver, Juliet found there was a letter from her father. Glancing absently at the other mail, she saw it was all for Christopher. On top there was an official-looking thing from London, and then her eye was drawn to the second letter, only partially covered by the first.

The envelope was lavender. Juliet could not see all of the writing, but she saw enough to know the bold hand was distinctly feminine.

Her father was a witty writer, but Juliet paid his letter only half a mind. Truth to tell, it served merely as a way to pass the time until lunch, when she could see if Christopher's mood was altered by the woman's letter. Juliet thought the florid hand could well have been Leslie's, it was in her style, and she could not help but wonder what it would mean.

Christopher looked no different as he bid her good day and asked after Charlie. Indeed, his manner was so much as usual that Juliet began to think she had mistaken the matter. But then, as they were being served the gooseberry tarts which were Christopher's favorites, he announced in the most casual manner, "I shall be leaving tomorrow for a week or so. I've been reminded that an age ago I accepted Carlisle's invitation to a house party at his estate near Leicester. You shouldn't have any problems while I'm away. I spoke to Cartwright, and he will come to mind matters in my absence. You are not to assist him, Juliet. The man has to begin to function in his normal capacity again, not wallow in his grief. Do I have your promise?"

Juliet nodded, and then, showing a great deal more resolution than she had known she had, she asked about one of the tenants who was behind in his rent. Christopher answered, and the rest of their meal continued quite normally. Only Juliet did not finish her tart. It had, she found, a sour taste.

She hoped that Christopher would not notice, or if he did, that the failure of her appetite would not strike him. In his dealings with her since he'd come to the Hall, Christopher had been fair, and with Charlie he had been marvelous.

That alone had earned him Juliet's favor. In return she would keep up her part of their marriage of convenience and act the untroublesome wife.

Never mind that it made her miserable, and it did, that he should respond so readily to Leslie's call. Or that the very words "house party" conjured up an image of wealthy, bored people and bedrooms. She would not let him know it.

Her thoughts not being the least pleasant, Juliet was pleased, as she would not have been only the day before, when Stokes came to tell her later in the day that all three of the Bridings had come to visit. As Juliet had had occasion to tell herself before, there was no use moping.

"Juliet! We are so glad to see you are looking well."

"May we see the baby, please!"

Juliet embraced Harriet Briding, the first speaker, and smiled at Becky, the second. "He is napping now, but when he awakens I should be delighted to show off my son."

At last she turned to Jonathan. "Jonathan—" she began.

"You are pale!" he proclaimed at once in an absurdly tragic way, his dark eyes searching her face. "But look, your beauty is intact! Indeed I believe your ordeal has only enhanced your looks. You are . . . matured."

Juliet's brow lifted at the irony of the description, but she managed a modest thanks.

"Is the earl truly at home, Juliet?" Becky asked breathlessly. "Mrs. Hodges had it from your cook that he is, and we did notice his flags flying."

"And have, with all those indications before you, arrived at the correct conclusion," Juliet confirmed wryly.

Becky fairly jumped from her seat with excitement. "Oh, I do hope I shall meet him! That is, I have met him, of course, but it was an age ago, and I was only a child. Now that I know how much the thing he is, I do want another chance!"

"And I hope you shall have it, Becky, but you must not get your hopes up greatly. Christopher has been taken up with matters here on the estate, and I do not know if he will come to tea."

Juliet bit her tongue before she could add that Christopher, in addition to his business affairs, had some packing to do.

"Now we have some news for you, Juliet." Though Harriet's tone was quiet, Juliet could see that her friend was excited, by the way her hazel eyes had widened. "Our Great-Aunt Porchester has written to say she will sponsor us this Season!"

"But that is quite wonderful!" Juliet smiled, for she knew how much the girls had longed for one. When their parents had died some years ago, they were left in such financial straits that without assistance they could never manage a Season in London on their own. Certainly Jonathan, who took no interest at all in his finances, had not saved up enough.

"I do hope she's not a dragon without any connections!" Becky exclaimed, the earl forgotten for the moment. "She must be ancient, for she was Mama's aunt. Did you ever meet her, Juliet?"

"No." Juliet shook her head. "But I did not go out much the brief time I was in London, you know. Surely your aunt cannot be too fusty, though, or she would not have offered to see to your come-out."

"That's right, Becky!" Harriet turned a severe look upon her sister. "You are being henwitted and mannerless besides. Here is Aunt Porchester willing to undertake all that sponsorship implies, and you . . ."

The Briding girls could, as sisters often do, fall to brangling. Thinking how much they sounded like Ros and herself, Juliet smiled. It was nothing serious, she knew. Though she had argued in much the same way with Ros, she would give a good deal to see her now.

Watching the two girls, Juliet did not notice that Jonathan had risen, until he had dropped down beside her and in the same movement had caught her hand in his. She did not like it, but, deciding it was time they had a talk, she left her hand where it was.

Jonathan, an uncomfortably admiring look in his dark eyes, gave Juliet the opening she wanted. "Tell me, Juliet, when will you be able to resume sitting for me?" he asked, seeming so much like a little boy, she was almost sorry to have to quash him.

A spoiled little boy, she reminded herself. "We agreed that after the baby came I would have to see about our sittings, Jonathan," Juliet told him firmly, ignoring the scowl forming on his brow. "And I find now that I truly have not the time."

To Juliet's annoyance, Jonathan's hold tightened on her hand. "But you cannot abandon me!" he cried. "How shall I capture your beauty? It is so rare, like a wildflower. I must have you before me!"

112

Juliet grimaced at the hyperbole, and tried unsuccessfully to withdraw her hand. "You are grasping me too tightly, Jonathan," she warned him.

Jonathan paid her no heed. "It is the earl, is it not?" he asked, his grip actually tightening.

Juliet ceased her struggling and left her hand to lie limply in his. All her determination she put into her voice. "It is not Christopher at all, Jonathan. It is, as I have said, Charlie. I have no time to sit for you, and you will not persuade me to it with this frantic behavior. Now, release me."

Before Juliet could see the effect of her words, the salon door opened, and Christopher strolled into the room. His eyes swept the group clustered about the tea tray, pausing imperceptibly as Jonathan reluctantly let go Juliet's hand, and then he was smiling his most charming smile at Harriet.

The shy, reserved girl was so undone she flushed bright red to her hairline. "Let me see," Christopher addressed her. "I do believe you are the older sister and that, therefore, you must be Harriet."

Completely undone by the thought that the famous Earl of Hartford actually remembered her name, Harriet stammered a reply. "Yes, yes, my lord."

"Ah, then you must be Becky Briding," Gallantly touching Becky's fingers to his lips, Christopher proceeded to devastate the younger sister as he had the elder.

Becky blushed, but, more intrepid than Harriet, she also managed a smile.

"How pleasant it must be to find yourself surrounded by such charming sisters, Mr. Briding." Christopher turned at last to Jonathan.

Juliet sighed to see Jonathan's mouth droop in the most petulant way. It would not have been easy for him to see the sisters whose adoration he had never had to share, won over so easily by a near-stranger.

"When Becky's not chattering and Harriet's not worrying, I suppose they're nice enough," he grudgingly allowed.

"Will you have some tea with us, my lord?" Juliet asked quickly, embarrassed for his sisters by Jonathan's appalling lack of manners.

As she poured his tea, Juliet wondered at the strange look Christopher had shot her in the moment it had taken him to say yes, he would like tea. Those keen eyes had seemed to search her intently, but then had glanced away before she could be really sure it had not all been her imagination.

Like a shot she recalled the letter he'd received, and it came to her that she had mistaken the intent of that glance. It had not been searching, it had been comparing. The thought brought her no pleasure, she knew full well she could never hope even with the best of goodwill to hold a candle to Christopher's mistress.

When Juliet handed Christopher his tea, he did not look at her again. All his attention was on Becky and Harriet, whose fears about their Aunt Porchester he was allaying. "She is a woman of consequence," Juliet heard him saying.

"I suppose I shall have to paint your portrait from the image in my mind." It was Jonathan's sulky voice which greeted her upon her return to the couch.

Immensely relieved that he had decided not to argue the matter further, Juliet smiled. "I am certain you will manage admirably," she soothed him. "You are too capable not to."

Jonathan looked as if the praise would cheer him, but then Christopher was addressing him.

"How are affairs on your land, Mr. Briding?" was the question which hung in the air for a moment.

Jonathan was renowned in the neighborhood for his lack of interest in his land, and now he allowed his scowl to return in full force. "I don't sully my hands with such matters," he proclaimed in such a querulous way that Juliet wanted to shake him. He then went on to pronounce, as if it were a challenge, "I am an artist, you know."

Christopher's brow arched a fraction, a slight cool smile playing on his lips. "No, I did not know."

Looking noticeably ruffled by the earl's air of faint amusement, Jonathan responded sharply, "I do portraits. My latest and certainly loveliest subject is Lady Juliet."

Very slowly Christopher's eyes traveled to settle upon Juliet. "I see," he said, and then turned to inquire if Harriet and Becky had had their portraits done, which of course they had, and which Becky at least was happy to describe in detail.

Juliet felt strangely disconcerted. There had been mockery in the look Christopher had dealt her, and, she thought, accusation, though what her crime was, she did not know. Nor was she destined to know. Christopher did not accompany the Bridings to see Charlie, and at dinner that night he said nothing.

It was not like Christopher to overlook any matter which displeased him, as Juliet well knew, and she decided she had been imagining things. If Christopher was being unusually taciturn as they ate, it was likely that he was preoccupied with thoughts of his coming week.

Juliet shivered and pulled her silk shawl more closely around her. She was being absurd to feel abandoned. She would do very well at the Hall alone; she had before.

"That is a most unusual shawl."

After his silence for most of the meal, Christopher's remark surprised her, and Juliet glanced up quickly. Oddly, he did not seem to be regarding the shawl with much favor, but Juliet liked it very well and looked down at it with pleasure.

"It is unusual, isn't it?" Of gray-blue silk, it was shot through with gold thread, which made it shimmer whenever she moved. "Ronald and Lutetia gave it to me for Christmas."

"Ah," was all Christopher said in response, and soon after, he had excused himself from the table, saying he would spend the evening preparing for his departure.

Really, her husband could be either the most charming or most odious of men, as Juliet observed the next day to Lutetia after she had recounted Christopher's strange behavior over her shawl.

"It is odd," Lutetia agreed. "Perhaps he was feeling badly at not having sent you a gift himself, as well he ought!"

Juliet did not think that at all likely, and said so, and then Lutetia cast her a shrewd glance. "But what really has you so blue-deviled is the Kit's hied off to this house party and left you behind."

Juliet's eyes widened at Lutetia's blunt speaking, but she did not argue the truth of it. She did, however, ask something she had long suspected. "Do you know about Mrs. Chester-Headley, Lutetia?"

When Lutetia nodded, Juliet sighed heavily. "I suppose you know it all, then?"

"All," affirmed the duchess imperturbably. "I know that Leslie acted the cat she is and that you administered the comeuppance she's deserved for years."

"Lutetia!"

"Don't look so shocked, my love. No one of any consequence can tolerate her. She's been too indiscreet over the years—long before her husband died—and she's been too acid-tongued. Her painted cheek has been begging for a good slap. As Kit must know—he's no fool, particularly with women."

"Oh no, Lutetia," Juliet said at once. "Christopher was furious with me, and I am certain at least a part of his anger was on her behalf. Besides, you should see the marks of favor he has given her—the carriage alone must be worth the price of a small estate."

"Tush, child, mere nothings—even the emeralds. Yes, my informants are thorough." She grinned, then continued airily, "Kit's always been lavish with his women, whether he stayed with them a night or a year, and he has never stayed above a year. Leslie's tenure was shorter than most, though."

"Leslie is no longer . . .?"

The duchess nodded knowingly. "I thought you might not be aware that Kit gave the widow her congé shortly

116

after you left town. He took up with others, of course, but no one for any length of time. And do you know what I think?"

Juliet looked at Lutetia's gleaming eyes with some apprehension. Lutetia plotting on her behalf—and that look indicated plotting of a high order—might well do more harm than good.

"I think we must get you to London, my dear. Kit will go for the Season, of course, and we must not leave him alone to fix his attention on another of Leslie's ilk. Instead, you must be there to give Kit a thing or two to think about when he sees all the young bucks clustered around you."

"Lutetia—" Juliet began, the warning in her tone quite clear.

"I know what you will say." Lutetia held up her hand. "You are afraid society will not treat you kindly. Needless fears! You were applauded, as you would know if Kit had not sent you away. And if that is not enough to persuade you, then remember"—and here the duchess drew her small but not undistinguished self up haughtily—"you will have my enormous credit behind you. People will line up to meet you simply because you are connected to the Duchess of Crewe."

"You are shameless!" Juliet could not help but laugh. "But it is not society's opinion I care about, it is Christopher's. Please heed me, Lutetia, for I know my husband, and he would not be pleased if he thought we had schemed up some reason to get me to town. Truly, my going without his invitation would do more harm than good. You will mind me, won't you?"

"Now, now, don't fret yourself, love. At least I've brought a smile to that lovely face of yours."

Impulsively Juliet crossed to Lutetia's chair and kissed her wrinkled cheek. "You spoil me unmercifully, Lutetia. I know full well that you have never stayed at Crewe Cottage so long before. You go on to London, and when you return, you can entertain me with your highly spiced version of what's gone on."

Lutetia only muttered that she had no intention of

going anywhere without her girl and her darling boy, but Sally came in just then with Charlie, and Juliet thought no more of the matter. It was only later, as she was eating her supper alone in the little dining nook, that she realized Lutetia had not actually said she would give up her scheming. Frowning at the thought, Juliet resolved to speak to her again on the matter.

17

"**M**y lord, we did not expect you back so soon."
Christopher cast Stokes a brief unfathomable look. "It would not do to refine on my relatively short stay at the Carlisles' overmuch, Stokes," he drawled. "Their French chef had caught cold and in consequence the food was not palatable. Tell me instead what has you in such a pelter. You *are* in a pelter, are you not?"

"Nothing so hasty, my lord," the old man replied with a ghost of a smile. "My old bones are not up to peltering. There is a fire at the Joneses' house. They're the tenants—"

"Yes, yes, man, I know where Arthur Jones lives."

"Her ladyship has taken most of the servants and the wagons— "

"Her ladyship?" It was asked in a róar and even Stokes, accustomed to his lordship's ability to shout when he took a mind, looked startled. "Blast it, man, it's freezing outside! With this wind it's colder still. She was only just getting her color back."

"One of the children is caught in the house and may be hurt."

As if that explained everything, Christopher thought disgustedly, flinging out of the house and shouting at the top of his lungs for Ajax. Damn the woman, could she not ever do what she was expected to do?

The scene at the fire was chaotic. Knots of men ran about seemingly at random, some yelling, others flinging small pails of water on the raging flames, and yet others doing nothing that Christopher could discern but standing and staring.

Christopher's attention narrowed on a group bending over a form on the ground. In an instant he was striding toward them, his eyes fixed upon the silvery head closest to the prone man.

"My lord!" a quavering voice wailed loudly, and Christopher's attention was jerked to another woman crouched on the far side of the man. Looking at her, Christopher did not see the combination of joy and relief that flared in Juliet's eyes when she heard Mrs. Jones hail him.

By the time he was looking down at her, Juliet's expression held only urgency. "One of the children is still in the house," she shouted above the fire. "Mr. Jones tried to go back, but a beam fell upon him. No one else will try now."

Juliet said nothing more, but her eyes held Christopher's, the plea in them unmistakable. What might have been a wry smile twisted Christopher's mouth briefly, and then he was shedding his jacket and calling for water. Three men came and soaked his flawless blue superfine beyond recognition, while Christopher consulted in low tones with them. Then, with the jacket wrapped over his head, he ran into the blazing house.

Mr. Jones moaned, and Juliet dragged her eyes from the empty doorway. His shoulder was burned, but not so badly as it might have been had he not been wearing a heavy jacket.

Working quickly, Juliet had him carried to a wagon, where she cut off his jacket and cleaned the area around the wound. After applying a salve to the burn, she bandaged his shoulder and wrapped him in a warm blanket.

As his eyes closed, his wife began to sob again, but Juliet, in a voice whose calm contrasted to the hysteria all around them, said, "Mrs. Jones, you mustn't fret so. Mr. Jones will mend nicely, and the earl will come out with Davey. Now, you must sit here with your husband, quietly, please."

Amazingly, Juliet's soothing was effective, and Mrs. Jones sank down with only an occasional moan to indicate how anxious she was. She'd forgotten her children, and when Juliet saw their frightened faces looking dazedly toward the house, she had them join their parents in the wagon. A neighbor woman agreed to watch them while Juliet went back toward the house, all the fears for Christopher that her activity had held at bay rushing to the fore.

There was no sign of him, and Juliet had to bite her tongue not to wail as Mrs. Jones had been doing. Suddenly a cry went up, and she saw, a cry of her own finally escaping her, Christopher hurtling out the door with a limp figure in his arms.

Disregarding the throng, Christopher made his way to Juliet.

The little boy was whimpering and looked quite pale with shock, but he was alive, and Juliet looked up to Christopher with a dazzling smile upon her face.

"He's suffering more from the smoke than anything, I think," Christopher shouted.

Juliet nodded, still smiling, and pointed to the wagon. "Please take him over there."

With Juliet following, Christopher strode in the directions he had indicated. His shirt was singed, his face was sooty, and his golden hair, covered with ash, resembled the color of mud. Nevertheless, Juliet thought she had never seen her husband look so vital.

He carried the boy as if he were a feather, not a twelve-year-old child brawny from work on a farm. After he'd laid Davey down and gone to help with the fire itself, Juliet stole a moment from her nursing to watch him. Standing a head taller than anyone else, he shouted orders with a natural air of command, and almost before her eyes, the chaotic activity around them took on a purposeful look.

As soon as Juliet had attended to young Davey, she had a footman drive them all in the wagon to the house of a neighbor, Mrs. Gregson, who had volunteered to shelter the family.

Aware of the dazed shock reflected on the faces of those around her, Juliet asked Mrs. Gregson to start some tea, and then got Mr. Jones and Davey into bed. A special concoction of herbs brewed into a tea soon put them both to sleep, and Juliet was pleased to find, when she came down to the kitchen, the other children and their mother looking, if not well, at least not so pinched as they had.

Juliet promised Mrs. Gregson extra rations of food, and left her the salve and herbal mixtures she would need, along with detailed instructions on their use. "Send for me if you need to," she said before leaving, and Mrs. Gregson nodded that she would.

Her duties fulfilled, Juliet realized how weary she was. She had not exerted herself so much since well before Charlie's birth, and felt so drained that she needed the footman's help to climb into the wagon. At the Hall she was surprised when Christopher came out the door. He was at the wagon before she could dismount, and with his hands around her waist, he lifted her easily.

"The fire . . .?" she asked, despite her intense awareness that his hands were still resting on her waist and that she was so close she could smell the clean-scented cologne he used. He had had time to bathe and change, but not to put on a fresh coat, she mused, looking dazedly at the cambric shirt which was open at the neck to reveal a great deal of chest.

And what was he doing here at all? she wondered confusedly. He had been gone only four days. Juliet shrugged slightly; she was too tired to think on it. She felt as if she might drop where she stood.

"Damn!" Christopher swore as Juliet swayed.

"Oh!" she cried as he swept her into his arms and carried her without effort into the house.

"Put me down," she protested faintly. "I can walk, I assure you. I am only a little tired."

"You are chalk white, and I've no intention of having you faint dead away at my feet," was the implacable reply.

"But I must see Mrs. Stokes. There's food that must be sent to the Gregsons'," Juliet continued to protest despite the grim set of Christopher's mouth. She could, of course, see it quite plainly, because she was so close. . . . She jerked her gaze from her husband's firm but sensual mouth.

"Mrs. Stokes has the matter of food in hand. There will be enough sent to Mrs. Gregson to last her the year, if she is careful. And the fire, to answer your question, consumed the house, but not the barn, the pigsty, or the chicken house. As soon as possible, Cartwright will have the house rebuilt, and the Joneses will be home before they know it."

"I am glad," Juliet sighed.

Her immediate worries answered, Juliet's mind was free once more to contemplate her proximity to her husband. His strong arms held her tightly against his chest. His breath ruffled her hair, and she could feel his heart beating against her breast. It would be lovely to lay her head against his shoulder.

"You can relax, you know," Christopher said suddenly, as if he had read her thoughts. "I don't bite."

Juliet darted a quick glance at him, but his expression gave no indication of his mood. He was looking ahead at Sally, Juliet saw, when she looked.

"Fetch water for a bath, girl, and some luncheon," Christopher ordered, and Sally darted away to do his bidding.

In her room, Christopher deposited Juliet none too gently upon the couch. Feeling a little ridiculous over all the fuss, she struggled to sit up.

"Stay still!" Christopher barked, and whirling around, picked up a thick shawl lying on one of the chairs. "Here, wrap this about yourself while I build up the fire. It's cold as ice in here."

"But . . ." Juliet began to say she was not cold, only tired, and that was why she had shivered, but swallowed her words when Christopher turned a "do-as-I-say-or-else" look upon her.

When the fire was roaring to Christopher's satisfaction, he strode back to scowl down at her.

"I distinctly recall telling you to leave the estate's affairs to Cartwright," he said, a flicking of his eyebrow indicating just how annoyed he was.

"Oh, do sit down," Juliet muttered, too tired to be placatory. The leaden feeling she'd experienced outside swept through her again, and she closed her eyes before adding, "You look entirely too energetic standing."

When she opened her eyes, he was sitting beside her, his disposition not much improved. He was still frowning, but at least he was not so overwhelming as he had been when he loomed over her.

"Cartwright doesn't know the first thing about nursing," she sighed after he had said "Well?" in a most imperious way.

"And if you are going to suggest I should have sent for Dr. Ramsey, then you cannot know he is as fond of spirits as he is of healing. He is nearly useless after ten o'clock in the morning. And I am not exaggerating, you may ask anyone," Juliet added rather petulantly, but she was tired.

Silence reigned while she lay with her eyes closed and wondered where Sally could have got to. Juliet peeped through her long lashes and saw Christopher was regarding her with what could only be termed a moody expression. She closed her eyes again.

"I'm surprised you didn't send for Briding," he said abruptly. "You could have used the help. Of the entire group, only O'Malley seemed able to think what to do, and he was taken up with organizing the men getting water."

Juliet frowned and looked at him oddly. "I certainly would not think to call upon Jonathan for help. He'd only say it was too tiresome a task and sooty besides."

Christopher's expression did not much change, and Juliet shut her eyes tiredly. It seemed as if he were searching for ways to fault her.

To her great surprise, she heard him sigh, and lifting her lashes slightly, she saw him run his hand through his hair in a distracted gesture.

She did not think she had ever seen her husband

124

look so at a loss, and though she did know why he should look so, she found herself saying softly, "You were quite magnificent when you went into that house. No one else would go, after they saw what happened to Mr. Jones. You saved Davey's life."

For a long moment Christopher said nothing. Then, just before Juliet's wavering smile could disappear entirely, his mouth pulled down wryly.

"It was nothing, Lady Juliet," he drawled, picking an imaginary piece of lint from his shirt. "I shall in future make a practice of saving the lives of my tenants' children. I felt quite feudal afterward."

For once Christopher's mockery was directed at himself, not at her. She smiled, and though she did not know it, it was a most luminous effort. "You are teasing me monstrously, my lord," she admonished, then, closing her eyes, gave in at last to the fatigue that assaulted her.

Christopher watched his wife's long lashes settle onto her cheeks, and though it occurred to him that he should tell someone the food and water he'd ordered would not be needed, he didn't move. He stayed watching her breast gently rise and fall. What a negligible slip of a girl she looked. Certainly too young and fresh for his tastes.

He grunted, a mocking sound directed at himself. Why was it, then, he was having difficulty dragging his eyes away? he asked. Perhaps he was only trying to understand how, when she had told him the boy was trapped, she'd only had to turn those enormous eyes upon him to get him to do exactly what she wanted. Only taking the time to observe how inevitable his response was, he had plunged inside a blazing house, risking his life for a tenant's son.

Abruptly Christopher rose and left Juliet to her sleep. In the hall he almost collided with Sally, who was hurrying with a tray.

His eyes flashed. "Your mistress has fallen asleep," he snapped gruffly. "Have hot food and water waiting for her when she awakens."

As he stalked away, Sally stared after him, wondering whatever had put his lordship in such a mood. She had hurried as quickly as she was able. Shaking her head, she hoped he had not been hard on her mistress. Lady Juliet had only been doing what she thought was right, and lucky it was for the tenants she was such a good lady.

18

Fool! Juliet snapped disgustedly at the reins of her dogcart. Once again, as it had been doing since the day of the fire, her mind had drifted from its appointed task and had occupied itself instead with recollecting how right it had felt to have Christopher's arms about her.

"Right henwitted." Juliet muttered, borrowing a phrase from the old cook at the vicarage. "And now we had best get right over, if we don't want to be run down by whoever this is pounding down behind us," she added, pulling on the pony's reins. Esmeralda, for that was the imposing name Ferdie had given the less-than-imposing creature, apparently saw the wisdom in Juliet's request and complied with a commendable if unusual degree of alacrity.

Juliet, looking back to see if the rider had enough room, experienced an altogether irritating thrill. The person approaching at such a furious pace was none other than the man who occupied her thoughts.

Christopher's stallion pranced fretfully as he reined in beside her, but there was no question who was in control. In a matter of seconds Ajax was quiet.

Exhilaration from his ride made Christopher's eyes sparkle, and brought color up in his face. The only thing marring his looks was the frown gathering on his brow.

"What is that?" he demanded, eyeing the cart and the fat pony askance.

Perhaps it was the lack of greeting, but Juliet willfully chose to misunderstand him. "The mistletoe and holly?" she asked innocently, looking to the back of the wagon. "Lutetia and I gathered it today. I needed some for the christening, and Lutetia maintains Crewe's greenery is the best in the county."

"Lutetia's the most arrogant person I know," grunted Christopher. "But the greenery is not what I meant. I can identify mistletoe and holly. I was referring to that thing you are riding upon."

"Ah, this," Juliet said unnecessarily. "Because I do not ride, I was forced to rouse an entire troop of people whenever I wanted to go anywhere, even if only to the Cottage. It was constricting, and O'Malley came to my rescue by fixing up this dogcart."

"You don't ride?"

The tone was exactly what Juliet had expected it would be.

"You needn't look so condescending," she burst out hotly. "I never had the opportunity to learn. A vicar's living does not allow for such an extravagance, particularly when he has eight children to support. There is no need for you to fear my failure will embarrass you, however. I want to learn, and O'Malley has agreed to teach me."

"How accommodating of him," murmured Christopher.

The irony in his tone was quite lost on Juliet. Completely unaware of how nicely her straw bonnet framed her face, and how her skin glowed rosily in the late-afternoon sun, Juliet glared fiercely at her husband, daring him to make even one disparaging remark about her plans.

The beginnings of a smile lurked at the corner of Christopher's mouth, but he made no further mention of the matter. Instead he startled Juliet by dismounting. "I've been to the Cottage to fetch you," he called over his shoulder. "Serena has arrived. Move over and I'll get that fat animal to maintain a respectable pace home. By the looks of her, you've never had her above a plod."

Before she could make a protest, if indeed she had

intended to make any, Christopoher swung up beside her and took the reins. One flick of his wrists raised Esmeralda's head and the next set her at a brisk trot.

Juliet's eyes widened considerably, and Christopher, seeing her expression, grinned. His teeth gleamed very white, and his eyes danced wickedly. Juliet looked hurriedly away, but ever so slowly her lips curved.

"It's in the wrists," Christopher explained unasked.

Tossing her pride to the winds, Juliet inquired earnestly, "Is it a trick I can learn?"

"With the proper teacher," he answered, leaving Juliet to wonder exactly what that meant.

He did not give her the chance to ask, for he was already telling her Lutetia would be joining them for tea. "She should arrive at the Hall to play your champion shortly after we do."

Juliet let the remark pass, only nodding to confirm she had heard it. There was no point arguing Lutetia's motives, as the duchess had told her only an hour ago she would lend Juliet support with Serena. "Not that you will need much. Serena's not like Eunice," she had mused.

Actually, because Juliet had gone so slowly, and Lutetia had set out immediately after Christopher left, they all arrived together, and while Christopher took the dogcart around to the stables, Lutetia and Juliet went to greet Serena.

The woman waiting for them in the drawing room was, Juliet saw at once, a softer, more feminine, and perhaps less striking version of Christopher. Her hair was a somewhat darker shade than Christopher's, and her eyes, though blue, were not quite so unusually light. Still, becuase she was tall, carried herself with authority, and dressed with good taste, Serena Satterwaite was a very handsome woman.

She extended the two fingers of her hand in a polite greeting, but it was, Juliet noted, a reserved gesture. Lady Satterwaite's attitude toward Christopher's wife was not icy as her mother's had been, but neither was it warm. When she recognized Lutetia, there was a fleeting but distinct flash of surprise in her blue eyes.

Juliet saw it and knew the reports of her which had reached Serena had not been good. Her chin lifted a fraction at the thought of what Lady Eunice had likely said of her.

When Christopher strode into the room some moments later, Juliet found herself experiencing another unwanted emotion, and that was envy. The unstintingly affectionate smile with which Christopher greeted his sister was one Juliet had heretofore seen him bestow only upon Charlie. Certainly he had never turned it upon her.

"Shall we allow Charlie to have his first formal tea, Juliet?" Christopher asked, turning to her with his arm still around Serena's elegant shoulders. "I think Ree's visit is an appropriate occasion."

"Are you certain, Kit? I wouldn't want to disrupt his routine," Serena said, frowning slightly.

Christopher grinned down at her and kissed her forehead. "Nonsense, Ree. You're worth it."

Juliet left to ready Charlie for his big occasion with a distinctly empty feeling in her chest. An absurdly empty feeling, she added sharply, for the woman was, after all, Christopher's sister.

"Oh, but he is perfectly beautiful!" Serena exclaimed at once when Juliet returned with Charlie some half-hour later.

Immediately—and she knew herself to be a really shallow person—Juliet felt herself melt just a little toward Serena.

"He is, isn't he?" Christopher agreed complacently as he came to take his son. At the sound of his father's voice Charlie waved his little fists and gurgled happily.

"Why, he knows you, Kit!" Serena exclaimed with no little astonishment. Her wide-eyed look did not diminish when she watched her elegant brother throw his infant son into the air simply to make him laugh unrestrainedly. When they repeated the game they had obviously played before, Serena could not help but smile.

Seeing that smile, Juliet could feel he thaw accelerate. A doting mother could forgive a great deal if the person in question was taken with her baby.

130

"Let Kit show you how to hold him, Ree," Lutetia trumpeted from her chair. "He's gotten to be a master at it, which is one of the greatest surprises of my life, I don't mind telling you!"

"And mine," Serena laughingly agreed. "Had I not witnessed it myself, had you only told me Kit handled his son with such ease, I'd have said you were bamming me shamefully."

Christopher grinned, completely unabashed. "I must say I am pleased to be able to startle two such women of the world. I thought I had lost that capacity ages ago. But there's really nothing to holding a child, Ree. You just need a good teacher, that's all."

Christopher so rarely complimented her, Juliet did not realize he had been referring to her until she saw Serena regarding her closely. Looking up quickly, she acknowledged his remark with a smile which lingered as she watched him painstakingly demonstrate how his sister should hold Charlie.

When Serena had him, Lutetia chuckled. "Don't worry, Ree, he's not china. Didn't you know babies are made to bounce?"

Serena clucked at the old woman, but did bring Charlie closer to her, cooing at him as she did, and was rewarded by a gurgling grin from the baby. "Why, he likes me!" she exclaimed in such awe that everyone laughed at her.

Sipping her tea as she watched the scene, Juliet was aware of a distinctly pleasant feeling. In Charlie's presence Serena had lost much of her initial reserve, and it seemed almost a normal family reunion of the sort her family might have had in the same circumstances. The thought cheered her, for she would never have thought such a thing possible.

That convivial feeling endured even without Charlie. Because Serena's husband, Hugh, was a diplomat, the two had lived in Lisbon and Parais as well as Vienna, and had led, by Juliet's standards, a vastly interesting life. Gregarious by nature, Serena could not help but respond to Juliet's unfeigned interest, and the two women were soon chattering like old friends.

"Juliet's curiosity will have you talking all night," Christopher teased lightly at one point.

"But I should like that above all things!" Serena responded immediately, making them all laugh and endearing herself to Juliet.

It was well that the two women had such a lot to talk about, for they were together a great deal. Christopher continued to attend to the estate's affairs for much of the day, and as the weather had turned cold and damp, they were prevented from escaping to the outside.

Several days after Serena's arrival, Juliet was alone in her sitting room when Stokes came to inform her that Jonathan Briding was below.

"I took the liberty, my lady, of saying you were indisposed this morning, but that I would see if you had recovered."

"Mr. S., you are my deliverer!" Juliet laughed. "And now that I think on it, it seems I still am not feeling at all the thing."

"Just as I feared, my lady," Stokes said gravely, though the twinkle in his eye made Juliet laugh again.

"I hope you are not sending anyone away on my account," Serena said, coming into the room.

"It's not on your account at all, Ree," Juliet assured her sister-in-law. She paused, and then, deciding Serena was the perfect person to confide in, she asked, "May I ask your advice, Ree?"

When Serena, looking mildly surprised, nodded, Juliet continued with a grimace, "I'm afraid Jonathan had decided to develop a *tendre* for me, you see. I'm not certain why, though I suppose he thinks it artistic to have a *tendre* for someone married. Anyway, whatever his reason, I've grown tired of his languishing glances and want him to turn them elsewhere."

Serena smiled to herself, for though Juliet was engagingly unaware of it, she had more than enough beauty to attract masculine attention. And she had something more, for what would hold that attention was a special radiance uniquely Juliet's. A result of her loveliness of spirit, it animated her face and made it a pleasure to look into her expressive eyes.

"You're doing the best thing by ignoring him, really," Serena told Juliet, and then shocked her by remarking casually, "You are unusual, you know. I and most of my friends would envy you an admirer, particularly one as handsome as I remember Jonathan Briding being."

"But he's so silly. Really, Ree, you'd not envy anyone Jonathan."

"Perhaps," Serena said skeptically. "But I think you probably do not much care for Jonathan because you do care very much for Kit."

Juliet, finding it difficult to admit she did indeed care very much for Christopher, did not know what to say, though her cheeks did heat.

Serena, seeing the blush, laughed. "Now I've embarrassed you, and I did not mean to do so. I am very glad you feel as you do."

Serena came to sit beside Juliet, and taking her hand, looked earnestly at her. "I admit that when I came, I was prepared to dislike you, Juliet. I was not at all certain you had not set a trap for Kit, but one hour in your company was all I needed to be convinced of the absurdity of that notion. Now I give thanks that fate put you in Kit's path. Sometimes I wonder if all his raving against marriage was not just a way of waiting for someone like you to come along."

Serena paused, and releasing Juliet's hand, looked toward the fire. Surprised by her friend's cryptic remarks, Juliet regarded her closely and saw that her lips had thinned into a bitter expression.

"It was Mother's doing, of course," she said softly, her face set. "You wouldn't know it now, but Mother was quite striking as a girl. Father, who looked like Kit and could have had his pick of any girl in London, fell deeply in love with her. After they married, he learned it was only his title and wealth that appealed to her, though she had led him to believe otherwise.

"She was rarely at home when we were children, and when she was, she only found fault with us. She succeeded in making me cower around her, for I am like Father in temperament. But Kit, though he inherited Father's looks, inherited Mother's will, and fought her every inch of the way. I can remember one particularly horrid time when she lashed out at him, telling him he was so mannerless no family of any merit would want him for its daughters. Kit stood it so long, then in that deadly cold voice he learned from her, he told her he had no intention of ever marrying. He had learned too well from her that wives only made life hell for their husbands. It was an oath he repeated over the years, though heaven knows he had the opportunity to marry anyone he wanted."

Serena looked up at Juliet then, a warm smile banishing the bitterness. "And that brings us to you, my dear, for you are utterly different from any woman Kit's ever known—or that I've ever known, for that matter. Perhaps it's the vicarage in you, but there is an undeniable air of sincerity and integrity about you."

Juliet blushed fiercely. "You make me sound like a saint!" she wailed.

Serena chuckled. "I did not mean to. I'm certain you would sin. Let's see . . . you would tell Mrs. Stokes she is an old dear, though she has you at your wits' end with her advice—"

"Serena! Am I really such a pattern card?"

"You are no pattern card, my dear. You are far too unusual for that. And I would never like you as much as I do."

"Oh, Ree, I must tell you how glad I am that you are . . . well, a friend."

"Thought I might be a younger Lady Eunice, did you?" Serena grinned as Juliet nodded guiltily.

"Can you be patient with Kit, Juliet?" she asked more seriously. "He must learn to trust in you. I know he can't have been easy to live with, but underneath that cool, mocking exterior is a very warmhearted man. I've reason to know, for it was Kit who shielded me from Mother."

"I shall be patient, for I've little choice," Juliet said, sighing. "But it is Christopher in the end who must decide what he wants of our marriage."

"You are right, of course." Serena nodded decisively. "And I've been thinking how to give him a nudge in the right direction. It's my belief you should come with me to London. . . ."

"You've been talking to Lutetia!" Juliet accused, causing Serena to look sheepish for the space of a heart beat.

"I have," she admitted. "And we both agree it's a marvelous idea. Besides, we'll have such fun! Hugh is a dear, but he is an old dear, and I would like to kick up my heels a bit before returning to him. And while I am shocking you, and don't say you aren't shocked, we shall show Kit how very well you go on in society."

Juliet's answer was the same firm no she had given Lutetia with the same reason. What Juliet did not tell either of her friends was that aside from her fear that Christopher would not take well to having her company forced upon him, there was another, perhaps stronger, motive for staying at home.

That motive was fear. She was only just coming to realize the extent to which she did, indeed, as Serena had put it, care for Christopher. She could feel as light as air when he only looked at her pleasantly, not to mention what a real smile did to her.

Even her body betrayed her, for ever since Christopher had come to Lincolnshire, Juliet had been disturbed by dreams of the night she had shared his bed. Her body bathed in sweat, she would start from her sleep, aware only of an aching need for her husband.

She was on dangerous ground, she well knew, for unlike Lutetia or Serena, Juliet was not the least sanguine about her chances with him. Oh, Christopher might take her up for a time. It was possible, but the idea that he would come to feel differently for her than he had for any other woman was ludicrous to her. If she went to London, she feared she would only be readying herself for a hard and unpleasant fall.

Therefore, she would not go. She would firmly resist her friends' lures and remain at the Hall, hoping absence would cure her perilous infatuation.

19

As a clap of thunder sounded in the distance, Mrs. Stokes, her lips pursed with determination, knocked firmly on the door of Christopher's study.

"My lord?"

"Yes, Mrs. Stokes?" Christopher frowned at the interruption.

"It's her ladyship, my lord."

When it seemed she might not continue, the earl said with more severity than he realized, "What is it about her ladyship, Mrs. Stokes?"

"She's not back yet, you see," Mrs. Stokes cried, her worry overcoming her.

"Not back yet?" Christopher repeated, his frown deepening. Looking out the window, he confirmed for himself that the sky had been prematurely darkened by thick black clouds. "Where on earth would she have gone with the weather threatening like this? Is Lady Serena with her?"

"No, my lord, she went alone. It was not so bad two hours and more ago when she set out. And you know how determined her ladyship can be. Said she wanted to see Mr. Jones and the lad who was hurt. She felt badly that she'd not had a chance to look in on them before, what with the company we have and all. Now, with this storm, I do fear the pony will bolt. O'Malley said he'd go to look for her, but I thought you ought to know as well."

"Have Ajax saddled for me, Mrs. Stokes," the earl said, already going toward the door.

The sky was even darker when Christopher cantered down the drive, and when he turned onto a shortcut which led through the woods, he felt the first splattering of large raindrops. Within seconds it had begun to fall in sheets, completely obscuring the path. Thunder cracked again and again, and Ajax, his eyes rolling with fear, shied and tossed his head.

"Hold, if you can, lad," Christopher shouted above the wind, knowing he could not go on until the storm abated somewhat. "There's a gamekeeper's hut close by."

Hating like the devil to give up his search for Juliet, he swore angrily as a vision of her lost in the cold rain rose in his mind, but when the rude hut materialized out of the rain, Christopher urged his animal into the shelter of its lean-to. Thinking the hut's door might be locked, Christopher threw his weight against it and burst inside with a loud crack.

"My lord!"

The soft, clear exclamation brought his head up with a jerk. Sitting before a crackling fire with a blanket around her shoulders for warmth, and looking entirely cozy, was none other than the person about whom, he admitted, he had been terribly concerned. Her boots having been placed neatly by the fire to dry, her slender stocking feet were extended toward the fire's warmth. Her wet hair was unpinned, allowing him to see that it had grown out to shoulder-length since it had been cut in London.

"My lord, whatever . . .?" Juliet began, rising to her knees.

Christopher's lean face darkened. "Mrs. Stokes sent me out after you. She was afraid you had come to harm."

Juliet essayed a smile despite her husband's glowering expression. He was, she could see, soaking wet. "Mrs. Stokes worries over me unduly. She is a dear, of course, but a fretful one. Still, I thank you for coming."

"It was nothing."

137

"On the contrary. This is not the sort of weather anyone would choose to be out in."

"Where are your cart and pony?" he demanded as, finally, he moved to shed his dripping coat and hat.

Juliet's mouth twisted ruefully. "I am afraid Esmeralda bolted at the first peal of thunder. I lost the reins entirely, but when she went around a corner, her pace slowed enough that I was able to jump free."

Christopher crossed to the fire and stood surveying her with not-very-friendly eyes. He took in the old blanket, the wet length of her skirt as it clung to her legs, and then her exposed ankles and toes.

"Coming out in this weather was a henwitted thing to do, no matter the reason," Christopher informed her tightly, his eyes frosty. "You have lost the pony and the cart, people have had to be roused to look for you, and I wonder what the gamekeeper would think were he here, as he might well have been, to see his countess looking as you do now."

A faint line of color had crept into her cheeks, but when Christopher mentioned the gamekeeper, there was a distinct flash to be seen in Juliet's dark gray eyes.

"Carter would think I was very clever to have started a fire by myself," she replied quietly but distinctly. "And he would treat me with all the respect with which he and everyone else on the estate have always treated me. I am the lady of the manor, my lord, not by virtue of what I wear, but by virtue of my marriage and the way I behave."

His arms crossed over his chest, Christopher stared stonily at Juliet. That she had the respect of everyone on the estate he knew was true. In the month he had been at the Hall he had heard nothing but her praises. And that those praises contained some criticism of his prolonged absence, he was aware. Even old Jake, the gardener at the Hall since before Christopher's birth, had observed tartly, "It weren't easy for her ladyship, bein' here alone so long, but she fair won our heats, she did."

"Would you care for some tea, my lord?"

Juliet's soft inquiry made Christopher aware he had been staring at her lost in his thoughts.

"You've thought of everything, I see." Christopher looked down to see that indeed there was a heavy water kettle sitting on the back of the hearth.

Juliet rose from her warm spot and went to the cupboard. Rummaging about, she found two cups and some tea.

When she reached for the tea, the blanket escaped her grasp and slipped down, allowing Christopher to see that her dress was soaking wet on the top as well as the bottom. It clung to her body, revealing her full breasts and a waist which was again the width of a handspan.

Shivering, Juliet wrapped the blanket more tightly about her.

"You are cold," Christopher said, his voice almost accusing.

Without looking up, Juliet knelt to place the cups in readiness by the hearth. "I got thoroughly soaked," she conceded. She looked up at her husband, a cha-grined smile curving her mouth. "I should have heeded Mrs. Stokes enough to bring a heavier pelisse, but please don't tell her I said so. I don't think I could live with her I-told-you-so looks."

The earl stood observing the way that half-smile and the flames from the fire made her eyes sparkle. "I should tell her," he replied lightly. "You are always taking care of others; perhaps it is time you allowed someone to look after you."

Briefly Juliet's eyes searched his, uncertain of how he meant that. Just as she had registered a faintly teasing gleam in his eyes, another draft assailed her, making her shiver again.

"If you continue to wear that dress, you'll take cold. Come here, and I'll unbutton you."

Juliet's eyes widened enormously, and she did not move. Undressing before him was unthinkable, but as she shifted nervously, her wet dress pressed against her, raising goose bumps and bringing on yet another uncontrollable shiver.

That brought Christopher to her side. "This is not, I think, the time for maidenly modesty," he observed.

Juliet looked quickly away from the amusement sparkling in his blue eyes, but when he took her by the arm, she stood and let the blanket slip to the floor. The many buttons fastening her dress were small, slowing Christopher's progress to what seemed a snail's pace.

When she finally felt the last button give, Juliet made to go immediately.

"Wait a moment," Christopoher said, his voice seeming lower than usual. "This chemise is wet as well. You'll need to remove it."

Without giving her a chance to demur, he began to unfasten the chemise's ties. As he worked, his fingers could not help but lightly brush her skin. Their touch was inadvertent, Juliet knew, but nonetheless her bare skin, where his warm hand touched her, tingled. It was less than useless for Juliet to try to pretend to herself that her reaction was from the cold; she only tried to keep herself from shuddering so that Christopher would not guess how he affected her.

"Thank you," she whispered when he had done and she had moved away. Her back to him, Juliet pulled with stiff, clumsy fingers at her garments, until she was almost completely unclothed. Total silence prevailed as she reached quickly to cover herself with the gamekeeper's rough blanket and then hung her clothes on a peg by the fire.

"The water is ready," she announced, simply to break the charged silence, but to her dismay, her voice sounded too husky. Biting her lip, Juliet knelt by the hearth. To lift the kettle, she needed two hands, which forced her to release the blanket. It slipped to her waist.

"Ah!" Juliet dropped the kettle and jerked the blanket up.

"May I?"

Juliet found Christopher kneeling close, far too close,

beside her. He was grinning, she realized when her eyes flicked to his face. Her heart began to pound, and she abruptly moved away.

"Thank you, my lord. This blanket makes it impossible . . ."

The nervous rush of her words stopped when Christopher chuckled aloud. "So I could see."

Juliet's cheeks turned a vivid red. She did not dare to look at him. Indeed he had to say, "Your tea, madam," in order to make her note that he was holding it out for her.

Still avoiding his gaze, Juliet watched from the corner of her eye as Christopher pulled a chair closer to the fire, then placed the rug she had been sitting upon directly in front of it. He did not sit down, but went to a washbasin by the cot. A towel hung there, and he retrieved it.

"Sit down," he commanded, though not ungently. Mystified, Juliet took a seat upon the rug as he had indicated. Christopher then sat behind her, and Juliet realized with a feeling akin to panic that his legs would be embracing her.

"I'll dry your hair. It is as wet as your clothes," Christopher murmured, already working the towel through her thick, wavy hair.

As she sat almost completely encircled by his very warm, decidedly masculine body, Juliet found herself for the first time in her life unable to think coherently. All her senses were assailed by his nearness. She could see him, hear his even breathing, feel his hands on her hair, smell a heady combination of rain, cologne, and man. The only thing lacking was taste, and if she turned her head even a fraction, her lips would graze his thigh.

The thought made her blush hotly. She lifted her cup, hoping the warm brew might slow her racing pulses.

"Juliet?"

"Yes?" Her breathlessness was too obvious not to be noticed.

"Will you always address me as 'my lord,' do you

141

think? It is not the custom any longer for a wife to be so formal with her husband, you know.''

Her eyes half-closed, Juliet could not trust her voice to reply. She shrugged slightly instead.

"Most people call me Kit.''

There was a soft, lazy quality to Christopher's voice which made it impossible for Juliet to think to say she'd never addressed him in so familiar a manner because he'd never asked her to do so.

His hands stopped working their magic on her hair and fell to her bare shoulders, turning her around to face him.

The blood began to pound in her veins at the sight of the half-smile that curved his firm mouth.

" 'Yes, Kit,' '' he teased her softly.

Entranced, Juliet stared, almost bemused, at the sparkle in his eyes. His mouth seemed to be coming closer. . . .

But then, to her confusion, he was looking away.

"My lord!'' she heard someone call at almost the same moment.

"Oh, my . . . Chr . . . ah, Kit!'' Juliet gasped, jerking backward. "Someone is here.''

"So it would seem,'' he remarked in a not-altogether-pleased tone as he rose.

While Juliet struggled to get into her still-rather-wet clothes, she heard O'Malley's Irish brogue through the door.

"We found her ladyship's pony and cart, my lord, and feared the worst. I've been lookin' everywhere for her, but had not thoought o' this place.''

"Lady Juliet is fine, O'Malley. In the future, however, you are not to harness the cart for her when a storm is threatening. Is that clear?''

"Yes, of course, my lord. I didna think it would blow up so quick.''

"Evidently. Thank you, yes, I'll take the cloak. You may go back now, I'll bring Lady Juliet myself.''

"Of course, my lord.''

When Christopher returned, Juliet could not look at him and stared mutely at the heavy cloak in his hands.

"Your minions are hard at work on your behalf," he drawled, holding it out.

"They are not my minions!" Juliet shot him a quick look and saw his eyes were twinkling.

"Your followers, then," he allowed with a beguiling smile. But just as quickly as it had come, it was gone, and he was frowning. "Let's get you home. The rain and thunder have subsided for the moment, and those clothes are not half-dry."

He buttoned her quickly and efficiently, and soon Juliet was sitting before him on Ajax. She felt very warm and protected in the circle of his arms, though as they made their way home she could not help but regret that O'Malley had remembered the game-keeper's hut.

20

"**I** do hope you plan to be on your best behavior, my love. You'll be the focus of attention for a good many people."

"He'll be happy with that, my lady!" Sally laughed, and Juliet grinned in agreement. Charlie had a decided partiality for being the center of attention.

"He'll have to share a bit of it with his mother, though. Her grace's dresser has fixed your hair in the prettiest way I ever saw."

"Thank you, Sally." Juliet straightened to look into the cheval glass. Her pale wheat-colored curls streamed prettily down from a knot fixed at the top of her head, some curling to frame her face and others to trail down her neck. "I only hope it will stay like this through the dance tonight. I've never worn such an intricate arrangement."

"Grace showed me what to do if it begins to come unpinned. Never you worry, you'll look fine as fivepence come the end of the dance."

It was not really a full-fledged dance they were having, just an informal dinner and entertainment for the forty-odd neighbors Christopher had invited to celebrate Charlie's christening. It was, however, Juliet's first formal outing in the neighborhood, and she did want to look presentable.

Making her way to the drawing room, Juliet smiled with pleasure. The Hall seemed to shine with the attention it had been given. When she spied Stokes, she greeted him warmly. "Everything looks very lovely, Mr. S. Please convey my thanks to the staff."

The old man beamed and said he would. "It seems quite like the old days," he added, which pleased Juliet. She knew from Mrs. Stokes that in the days of Christopher's grandmother the Hall had been a place of much gaiety and warmth.

In the drawing room Lutetia and Serena were seated on the couch discussing something with serious expressions on their faces, while Ronald and Christopher chatted by the fire.

Lutetia was the first to see her, and called out in her raspy voice, "Grace has outdone herself, Juliet! You look quite charming. Come and kiss this old cheek, and let me marvel over that dewy complexion of yours. I do wonder if my skin was ever so soft."

"Lutetia, you are the greatest cozener alive," Juliet laughed, coming over to greet her friend.

"She speaks no more than the truth, Juliet." Serena smiled her welcome. "You look lovely. I vow you and Kit will be almost sinfully handsome together. What do you think, Kit?" his sister asked, looking across at her brother.

Juliet turned toward him as well. He did look extraordinarily fine in his formal dark attire. Perhaps it was the contrast, but his blue eyes seemed particularly crystalline.

"You would add immodesty to my already lengthy list of sins, Ree," he said with a wry smile for Serena. "Suffice it to say I think it would be difficult to improve upon my wife."

"As do I!" exclaimed his grace, coming forward to raise Juliet's slender hand. "I don't believe I've ever seen you look lovelier, my dear."

Even as Juliet smiled at the older man's flattery, she thought the duke had only chosen to take Christopher's words as complimentary to her. He might as easily have meant that because she was a hopeless cause, there was no way to improve her.

Perhaps she was only being sensitive, but ever since they'd returned after the storm, Christopher had been reserved with her, almost as if he regretted their moment of intimacy. Though she would look up to find his gaze was upon her, it would, invariably, be too veiled for her to read.

"But, Kit!" Serena exclaimed suddenly. "You haven't given Juliet her gift."

Juliet looked with surprise from brother to sister. "Gift?" She addressed Serena, not her unfathomable husband.

Nevertheless it was Christopher who answered, his deep voice bringing her attention back to him. "In commemoration of the son you've given me," he said, extending a large flat rectangular box of wood he had lifted from the mantel.

The catch was old and resisted Juliet's suddenly clumsy fingers, but when it gave, she gasped aloud. A necklace, brooch, bracelet, and long dangling earrings, all of silver filigree so thin and intricate it looked like lace, lay upon a bed of black velvet. At the center of each joint—and the necklace alone had more than a hundred—a perfect diamond gleamed brightly.

The effect of the whole was dazzling, and Juliet, her eyes enormous, gazed wonderingly at the gift.

"They are . . ." she began, looking up at Christopher.

"The St. Charles diamonds," he finished quietly, his blue gaze locking with hers. Something flickered briefly at the back of his eyes, but almost before Juliet could register it, he was lifting the brooch from the box.

As he pinned it on her, Juliet was wondering what the gift meant—if, indeed, it meant anything at all. Was it only another example of Christopher's penchant for giving women extravagant gifts? Leslie Chester-Headley's emeralds came to mind. But these were the St. Charles jewels. Juliet searched Christopher's expression. Was he telling her she was worthy of the title countess now? His face told her nothing, for he was listening to Lutetia tell him about a time she'd seen his grandmother wear the necklace. Juliet ran her finger over a long, exquisite earring. She was refining too much on the matter; likely the gift was, as he had said when he presented it, to acknowledge the mother of his heir, nothing more or less.

To everyone's approval, that heir was the very model of infant decorum throughout his christening. The supreme effort took its toll, and as soon as he was home and fed, he yawned hugely and fell fast asleep.

Chuckling, Juliet kissed his cheek. "He should sleep for some time now, but fetch me when he awakens, Sally."

After Sally said she would, Juliet, her silk skirts rustling softly, hurried from the room. Even now she could hear the first of the carriages arriving.

At the foot of the stairs she took a deep breath. It was the first affair she had ever hosted, and though it was a relatively small one, she felt anxious. Would she remember all their names, would they enjoy themselves, would they think her absurdly young to be the Countess of Hartford?

"This is always the worst moment."

Juliet whirled at the sound of Christopher's voice.

Unbelievably, he was smiling. "You needn't worry, everyone will be thoroughly charmed."

Juliet did not have the time to decide whether he meant charmed by her or by the Hall, for Mr. Stokes was already opening the door, but she did know that her husband had been kind. The effect was immediate. The vicar's wife summed it up nicely when she remarked later to her husband, "I don't believe I ever saw anyone's eyes shine so brightly as the countess's did tonight when she received us."

The evening, after starting so auspiciously, continued in the same way. It was with great relief and some surprise that Juliet found that Christopher, when he wanted, could play the affable host very nicely. Of course all the ladies were fluttering delightedly when they left him, but it was a measure of Christopher's charm that with a deft word or two he could bring a broad smile to the faces of their husbands and brothers as well.

Country gentry from the near neighborhood, all Juliet's guests were delighted to be attending a dinner

147

party at Hartford Hall. Everyone, it seemed, exclaimed over something, whether it was her lovely brooch, or the way the Hall gleamed, or her dress, or Charlie's impeccable behavior. Won over by the universal friendliness, Juliet soon relaxed and was able to enjoy herself and the meal she and Mrs. Stokes had worked so hard to arrange.

After dinner, when the ladies were happily ensconced in the drawing room and the gentlemen were at their port, Juliet left her hostess duties in Serena's vastly capable hands and went to attend to Charlie. As she was returning, she was not pleased to see that Jonathan was waiting for her at the door to the library.

Nodding, she made as if to pass by, but he caught her by the arm, saying plaintively, "Juliet, I've been waiting for you."

Juliet's brow lifted with impatience. "I have guests to attend to now, Jonathan."

"Please, this won't take a moment," he said, pulling her into the room and closing the door before she knew what he was about. "I remembered that yesterday was your birthday, and I wanted to give you this." As he spoke, Jonathan held out a box in which lay an old and lovely cameo.

Even as she had the irrelevant thought that for someone who had heretofore received only a string of not-very-fine pearls from her grandmother on her sixteenth birthday, she was certainly making up for lost time, Juliet shook her head exasperatedly. "Jonathan, this will not do! I am married and cannot receive gifts from you or anyone else. You must see that you place me in an awkward position with these attentions."

The crestfallen look on Jonathan's face almost made her relent, but she did not. It was time the self-centered young man thought about another's feelings. Resolutely she turned on her heel to go.

"But—"

The ardent reply Jonathan was about to make was cut short by the opening of the door. "Ah, here you are. Sally said you had left Charlie some little time ago."

Juliet bit her lip, entirely put out to be found closeted with Jonathan. It made her feel almost guilty.

It did not help when Christopher's blue gaze impaled her and then moved in the most accusing way to Jonathan, who stood with the box in his hand, the large cameo quite plain for all to see.

"Jonathan was only just showing me a gift he bought for Harriet, Christopher."

Juliet heard the calm, assured lie as if it had come from another's mouth. Her father would have scolded her for it, but it seemed the most graceful way to extricate them all from Jonathan's foolishness. Not that Christopher would be jealous. His affections, of course, were not engaged enough for that. But he did not seem pleased to find Juliet neglecting her other guests to hold a tryst with Jonathan. There were rules for these things, she supposed, and from the look on Christopher's face he had little regard for a young puppy who did not abide by them.

With a composure she had never imagined she would have, Juliet added, "But we have just finished our chat, my lord, and I hope you will escort me to the ballroom. It is time to open our dance, I think."

"Precisely why I came in search of you, my dear," Christopher drawled with just enough mockery in his tone to bring a flush to Juliet's cheek.

It prompted her to lift her chin, and because she had done nothing to be ashamed of, she turned to Jonathan with great deliberation and reminded him that he had claimed a dance from her.

"Very smooth, my dear," Christopher whispered after the library door had closed behind them. "You have learned a great deal here in the wilds of Lincolnshire. But I wonder why you thought it necessary to protect Mr. Briding. If he is presumptuous enough to present my wife a valuable gift while he is enjoying my hospitality, he should be man enough to listen to my thoughts on the subject."

A delicate pink tint rose in Juliet's cheeks, but her gray eyes, when she raised them to Christopher's, did not falter.

"I cannot see that it should matter to you if Jonathan Briding wanted to present me a cameo for my birthday. Before we married you told me we should go our own ways, and you have not since then indicated that you have changed your mind. If I told a lie in the library, it was because Jonathan presumed upon me, not you, and I thought it was I who should set him straight."

Her breast heaving slightly with emotion, Juliet steeled herself for a cool set-down.

She was taken off guard, therefore, when Christopher, regarding her with narrowed eyes, said, "Today is your birthday?"

Juliet blinked. "No, no." She shook her head. "Yesterday was."

"Lord Christopher!" It was Major Bromwell, standing just inside the ballroom door, who hailed them. "You've got your lovely wife where you want her, I daresay. The kissing bough, as we called it in my day, is just above you!"

The mistletoe had been Becky Briding's idea, and Juliet had quite forgotten it until now. No one else had, it seemed, for she heard the cry "A kiss! A kiss!" raised by all the people clustered nearby.

If Christopher was disconcerted to find himself the object of attention at so inopportune a moment, he recovered quickly. With a sudden entirely boyish lopsided smile, he bowed to the group.

"It is my duty to keep my guests satisfied, but I confess I have seldom found the task so . . . ah, pleasant."

His easy jest earned him great shouts of laughter, and when he turned back to Juliet, he was still smiling. It seemed so strange to Juliet that Christopher should be about to kiss her here before the world when he had scarcely touched her since their marriage, that she felt quite dazed.

As if in a dream she watched as his long thin fingers came to tilt up her chin, forcing her to look at him. His smile had faded, she saw, and had been replaced

150

by a look she did not recognize, though it made her shiver.

Normally kisses stolen under the mistletoe were short, brief salutes. This one was not. After only the briefest hesitation, Juliet's mouth, surrendering to her husband's lips, opened softly. She was aware of nothing but the sweet, demanding, thrilling feel of him. Dimly she did hear a cry go up, then felt Christopher pull away. Just in time she kept herself from crying out for more.

"Well done!" cheered the major.

Wretchedly aware of the blush staining her cheeks, Juliet did not know where to look. She felt exposed to everyone, but most of all to her husband.

Concentrating on keeping her head up, Juliet allowed Christopher to lead her through the crowd onto the floor.

Her hand, raised to acknowledge the ripple of appreciative applause their entrance had set off, faltered slightly when Christopher, out of the corner of his mouth, whispered, "Happy Birthday."

When she registered the ghost of a chuckle accompanying his words, her cheeks colored visibly. Their audience, whose members thought they were the reason the countess blushed so prettily, applauded more loudly. The music started, and on cue Christopher swept her into his arms.

Unable to avoid it now, Juliet looked up into her husband's face. Whatever it was she had expected, it was not the beguiling, roguish grin with which he was regarding her. And without thought for the morrow, for in fact she could not have kept from it if she had thought what she was about, Juliet returned that smile measure for measure.

21

All the ladies watching—and that was all the ladies in the room—breathed a collective sigh of delight as the earl, smiling the sort of breathtaking smile they had only dreamed about, whirled his lovely young wife in the figure of the opening dance. Two of those ladies, after they had sighed, also exchanged a significant glance. Juliet, too taken up with the delight of dancing her first dance with her husband, did not notice. She did learn the next day, however, what it signified.

"A delightful evening, my dear!" the duchess pronounced at luncheon. She and the duke, not wanting to travel late, had stayed the night and now Lutetia's black eyes were sparkling as she glanced around the table.

Juliet, not in her husband's arms now, saw that sparkle and wondered at it.

"I declare I had almost forgotten how very much I enjoy the social whirl," Lutetia continued. "I believe that while the sociable mood is still upon me, I shall prevail upon Crewe to take me to town."

"But that is wonderful!" exclaimed Serena as if on cue. "Now I shall have someone to keep me company when I go."

Juliet's eyes narrowed. There was of a sudden a great deal of talk about London. When she saw the duchess's gaze settle upon her, she shook her head, silently imploring her not to say what Juliet with dreadful certainty believed she had it in her mind to say.

Lutetia, never easily deflected from her course, was not now. "I know!" she cried wide-eyed, as if the thought had just come to her. "You must come as well, Juliet! I am persuaded you will be lonely without Crewe and me or Serena for companionship."

Juliet's gaze flicked briefly to Christpher, but he was regarding Lutetia with a veiled expression. Her smiling, teasing dance partner of the night before was gone.

"I am getting old, you know," Lutetia continued, her face taking on such a pitiful expression that Juliet, despite the circumstances, choked. Lutetia waved her hand loftily. "You may laugh all you like, but it is true. I am how old now, Crewe? No, never mind, it never does any good to exactly know one's age. It is better by far to ignore the matter and enjoy yourself. And it would be my greatest pleasure, child, to take you around. All my connections owe me favors—I've seen to enough of their whey-faced chits over the years!"

"Lutetia, you are a complete hand, you know," Juliet chided, though she was grinning. "I cannot possibly—"

"Of course you can," Lutetia cut in imperiously. "That boy of yours can come right along with us. We won't leave him here to starve. You and Serena can do the shops by day, and in the evening we shall all join forces. Crewe can escort us about. I think I might even give a ball in your honor."

"Lut—"

Lutetia held up her hand, and though it was quite small, the gesture was authoritative. "You cannot deny me, you know, Juliet. I stayed beside you in your time of need, and now it is your turn to do something for me."

"Lutetia!" Juliet cried, aghast at such ruthlessness.

"Lutetia is shameless when she's trying to get her own way, Juliet." The duke smiled at her in his gentle way. "She will use every weapon at her disposal, and you must disregard her completely. Only remember that it would indeed make us both very happy if we

153

could take you about in society with us. And, too, if you come, we shall be able to see Charlie. You know very well that we dote on the lad."

"You really are too kind, your grace, and you are every bit as bent on getting your way as Lutetia! I must refuse, however. There is a great deal for me to do yet here on the estate. I've flowers to plant, and O'Malley is going to teach me to ride."

"Nonsense!" It was, of course, Lutetia. "You have gardeners for the flowers, and you may learn to ride anytime, even in town, if you must. What say you, my handsome lord? Surely your plans include the Season. Persuade Juliet to come along with us so that we can all have a grand time together."

Along with everyone else, Juliet turned to look at Christopher. Her heart sank at what she saw. With his lips curved slightly in the mocking smile she feared, Christopher flicked his cool gaze from Lutetia to her and back again. His voice no warmer than his gaze, he said, "Juliet is a grown woman, she may do as she likes."

Though if I do, I'll pay for it with your displeasure, Juliet added to herself. He did not want her. She had known he would not, but to have it said so openly before company hurt. His lingering kiss and teasing smile had meant next to nothing. He still wanted free rein in town, and to see her only when it suited him.

Was she, then, because Christopher could not be bothered with her, never to go to a play, visit Vauxhall Gardens, or again see the Elgin Marbles? It did not seem at all fair.

"Well, I suppose going to town would not be such a burden," Juliet allowed, smiling at Lutetia and studiously avoiding her husband. "When had you thought to leave? I presume you mean to move quickly for fear the Grim Reaper may catch you first."

Ronald and Serena laughed, but Lutetia, less modest as always, gave a great hoot. "Minx! You mustn't tease your elders. It won't do. But, to answer you, I think five days would be ample time in which to do our packing."

154

When Juliet, Serena, and Ronald had agreed, Lutetia, who did not lack for audacity, turned to Christopher. "And you, Kit? Will you be coming with us, or will matters at the Hall keep you in Lincolnshire yet awhile?"

Lutetia, both a duchess and old enough to be his mother, found reason to look into her teacup when Christopher did not answer at once, but only regarded her with a narrowed icy look. "Five days should be sufficient for me as well," he said after he had made her squirm long enough.

It had been an unpardonably rude thing to do, Christopher knew, but he felt angry enough not to care. He hated having his hand forced by anyone, whether a duchess or his wife. Not that he thought Juliet the author of this scheme to get herself back to town without his invitation. She was too honest to have played the reluctant party so convincingly. But, he thought, abruptly excusing himself from the table, she could have held out, if she had really wanted.

He had thought she was content. . . . Well, never mind what he'd thought. He'd obviously been wrong. She'd agreed to leave the Hall (and him as well, he could not help adding) readily enough.

Damn! He should be glad to be going to London. He was in danger of becoming maudlin. Still he did not have to be pleased to have had his decision made for him. He would have to go, if Juliet did, for he could not trust her not to make another disastrous misstep without him; but, he swore grimly, she would pay a price for cutting up his peace.

Later that afternoon Serena knocked on Juliet's door, interrupting her as she consulted with Sally on what should be packed. "That will be all for now, Sally," Juliet said at once. It was the first opportunity she had had to speak with Serena alone.

"Serena!" she said the moment the door had closed. "I wish you and Lutetia had not done this—and don't bother to deny your part. I saw your eyes encouraging her grace. I know you mean well, but Christopher is furious at being maneuvered in this way. I only wish I

155

had not given in to my own base impulse to goad him."

Serena chuckled at Juliet's mournful expression. "Kit, when he wants, can be odious enough to try even the most saintly person."

Serena laughed as Juliet groaned aloud, and then added with a militant gleam in her eye, "But I have taken it upon myself to give my brother a thing or two to think about."

"You've talked to him?"

"Indeed I have, and you needn't look so anxious. I only informed him that it would be of little use to his son for society to think his mother so wanting she could not be allowed an occasional visit to town. I am in the right, and he knew it. There was nothing at all he could say."

"What else did you say, Serena? I can tell by that smug look that there was more."

Serena grinned then. "I told that imperious brother of mine what Lutetia told me, that if he thought you should be kept from coming to London simply because you had dealt Leslie what she deserved, he was fair and far out. For every one person scandalized by the incident, at least a dozen applauded you."

"Oh, Serena!" Juliet cried. "Was he very angry?"

"Well, he was not much pleased," Serena conceded dryly. "But it did him a world of good to hear it anyway. Now let's forget my brother for a bit, for I know that we shall have a glorious time in town! Just think of the shopping we can do. I've brought along all the latest copies of *La Belle Assemblée* so that we may decide what we'll have made up first."

Juliet listened, comforted by Serena's enthusiasm. It would, she hoped, lend her the courage to face Christopher and his cold displeasure.

22

"I do hope Kean is at his best tonight! He can be flat sometimes, you know, and I should be so disappointed if he were."

Lutetia, looking quite dashing in a deep lavender dress and matching turban, addressed Juliet and Serena, who sat opposite her. They awaited the duke, Christopher, and Arthur Coleman, a friend of Serena's, who were still in the dining room savoring their port.

"Well"—Serena grinned happily— "whatever takes place onstage, at least we three can be assured that we look magnificent for Juliet's debut."

While Lutetia laughed, Juliet rolled her eyes. "Not being as complete a hand as you, Serena, I hesitate to say I look magnificent, but I can say, thanks to you both, that I look passable."

"You like Prym, then? Gad! What a name." Lutetia shook her head, the plume on her turban waving excitedly.

"She is a dear creature." Juliet smiled. "As unlike the dresser I had last year as possible. You must thank Grace for finding her."

"I shall," Lutetia assured her. "But where did you two find such perfect dresses on so short notice?"

"We visited Mrs. Henry," Serena spoke up, waving her hand idly. "I made it clear it would be worth her while to accommodate us."

Juliet chuckled dryly. "The order Serena promised

the poor woman, if she would rush our gowns, lifted her brows to her hairline."

"My dear, we are here for the Season," Serena said, as if that explained a great deal. "Furthermore, even had the clothes you bought last year been in a suitable style, they would still be outdated."

"That is what she says every time I protest another purchase." Juliet shook her head. "But I will say, you do make shopping a sight more fun than ever Trask did, Serena, and that does not even mention your better eye."

"Which is scarcely any compliment at all. Even a blind person could have seen you didn't need those light colors. And if I do say so myself, I did especially well when I chose that particular dress for you."

Serena, her head tipped slightly, admired the picture Juliet made in a dress of silver net over a midnight-blue underslip. The combination of colors had lightened Juliet's eyes to the color of the net, while the wide neck, though of a depth Juliet could accept, exposed just the right amount of her fine creamy shoulders.

"And Charlie is getting on well with his new nurse?" Lutetia asked Juliet.

"Mrs. Adams is a gem! With Mrs. Stokes as her sister, you know she must be a kind soul. It helps having Sally there as well, of course. She's a familiar face for him."

"So you've no regrets about coming?"

"I've enjoyed myself immensely," Juliet temporized.

But Lutetia did not let her off so easily. "And Kit?"

Juliet flashed her a wry look. "If you are asking has Christopher forgiven me for coming—no, he has not. He speaks only when he must, and then only as briefly as possible."

"Well, he has come tonight, at least."

Juliet made a face. "Only because you asked him directly, Lutetia, and, I daresay, to be certain I don't do anything disgraceful."

The gentlemen came in then, with the duke and Mr. Coleman leading the way. Juliet's eyes unerringly went

158

to the figure strolling in last. In a superbly fitting coat of dark blue, a white satin waistcoat, and dark blue pants of as close a fit as his coat, Christopher would draw any woman's eye.

His gaze touched hers and as quickly he looked away. It had been thus ever since Juliet had said she would come to town. He was not actually impolite, and as Serena was staying with them, he was even at home a good deal of the time, but his manner toward her was the equivalent of a slap.

Only once, when she had been nursing Charlie and he had come upon her unawares, had she caught a flash of warmth in his eyes. And then, of course, it had been impossible to determine whether she or Charlie was the cause of that brief arrested look. The odds, Juliet thought, favored Charlie.

"It is time we were on our way," she heard Lutetia say, and Juliet sternly quelled an attack of nerves. It was her first outing in society since her ill-fated attendance at the Darnsbys' ball.

"Why, thank you, Mr. Coleman." She smiled at that gentleman as he assisted her with her wrap. He smiled in reply, but it seemed as if he were directing that expression to her shoulders, so difficult did he find it to tear his gaze away.

"Very lovely," he murmured when he did at last look up.

Her eyes sparkling at this conformation that she did indeed look nice, she thanked him prettily. Then, chancing to look to the door, she saw that Christopher was watching them and not looking vastly pleased, it seemed. Of course, he was of late never looking particularly pleased, but the degree of frown did seem more intense. For some unknown reason, the thought cheered her immensely and sent her to the carriage in higher spirits than she had been since her arrival in town.

The first intermission at the theater proved that Lutetia knew society a deal better than Juliet. Just as Juliet was telling herself that if no one came to their box, it would not matter to her, she would simply go home to the Hall, the door opened upon a steady stream of visitors.

Crowding into the small space, they paid their respects to the duke and duchess, greeted Christopher and Serena, and were introduced to Juliet. No one, and Juliet watched closely, so much as lifted an eyebrow when they learned who she was.

Christopher patiently stood by her at the first, making one presentation after another, and she was grateful to him. His presence seemed a public confirmation that she had been forgiven. The situation did not last for long, however, for an old friend of Serena's, a very pretty redheaded friend, was soon turning him away from Juliet by the simple expedient of firmly grasping his arm.

Juliet was scarcely given the time to notice, however, for almost at the same moment, she saw a familiar auburn head weaving its way through the closely packed crowd.

"What a pleasant surprise, Lord Darnsby!" she exclaimed sincerely, for it was Hal Darnsby, looking very handsome in his regimentals, who was lifting her hand to his lips.

Hal's eyes twinkled merrily. "The pleasure is all mine, Lady Juliet. By Jove! You are in looks tonight!"

Juliet smiled at him with real pleasure. "I am pleased to see the army has not affected your ability to flatter, Lord Darnsby. If I recall correctly, you were extremely generous the first time we met, when I was, to say the least, not at my best."

Hal grinned. "You were more . . . ah, shall we say, informal on that occasion, perhaps, but no less charming."

"And discreet!" Juliet grinned back. "I would wager that with your sweet tongue and that uniform you'll break all the girls' hearts."

"Or die in the attempt," Hal swore in mock solemnity, his hand over his heart.

When someone in the crowded box jostled him, Hal made a face at Juliet. "I'm taking too long at your side, I suppose. Everyone wants to meet you, you know. The entire theater is abuzz with talk of Kit's beautiful wife."

Juliet was amazed and looked it. "Well!" was all she could think to say, causing Hal to laugh delightedly. "Your dress may have changed, Lady Juliet, but I can see you are still not the least puffed up about your looks." He laughed again, for Juliet still did not know what to say, and indeed was looking uncomfortable. "What do you say to a ride in the park tomorrow in my new phaeton? I can regale you with my adventures in the army, and you can tell me how it is to be a diamond of the first water without knowing it!"

Juliet did not try to resist his charm, and, her eyes sparkling at him, she told him she would like it above all things. Firmly putting aside all memories of her last trip there with his sister, she added, "I've never been perched up high in a phaeton, you know."

Hal expressed his horror at this lapse in her experience, and then ceded his place at her side to a balding man who, though as flattering, was not half so much fun.

At the second intermission Serena suggested they go for a walk in the lobby. "It was a little warm here before, with half the theater trying to crowd in," she observed with a grin at Juliet.

Lutetia, not to be outdone, shot Juliet a triumphant look, and Juliet, seeing it, smilingly bowed her head in acknowledgment of the duchess's superior wisdom.

Superior wisdom in regards to society, not Christopher, Juliet added to herself as she descended the staircase to the lobby. Serena on one side with Mr. Coleman was all volubility, while Christopher on the other was absolutely silent.

When they reached the lobby, their little group was quickly surrounded. There were friends of Serena's, friends of Lutetia's, friends of Christopher's, and young bucks who could only claim to be friends of friends. Chritopher eyed the scene with an arched brow, and then, saying he would fetch them all drinks, departed.

Juliet could not much blame him, really; it was close with so many people about. Still, as she watched his broad shoulders disappear into the crowd, it was impossible for her not to recall how the last time he had gone to fetch her a drink he had never come back.

"Lady Crump! I've someone I'd like you to meet!"

Lutetia's voice recalled her to the present, and though it took a great deal of resolution, Juliet put Christopher from her mind. Or at least to the back of her mind. There was little else she could do, she reasoned.

When she had been introduced to so many people she was beginning to forget faces, not to mention names, Juliet decided she too would escape. Ronald had elected to remain in the box rather than attempt the lobby, and Juliet, after telling Lutetia where she was bound, headed eagerly toward his calm company.

She had gone about halfway up the stairs when an unfamiliar voice hailed her. Turning, she saw a gentleman approaching, puffing in his hurry to reach her. His appearance rang a distant chord, but it was not until Juliet saw the woman accompanying him that she was able to put a name to the young man.

He was the Marquess of Hightower and the woman with him was Celeste Darnsby. Celeste's eyes narrowed sharply as they swept Juliet.

It was, Juliet knew, the highest compliment she had received all evening, and she experienced a most delicious, if unworthy, feeling of triumph.

"Lady Hartford! I say, this is luck! You have been so surrounded I thought we never should get the opportunity to speak to you! But I told you that if we kept our eyes open, an opportunity would present itself, didn't I, dearest?"

The marquess beamed fondly at Celeste, who, when his attention was returned again to Juliet, slanted him a disgusted look. Celeste, Juliet surmised, had not been as eager as the marquess to see her.

"Celeste." Juliet nodded coolly when their eyes met.

Celeste made some reply, and then the marquess was saying, "Your beauty shining from Crewe's box was like a beacon, Lady Juliet," and because that phrase caused Celeste's lips to thin with annoyance,

162

Juliet quite forgave the young man for forcing her into conversation with the girl.

She smiled nicely at him and was not displeased when his rather distinct Adam's apple began to bob up and down.

"And how is your mother, sir? I hope she is well?"

"Why, thank you, yes, Mother is quite well. She is eagerly awaiting the day I bring Celeste home."

So Celeste had come off with a high title. "I take it congratulations are in order, then?" Juliet inquired politely, looking from Lord Hightower to Celeste.

"Yes." Celeste's chin went up. "We've set a date in August."

"How nice."

"I was not aware you were acquainted with the duke and duchess." The remark seemed to burst from Celeste, as if she had not meant to say it.

Juliet might have pointed out that there was a great deal Celeste did not know about her, but she restrained herself. "I met them in Lincolnshire," she explained.

"Didn't you know, dearest, that Crewe has an estate in Lincolnshire?" asked Lord Hightower, seemingly scandalized by his beloved's ignorance of so weighty a matter.

Juliet nearly laughed aloud at the irritated look that crossed Celeste's face, but then the young man was asking if the duke's estate was close to Hartford, and she was called to satisfy his curiosity as to Crewe Cottage's exact location.

"I wonder where Kit could be," Celeste asked when the marquess had finished talking. Her tone was innocent, but her eyes were not. "I did see him in your box, did I not?"

Juliet's expression did not alter. "Christopher? Yes, he's here somewhere. He went to fetch punch, but I found I could not withstand the rigors of the crowd in the lobby long enough to wait for him."

"The crowd around you, Lady Juliet," the marquess corrected her, his throat working again. "We spent the devil of a time trying to break through all the people surrounding you, and still were not able to. But with you and Lady Serena at the center, one can quite understand the crush."

Juliet looked hard at the marquess, wondering why Celeste's betrothed would be making such an absurd to-do over her. Little more than a second later, she got her answer.

"Oh, look! Here is Hartford now!" the marquess exclaimed, his face flushing with excitement as he looked down the stairs.

Juliet understood then that the goal for both the people detaining her was Christopher. Celeste's reasons she already knew, and she surmised that Lord Hightower was one of those young men Serena had told her about who took the Earl of Hartford as their pattern for behavior in all things. He seemed so beside himself now that Juliet hoped he would not have apoplexy before Christopher got to them.

Christopher, when he did arrive, only tossed Lord Hightower a nod of acknowledgment. Juliet thought the scarcely civil greeting would surely crush the young man, but from the beaming smile on his face she gathered it was sufficient. Celeste got her name said, nothing more, and, not as easily pleased as her husband-to-be, she visibly pouted.

The bare civilities accomplished, Christopher turned to scowl at Juliet. "I struggled through that damnable crush with your glass, only to find you had gone."

Juliet searched his eyes a moment, wondering what to make of this heat over so small a matter. She tried for a level, easy tone. "I am sorry you were put to such trouble for naught. I'd had enough of the crowd, however, and was on my way back to our box. And then Celeste and Lord Hightower chanced to see me," she finished, turning to look at them in the hopes that Christopher would do so as well.

He did not. She could see from the corner of her eye that he was still regarding her grimly.

He might have said more, but the marquess, happily, did not give him the opportunity. In his breathless, eager voice he said to Christopher, "When I met

Lady Juliet last spring, I knew she would be a sensation!"

Juliet thought this such a whisker that her eyes widened, and Christopher, who had still been watching her, made an odd, choking sound. But the marquess had succeeded at last in getting the earl's undivided attention, and swelling with delight, he rushed to add, "And this evening she has proven me right. The talk of the theater is how much more profitable it is to look at your box than at the stage."

Juliet almost felt pity for the young man. If his object was to impress Christopher, he had gone about it entirely the wrong way. Praising her was likely to earn him a set-down.

It did not, but Christopher only inclined his head, acknowledging the remark, nothing more. Though Juliet would have liked him to shout "Hear! Hear!" she could not blame him. Lord Hightower was so obviously currying favor.

Celeste, though she must have sensed Christopher's cool reaction toward her betrothed, did not allow it to deter her from playfully poking Christopher with her fan. "But what a box you are in, Kit! I vow, I never thought to see you in such aged company as that of the Duke and Duchess of Crewe. Why, they are your mother's age!"

"But they are the very best *ton*!" cried her betrothed, clearly scandalized.

Christopher took no note of him, but did turn to look at Celeste. He was not, Juliet saw, smiling. "Actually Ronald is older than Mother, Celeste. But their age does not signify, you know. Few people half their age have even a quarter of their wit."

The lights dipped then, calling the intermission to a halt, but Juliet nonetheless saw Celeste wave her fan hastily to and fro and heard her say, "Well!" in the most put-out way.

Taking Christopher's arm to go back to their box, Juliet thought it served Celeste right for saying Lutetia and Ronald were aged. And then the thought of

Lutetia's probable reaction to such a remark made her chuckle aloud.

"Not thinking you're glad Lutetia wasn't present, are you?"

Juliet turned quickly, amazed that he should have guessed her thought. Her heart seemed to stop as she took in his wry grin. "Only for Celeste's sake," she whispered as they entered the box just in time to see the lights go down.

23

"**L**ord Halsey to see you, my lord," Morton announced gravely from the door of Christopher's study.

Christopher, his booted feet upon his desk, lazily saluted Tony with the glass of brandy in his hand.

"I didn't think you were expected back from your mother's for another week or so. Is she doing so much better, then?"

Tony went directly to the tray which held a bottle of brandy and some glasses, and after pouring himself a liberal portion, eased into the large leather chair opposite Christopher's desk. "Mother is better," he acknowledged after he had taken a long draft from his glass. "How long her recovery will last is another question. I daresay I'll be called down to Hampshire in a month or so to hold her hand all over again. It's been that way since Father's death. I just settle down again in town, and then I get an urgent message saying she's fallen back into melancholia. I suppose I can scarcely blame her. They were very devoted, as you know."

"Hmm." Christopher seemed mesmerized by the golden liquid swirling in his glass. "Your parents' obvious care for one another was always something I envied you."

Tony cast Christopher a suddenly keen glance. After a moment he said casually, "I trust the situation you found at the Hall was felicitous?"

It was some little while before Christopher repeated

"Felicitous?" very slowly. "Was it felicitous, I wonder, to find my own servants upbraiding me?"

Tony's generous eyebrows shot skyward.

"You are incredulous, I see," Christopher drawled with a crooked smile. "Perhaps even doubting. I assure you that Mrs. Stokes told me to my face that my failure to be present for my son's difficult birth was disgraceful. Her husband, more discreet by nature, contented himself with a glacial 'My lord' for welcome after he had not seen me for over a year."

Tony first choked, then coughed, and Christopher observed his spluttering with an ironic half-smile curving his mouth. When Tony was once more breathing easily, he resumed his story as if he had not paused.

"And if that were not enough, Lutetia and Roland, in residence at Crewe Cottage as usual in the summer, met Juliet and in essence adopted her as their daughter. Roland never actually took me to task, but Lutetia, as you can imagine, did not spare me."

Tony, wiping his eyes, managed a chuckle. "And what did the lady herself have to say? Did she play the martyr?"

Christopher's gaze returned to his glass. "She acted as if the universally grim stories of her lying-in were entirely exaggerated. She could not quite hide her fatigue, but other than that she was . . ." He shrugged, leaving the thought unfinished.

A long silence ensued, each man lost in his thoughts, and then, as he stared idly out of the window, Christopher spoke again. "You will not credit it, Tony, but that girl ran the estate virtually alone. Cartwright's wife died, and the poor man was so distracted, his work fell off entirely. There are almost no entries in the books for the month of May. When Juliet realized the situation, she took over the books and put Cartwright in the position of counselor until he could pull himself together."

"Good Lord!" Tony exclaimed. "Well, your problems must be solved, then."

"Oh?" Christopher's brow arched quizzically.

"Lady Juliet must be content with her lot at the

Hall, I mean. She'll not mind staying there while you come to town. But, good Lord! I've forgotten to ask after your heir."

A broad, genuine smile lit Christopher's face. "Charlie's very well, thank you. He's the spitting image of his father, if I may say so."

Tony laughed. "A handsome devil, then. I'd like very much to see him."

"Would you?" asked Christopher, his smile becoming wry. "You should have that opportunity, if you stay to tea."

"What? Your son is here? But that must mean Lady Juliet . . ."

"Quick as ever, I see," drawled Christopher with a lazy grin. "No, my wife did not remain at the Hall content with her lot. As I said, everyone who met her in Lincolnshire became entranced with her. Perhaps it was the air. Serena proved no exception. When she and Lutetia were coming to town, it was obvious to all that Juliet should come as well."

"To all?" Tony asked with a shrewd glance.

Christopher's expression darkened, and he threw down the rest of his brandy. "There was nothing I could do," he said over his shoulder as he went to replenish his supply. "Even Ronald supported her. With the Duke and Duchess of Crewe declaring it would be their greatest pleasure to sponsor her, it was impossible to refuse. Anyway, she had to come to town sometime. You're just in time to attend the ball Lutetia's holding in her honor. It's next Tuesday."

"Good Lord, Kit, how long have you been in town?"

"Two weeks."

"So long? But how has it been? Has Lady Juliet had any better time of it?"

"You mean has Juliet appeared dressed as a Gypsy waif, fallen into a brawl on the street, or slapped Leslie? No. She is still doing good works. She'd not be Juliet, I suppose, if she weren't. However, she is confining herself to accepted charities. She and the duchess give their time at an orphanage which Lutetia has long sponsored. As of yet Juliet has not tried to adopt one of the children unfortunate enough to live there."

Christopher paused, once more taking a swallow of brandy. When he resumed again, he spoke slowly, almost as if he were speaking against his will. "As for her appearances in society, Juliet has behaved as she should. And is, it seems, enjoying some success. Hal Darnsby and his cronies have made it quite the thing to be seen escorting the beautiful Countess of Hartford about town."

"Beautiful?" Tony knew he was echoing Kit, but he could not help it.

To Tony's surprise, Christopher looked slightly uncomfortable. It was a fleeting expression, but there was no mistaking it.

"She has a new dresser," Christopher said, a shade of impatience creeping into his tones. "Lutetia sent her over when we arrived, and Juliet's looks are more fashionable now."

Tony did not find Kit's answer very satisfactory. Did he mean Juliet was more fashionable or, as he had first said, beautiful? Kit, however, was looking too grim for Tony to pursue the matter.

"And Lady Corinne?" he asked instead, referring to the wife of a much older baronet whom Christopher had seen more than a little of after Christmas. It was she who had written to Christopher to remind him of the Carlisles' house party. "How is she taking the news of Lady Juliet's arrival?"

Christopher shrugged in a way Tony thought told a great deal. "Actually I've seen very little of Corinne. Serena has had me dancing attendance on her and my wife."

"I see," said Tony, taking a swallow from his glass, though in fact he did not see at all. If there was one thing he knew about Christopher St. Charles, the Earl of Hartford, it was that no one ever had made him do anything he had not wanted to do. Kit loved his sister, he knew, but even so, Tony would have wagered a staggering amount on the proposition that Serena could not bend her brother to her will, unless for some reason he actually wanted to do what he protested he did not want to do.

A slow smile spread over Tony's face. Remembering the Countess of Hartford's lovely, expressive eyes and the short but lively conversation he had had with her, he broadened his smile perceptibly. How delightful, he thought to himself, that just when he had decided this Season would be like every other, he should be provided with the sight of Kit trying to come to terms with his young wife for entertainment.

24

Not many days later, Juliet came down to breakfast to find Christopher was the only one there before her. She was not surprised to find him there alone, for Serena was the latest riser of the three. Nor was she surprised that he did not so much as raise his golden head when she entered.

She helped herself to toast and damson preserves, accepted coffee from the footman, stirred in some sugar, and still there was not the least sign of acknowledgement.

When the footman left, Juliet decided she could not accept such a state of affairs any longer. For two weeks she had tolerated it, and now she had had enough. "Christopher? May I speak with you?"

His blue eyes lifted slowly, as if Juliet were asking a great deal to tear him from his morning paper. He said nothing, only looked at her with indifferent eyes, waiting.

Juliet held her temper, though it took some effort. Really, he could be insufferable at times!

"I won't pretend I'm not glad I came to town. I have enjoyed myself a great deal. However, I cannot help but know you are displeased that I have come. I would have relations between us better than this, if it is possible. Would it make any difference to you if you knew I did not put Lutetia up to inviting me?"

Christopher, without the least change of expression, folded his paper carefully. "I am not such a fool as to think that Lutetia would make her plans without any encouragement from you at all."

Juliet's breath caught. "You would think me a liar, then?"

The door opened noisily before Christopher could reply. It was the footman with more coffee, and when he stood between her and Christopher, Juliet furiously blinked back angry tears. It had seemed such a simple thing to tell him the truth, have him believe it, accept her presence with a wry laugh for Lutetia's interfering nature, and be her friend again. She should have known that nothing with Christopher would be so easy.

When the footman was gone, her husband, his penetrating gaze upon her, resumed the conversation in an impatient tone. "I believe you did not actually put Lutetia up to her scheme. But can you honestly say that you knew nothing of her intentions?"

Juliet began to say that of course she had not known, when, remembering the conversation she'd had with Lutetia on the subject, she snapped her mouth closed.

"I see you've refreshed your memory." It was Christopher at his most biting.

"I told her not to invite me!" Juliet cried, stung. "I told her you would be furious if I came."

"And yet you did come, did you not? You might have refused Lutetia, but no, you wanted to enjoy society. And now you tell me that you are enjoying it. So where is the rub, Juliet? Is it that you want me to be pleased that you've come? Like most women, you ask too much. I did not invite you. You forced your company upon me. I am doing my part now that you are here, playing the attendant husband. I do so for the sake of my son. And with that you'll have to be satisfied, because it is all you'll get."

Christopher's napkin landed in a heap on the table, followed by his paper, and the next moment Juliet was staring at the door that had slammed sharply behind her husband.

"Juliet, you look far too blue-deviled for someone who is one of the successes of the Season! I do hope it

173

is not my brother who has put that dreadful frown on your face."

Serena's high spirits only served to cast Juliet's further down. It seemed unfair that this morning of all mornings, her sister-in-law should choose to rise early. "We had something of a . . . ah, clearing of the air, you might say," Juliet allowed with a wan smile. "But please, let us not dwell upon it. Tell me instead what has served to put you in such a good humor at so early an hour."

"For pity's sake don't tell me you've forgotten we go to Mrs. Henry's for the final fittings on the gowns we'll wear to Lutetia's, Juliet! Or that we've the Abernathys' rout this evening! I know Caroline Abernathy is a trifle rackety, but that makes her affairs all the more entertaining. One never knows exactly who might be in attendance."

Juliet, whose very being felt leaden after her disastrous conversation with Christopher, was about to protest she could not go. She would say she needed to rest for Lutetia's ball the next evening. Her mouth opened too late, however. Serena was already speaking.

"Before he slammed out of the house, looking, I might add, as out of sorts with the cleared air between you as you do, Kit informed me he'd had a change of plan and would not be able to accompany us this evening. It is of little moment, though. I'm certain I can prevail upon Tony to do the honors."

Juliet never doubted her immediate assumption as to where Christopher would be spending his evening. He had made it plain enough that he had been her escort out of duty, not pleasure, and she was certain he had decided he was due a little of the latter. A vision of his former mistress's voluptuous charms clad in revealing dishabille rose in her mind. It was followed by a vision of herself eating dinner alone off a tray in the library.

"Tony would be a delightful escort," she heard herself saying to Serena.

Before she was even inside the door of Mrs. Abernathy's elegant town house, Juliet knew it was a mistake to have come. There were so many carriages lined up before the house that it took half an hour merely to alight. Of course their hostess was vastly pleased with the dense crowd, as it proclaimed her affair a success, but Juliet could scarcely hear above the roar of voices and found it difficult to move besides. Images of Christopher ensconced in a bed with satin sheets did little to ease the tediousness of the crush.

To her further chagrin, the third person to accidentally elbow her was none other than Jonathan Briding.

"Juliet!" he cried, taking her arm without her permission. "I knew I was charmed! But to have found you in such a crowd at my first affair in London is more than even I had hoped for."

"Yes, yes, it is quite a coincidence." Juliet just kept herself from sighing. "You do remember Lord Halsey?" She turned to indicate Tony, but found he had moved away to greet an elderly couple.

Nor would Serena be of any assistance. Juliet saw she was already making her way to the dance floor. "Are Becky and Harriet here?" Juliet asked, looking around with some hope.

"No, Aunt Porchester thought the crowd here would be too fast for them. They are attending a soiree with her. I am glad I decided to forgo it and come here instead. I'd have missed you otherwise."

Jonathan's look was so ardent she knew she could not let it pass. Waving her fan vigorously to cool her cheeks, Juliet implored quietly, "Jonathan, please do not look at me in quite that way, I beg you. I am glad to see you as well, of course, but you are embarrassing me. People will begin to wonder."

"Let them wonder," Jonathan retorted arrogantly. "My eyes have been opened since I came down to London, Juliet. The way society carries on shocked me at first, but now I'm glad I know. I've been a fool, acting so properly, only to find the accepted behavior is to be as free as one likes. Do you know that few wives feel any obligation toward their husbands once they have provided him an heir?"

"Jonathan!" Juliet's eyes flashed angrily. "I do not know who feels that way, nor do I care, for I feel very differently about marriage—"

"Well, well, if it is not the Countess of Hartford, holding a *tête-à-tête*."

If she lived to be a hundred, that particular voice was not one Juliet would ever forget. Had Jonathan not had hold of her arm, Juliet would have walked away without even looking around, but before she could ask him to escort her away, Leslie Chester-Headley had moved deliberately into their path.

The widow's face, Juliet decided in the time it took to take a breath, looked older than it had only a year before. Her green eyes, however, could still narrow menacingly. Tonight there was a feverish sparkle to them, perhaps because she was aware a good many in the crowd had turned to watch another juicy confrontation between the Countess of Hartford and Mrs. Chester-Headley.

"You are returned from your confinement, I see," she said insolently.

Juliet thought it a rather clever play on the word "confinement," but decided this was not the time to remark upon it. Summoning every shred of assurance she had developed at Hartford Hall, she did not by so much as a flickering eyelid acknowledge the remark or the speaker. Keeping her gaze so cool it put more than one person present in mind of the Earl of Hartford himself, Juliet stared through Leslie Chester-Headley as if she were thin air.

With slow deliberation she then turned to Jonathan. "I declare, one can never tell what common sorts one may stumble upon with the floor so crowded, Jonathan. I believe I would prefer a lemonade to enduring this crush. Would you mind?"

With no more ado, they moved away, the crowd parting easily for them.

"You were magnificent!" Jonathan's eyes blazed with admiration. "I don't think Brummell could have done better."

Juliet smiled faintly. She had carried it off well, she

knew, but she had not enjoyed it. The hatred the other woman bore her was too unnerving.

"Jonathan, I must go," Juliet said at once, looking around for Tony. "I really had no desire to go out tonight, and now . . . well, I'm certain you understand. Do you see Lord Halsey?"

"But I will take you home myself," Jonathan said, leaping at the chance to be alone with her.

She would have none of it. "No, no, please."

Eventually Juliet prevailed with everyone. Tony, of course, offered to take her as well, but Juliet pointed out what a shame it would be to make Serena, who had so looked forward to the evening, leave for such little reason.

Jonathan proved a more stubborn case, but at last they hit upon a compromise. He had finished her portrait, and Juliet agreed to receive him the day following Lutetia's ball. She firmly included Harriet and Becky in the arrangement.

"Oh, all right, I shall bring them," he agreed snappishly, after more than a little argument. Under his breath Juliet heard him add, "Though why you are such a high stickler after your husband's doxy insults you in public is more than I can understand."

That the widow was most likely not Christopher's mistress now, Juliet did not bother telling him. It seemed a small point. That night sleep eluded her as she tossed about wondering how lovely Leslie's successor might be.

The slamming of a door close by jerked her from a fitful doze. When something fell to the floor with a crash, she sat up, and at the sound of something else heavy going down with a thud, Juliet left her bed. The noises had come from Christopher's room, which, of course, adjoined hers. Because the connecting door had never been used, Juliet was slightly surprised to find it unlocked.

Slowly opening the door, she found that a candle-holder hanging on the wall by the bed illuminated the room. It was a masculine room, she noted almost absently as she scanned it. The colors were dark, the

177

furniture, though surprisingly sparse, was heavy. A beautiful rug from Persia lay on the floor, and on it Juliet could see a heavy silver tray lying upside down. All the odds and ends it had held were scattered about at random. Anxious now, she looked at the bed but saw no one; then finally, glancing down at a chaise just out of sight behind the door she had opened, she saw one well-booted foot dangling off it.

Peeping around the door, she made out the rest of Christopher's elegant form. His eyes were closed, and after a moment she realized he was snoring softly.

He was in his cups! she decided with no little amazement. He must be, or else, surely, he'd have undressed and gotten into bed. She hesitated a moment, wondering if she should call for Harkins.

She would in a moment, she decided, drawn like a magnet to her husband. Somehow he looked so innocent in his sleep, with no lines to mark a scowl or mocking smile. And so handsome. He was Apollo tonight, just as he had been when he had served her so badly that night almost a year ago.

Perhaps if she just took off his boots and put a cover on him, he would rest just as well on the chaise as he would in bed. Harkins could sleep on undisturbed then.

Juliet pulled the first boot off with no trouble and had begun to tug on the second.

"What the hell . . .?"

The boot came off, and Juliet turned to find Christopher's eyes were open, a frown creasing his brow.

He closed his eyes, but said distinctly enough, "Is that what you sleep in?"

"If you will lean on me, I think I can get you to your bed," Juliet said, ignoring the fact that he had reopened his eyes and was again frowning at her gown.

"You must have had it since you were a girl," he said a trifle peevishly.

"I *am* a girl, or so you are always at pains to tell me."

Juliet's tone was distinctly snappish, but surprisingly, Christopher took no umbrage. Far from it, in fact, he smiled. Before she knew what he was about, he had reached for her hand and pulled her down beside him.

There was not much room on the chaise, and Juliet landed with her face only a few inches from her husband's, her breasts pressed close to his chest and her legs entwined with his.

"You're not chiding me for neglect, are you, my sweet?" He grinned, his face very close to her. So close she could smell that he reeked of brandy.

"Mmm, I'd forgotten how soft flannel can be," he murmured, his hand stroking the side of her body.

Juliet remembered too well how he had regretted what had happened the last time he'd had too much to drink and had encountered her in his bedroom. "Christopher, please!" She struggled against him. "Whatever are you doing?"

"What I should have done from the beginning, most likely," he said softly, and tipped up her chin.

Their eyes met, and suddenly Christopher was grinning a wonderful lopsided grin. "Did you really set Les down as royally as they said at White's, Juliet? And I thought you had such a soft heart. . . ." His eyes traveled to her mouth, and then, no longer smiling, he kissed her.

When he released her, he sighed, and laying his cheek upon her head, fell quite fast asleep.

It took Juliet some time, but finally she pried herself from beneath her husband and got a blanket from the bed to cover him. "Ask me to stay when you're not foxed, my lord, and we shall see what I say," she told him softly after kissing his brow.

This time, when she lay down in her bed, sleep came almost instantly.

25

"**D**id you really not hear her hiss, Juliet?"

"For all I know, Ree, the woman stood on her head. I was too concerned with getting away as quickly as possible to take note of anything she did."

Serena sighed, vastly disappointed. It was teatime, and as she had been doing a great deal of the day, Serena was quizzing Juliet mercilessly about her scene with Leslie. "Well, I think it is really too bad that I should have missed all the excitement. Within minutes—minutes, I assure you—no one at the rout could speak of anything else. You are a sensation for dealing her such a set-down. You know she left soon after you did? She couldn't hold her head up!"

"Well, I cannot say I'm sorry," Juliet remarked, frowning a little. "She has been both cruel and insulting to me. Still, it seems almost ghoulish the way society takes people up, only to turn on them."

"Saint!" Serena cried, her eyes alight. "You see, you are a saint to feel the slightest shred of pity for that witch."

"I stand accused." Juliet grinned, hanging her head contritely. "And you must try to make a sinner of me by telling me the shocking story of how you passed your time at the Abernathys' rout."

"My time was not half so interesting as yours, I'll have you know: accosted by your husband's former mistress while deep in conversation with an admirer. All right, all right. I'll desist." Serena laughed, casting up her hands as Juliet turned a most threatening look upon her. "Actually your excitement has made me almost entirely forget that Letty Carstairs, an ancient friend of mine, has invited me to a house party she's got up out at her home in Richmond. You'll get on well enough without me for a few days, won't you?"

Juliet gave her a wry look. "I shall try to maintain my decorum in your absence, Ree. But how long shall I be put to the test?"

"Only a few days. Letty's other guests are unexceptionable, to be sure, but not worth a week of my time, I think."

Juliet laughed, and Serena, who had been serious, giggled when she realized how toplofty she sounded.

"Ma'am?"

"Yes, Morton?" Juliet looked up to find Morton looking down his decidedly raised nose at them. She was a little surprised, for since she had added Mother of the Heir to her credentials, his nose had not once tilted up at her. It still did not bend before her as it did to Christopher, but its present angle seemed a severe setback.

"Is something amiss?" she was moved to ask.

"The lad, Ferdie, wishes to speak to you."

"I see," Juliet said, asking Morton to show the boy in. And she did see, for Morton was still offended by the lad and had looked most unpleasantly surprised to see him among the servants arriving from Lincolnshire.

"Hello, Ferdie." She smiled assuringly, for he was darting anxious looks toward Serena. Then, with Morton in mind, she asked, "I've not had the chance to ask how you are getting on. Are you glad you asked to come to town?"

The young boy shrugged his shoulders lightly. " 'Appens I like the country better, m'lady. It's cleaner there."

Juliet chuckled at the idea that Ferdie had grown too fastidious for London. "I confess that I think so too, Ferdie. But what did you wish to speak to me about?"

Again he looked uncertainly toward Serena, but Juliet told him not to mind the Lady Serena and to say

181

what he had come for. "It's like this, m'lady," he said, shifting back and forth. "Yesterday and again today, when I was out in the mews, I saw a bad man watchin' the 'ouse."

"Was it your former master, Ferdie?"

Ferdie shook his head. "Not 'im, but another bad 'un I saw with 'im once or twice."

"I see. Does anyone else know?"

"Mr. Wickam, ma'am. He said we should keep an eye on 'im."

"Well, that sounds good, Ferdie..I can't think what he would want here."

"Knowin' the likes of 'im, 'e means to make off with your jewels."

It was a childish suggestion, for when she went out, Juliet was protected by at least two postilions and the coachman. One look at the serious expression on Ferdie's face, however, and Juliet suppressed her smile. Instead she reached out to smooth back a lock of ginger-colored hair that had fallen onto the child's brow.

"Thank you for the warning, Ferdie," she said gravely. "I shall be very careful when I go out now."

Apparently satisfied with Juliet's assurance, Ferdie nodded once and then sped toward the door.

"I knew the child adored you, but to make up a bogeyman to protect you from seems a little extreme," Serena observed when the door had closed on Ferdie.

Juliet frowned. "You think it was only his imagination, then?"

"Undoubtedly," was the staunch reply, and so when Juliet went to take her bath and dress for Lutetia's ball, she did not think again about Ferdie.

It was Christopher she thought of as she slid into the scented bath that her dresser, Prym, had ready for her. As she thought of his kiss the night before, her pulse raced. Immediately she told herself not to be such a fool. Without all the drink in him he had likely turned back into the Christopher who kept her at arm's length.

What accounted for the way he had behaved, she

did not know. Nor could she know without asking him. One thing was clear, however: he deeply resented having her presence forced upon him.

Nursing Charlie after her bath, she kissed his golden head and mused softly, "We must go home, Charlie. To stay will not help matters with your father. Perhaps, if he has the opportunity to choose to come to us, he will. I pray so, at least."

"My lady, you are a pleasure to look upon," Prym said, some hours later, when Juliet, but for her shawl, was ready.

"If I do, Prym, it is entirely due to your cleverness." Juliet smiled. "The coronet you've woven with my hair is lovely."

"It is the diamonds that make it look so nice," replied Prym modestly.

Juliet chuckled, for she thought the diamonds sprinkled throughout the smooth braid pinned atop her hair looked rather more than nice, but her amusement disappeared when her eyes fell to her dress. What her mother would say about its neckline, she did not want to think. The high waist, actually a row of brilliants just under her breasts, only seemed to emphasize the amount of creamy skin displayed. Serena had insisted the décolletage was absolutely perfect for Juliet's necklace, and she had been right. The neckline's square cut displayed the St. Charles diamonds perfectly. Unfortunately it displayed a great deal of her as well.

Still, that was the only thing about her dress which Juliet did not like. Made of nile-green silk, it was cut to flow with the contours of her body, actually narrowing just slightly below the knee. With her long white gloves, the magnificent diamonds in her hair and at her neck, and such a superb dress, Juliet thought it was not being vain to say she looked quite elegant.

Christopher was the only person in the drawing room before her. He stood with one arm resting on the mantel, gazing into the fire, a glass of brandy held idly in his hand.

Her heart skipping a beat, Juliet stopped to admire him before he became aware of her. The firelight played over the perfectly formed planes and angles of his face, accenting its strength as well as its beauty. There could be no mistaking the strong will of this squared-jawed, golden-haired, elegantly clad husband of hers.

"Ah, Juliet," Christopher began, turning when he realized of a sudden that he was not alone. "I'm not certain . . ."

For a long, nerve-racking moment, he stared at her without completing his thought. Juliet searched his eyes, but whether he was struck speechless in horror or in admiration, she could not fathom.

"I hope you approve." Juliet could have bitten her tongue over the entreaty she could hear in her tone.

"I had forgotten about the pins for your hair," Christopher said abruptly.

It was so far from the answer Juliet wanted that something of her disappointment flashed briefly in her candid eyes.

Christopher, his keen, cool gaze upon her, must have seen it, for he added after a moment in a softer voice, "They suit you."

It was not much in the way of praise, but from Juliet's smile an onlooker might well have thought she'd just been told she was very beautiful indeed. "Thank you, my lord," she said.

Their gazes held, and then Christopher said, "Juliet . . ." before abruptly swinging back to the fire. To her amazement, Juliet thought the expression on his face when he'd turned away had been sheepish.

He took a long draft from his glass before coming about again to address her face-to-face. "I am not at all certain what happened last night," he said, getting at length to his point. "I've not been so far gone since I was a boy just down from school, and that was quite some time ago. I do seem to remember you, however."

He looked wretchedly uncomfortable, if Christopher could ever be said to look wretched. Juliet took pity on him. "Yes, I came to your room. I heard the tray fall and thought you were hurt."

"I see." The reply was stiff, and Christopher's eyes

flicked briefly away to the window. "Then it was you who took off my boots."

"Yes, and put the blanket over you."

"Ah, yes, well, thank you."

Juliet clenched her hands tightly, anything to keep her laughter contained. If he had been the sort of man to blush, he'd have been red. He was not. His voice, instead, had become terribly severe. "It was nothing," Juliet said when she was certain her voice would be level.

"Was it?"

Juliet looked surprised at that.

"I mean that I am not certain how I acted," Christopher confessed at last, scowling his disgust for the position in which he found himself.

Juliet's eyes lit. She could not prevent it, though she did try. "You were very charming," she assured him, a faint smile tugging at her mouth.

Christopher, of course, saw that smile. "So I've nothing to apologize for?" he asked.

"Nothing at all," Juliet assured him softly, daring to hold his gaze.

"More fool I, then," he said after a moment in a very low voice. Indeed he spoke so quietly, and Serena, who had just flung open the door, spoke so loudly that Juliet was not certain what he had said at all. Nor did her sister-in-law give her the time to think on it. Serena clasped her hands together as soon as her gaze fell upon Juliet.

"Oh, my gracious!" she exclaimed theatrically. "You look just like a princess, Juliet!" Her reverent attitude was brief, for she went on almost immediately, "I hasten to add that I do not mean like Caroline. I mean one of those fairy-tale princesses."

"Serena, you are a gudgeon!" Juliet laughed, her eyes resting fondly on Serena's handsome figure. "A fairy-tale princess, indeed. Well, if that's the case, then we must be off, for my carriage is likely to turn into a pumpkin if we wait too long."

26

"**I** declare, I never thought to see such a beautiful sight as Lady Lutetia's ballroom last evening! It looked as if all the stars in the heavens had fallen into the room, there were so many tiny candles. And, Juliet, those diamonds! You must have been in alt wearing such magnificent jewels! I had to pinch myself when Lord Christopher led you out at the first. You were such a handsome couple, I thought I must be dreaming!"

"Thank you, Becky." Juliet smiled. "I am glad you enjoyed yourself as much as I did."

And Juliet had enjoyed herself. Being the center of attention at a glittering London ball, though not something she would want to do often, had been a decidedly heady experience. As Becky had said, she and Christopher had opened the ball, although according to custom her partner should have been Ronald, her host. Lutetia, the black plumes in her hair waving emphatically, had decried such nonsense.

"It will be so much more the thing if you, my handsome lord, lead out your lovely lady. The romantics will be talking of the sight for years to come."

More momentous, however, had been her second dance with her husband, for it was the first dance he had ever asked for. Actually, he had done more than ask, he had cut out a young buck who had already bespoken the dance. "Did my wife forget to say all her waltzes are mine?" the earl had asked in such a way that the young man had immediately given up his place. To her he had whispered with his eyes sparkling mischievously, "A pity your memory is so notorious, my dear." Not giving her time to reply, he had drawn her close to him, closer than was strictly proper, and had led her in her first waltz.

"And, Harriet, I hope you enjoyed yourself last evening?" Juliet asked, dragging her thoughts away from her husband. "I believe I saw you stand up twice with Mr. Cousins, did I not?"

Harriet's cheeks turned pink, revealing far more about that young lady's thoughts on the subject of Mr. Roderick Cousins than she could allow herself to put into words.

It was left to Becky to say in crowing tones that Harriet had also sat out a dance with Mr. Cousins, when Lady Porchester had unequivocally refused his request for a third dance.

"Becky!" Harriet cried, her blush becoming fiery red.

Becky's nose wrinkled. "I cannot see why you are so reticent on the matter, Harry. If a young man were pursuing me in that way, I declare I'd be proclaiming my good fortune from the rooftops!"

"That, Becky, love, is because you are now and always have been shameless," said her brother. "But," he continued, loftily ignoring the face Becky made at him, "I have never known you not to keep a promise, and I distinctly recall that you both promised to allow me to present my portrait to Juliet in private."

"Oh, Jonathan, must we go? I should so like to see it!" Becky exclaimed before Juliet could say anything.

"We have been over this before, Becky," Jonathan snapped. "You know how sensitive I am about my work. I couldn't bear to have anyone else see it before Juliet has approved of it."

Harriet, ever the diplomat, spoke up then. "It is true, we did promise, Becky. May we go up to see Charlie, Juliet? We've not seen him since we came to London."

"He would adore it." Juliet laughed, crossing to the

bell pull. "Mrs. Adams took him to the park for a walk, but they should be back any minute now."

As the girls dutifully trooped out with Morton, Jonathan lifted the portrait, still with its covering, onto a chair by the window.

Juliet watched as he arranged it to his satisfaction, turning it this way and that in the light. His face reflected a disquieting intensity as he worked, and Juliet was of a sudden glad there was no audience for the unveiling.

"It is ready," he said at last, looking to Juliet with such solemnity that she wished she could laugh to dispel the tension. She restrained herself, however, and walked rather slowly to look at what Jonathan had done.

"Oh no, Jonathan!" she gasped when she was able to speak. "I never wore anything so . . . flimsy!"

Jonathan's mouth tightened, but Juliet, still gaping at the picture, paid him not the least mind. "It is the way I see you. It is artistic license!" he muttered.

Juliet's head jerked around at that, and she regarded him with an incredulous expression. "Artistic license indeed!" she retorted so angrily that Jonathan took a step back from her. "You have taken advantage of me, Jonathan Briding, in the most unforgivable way. Under the guise of friendship you have compromised me!"

The sparks still flying from her eyes, Juliet looked again at the portrait. She could not fault his technique; it was, for an amateur, a very good likeness of her, even catching exactly the luminous gray of her eyes. Juliet scarcely noticed. She was far too infuriated to see anything but the liberties Jonathan had taken.

When Juliet had sat for him, indeed anytime she had ever seen Jonathan, her hair had always been pinned up quite properly. In the portrait, however, her unruly waves cascaded wantonly about her shoulders, glinting like silver in an afternoon sun.

But that was not all, nor even the worst. Juliet's cheeks reddened as she took in the costume Jonathan had painted her wearing. In truth it was not a costume at all, but only a flimsy scarf! Thank heavens she was sitting down in the portrait, with only her head and torso exposed, though even so the effect was indecent. The thin, gauzy scarf clung just to the tips of her breasts, leaving very little to the imagination.

It stunned Juliet that Jonathan could so accurately imagine how she would look. No one would believe she had not sat for him draped just as he depicted her. Groaning aloud, Juliet tried not to consider how furious Christopher would be to think she had behaved so improperly. And then to have that impropriety recorded in such minute detail for all the world to see!

"I thought you would be pleased," Jonathan began, his voice sounding suspiciously close to a whine.

"Well, you were very wrong!" Juliet said, scarcely able to look at him. "I want you to cover it again, and then I shall have Morton take it to my room, where I shall decide what to do with it."

"You can't hide it, Juliet! It is my masterwork. If you are only going to stow it away, I'll take it home with me."

"No, you will not, Jonathan Briding. This is my portrait. I am the one whose reputation would be in tatters if anyone else ever saw it. Now, unless you want me to do it for you, please do as I ask."

"Oh, all right." Jonathan's mouth twisted in an angry, petulant grimace as he attended to the task Juliet had set him.

Just as he finished draping the cloth, there was a knock at the door.

"Are we too soon, Juliet?" called Harriet.

The more impetuous Becky tumbled into the room before Juliet could answer, crying, "May we see it?"

"No!" Juliet had no difficulty finding a response to Becky's question, and even had the presence of mind to move into Becky's path.

"It is a very private work, you see, Becky, and your brother and I have decided it is best if it remain so."

Becky began to object; she even opened her mouth to do so, but something in the atmosphere deterred her. Perhaps it was the paler-than-usual color of her brother's face. More likely it was the determined sparkle in Juliet's eyes. Whatever the reason, Becky's mouth, for once, closed without uttering a sound.

Relieved to see Becky's gesture of acquiescence, Juliet turned to Harriet. "Did you leave Charlie napping?" she asked, more to deflect conversation from the portrait than anything.

Harriet's glance flickered briefly from Jonathan to Juliet; then, as if she had only just heard the question, her gaze focused on Juliet. "Actually, we did not see Charlie at all, Juliet. Sally is quite beside herself with worry. She says Mrs. Adams is almost an hour late."

"As Mrs. Stokes's niece, Sally comes naturally to worry," Juliet murmured half to herself. She had no more than voiced the thought when the conversation she'd had with Ferdie the day before popped into her mind. It seemed preposterous that there was any connection, but Juliet found herself announcing that she herself would go to the park to look for her son and his nurse.

When all three of the Bridings said they would come, she only nodded absently, though she was a little surprised Jonathan had not stalked off in a miff. The thought reminded her to ask Morton to have the covered portrait taken to her room.

Unfortunately, Morton, normally efficient in seeing to his mistress's wishes, was delayed on this particular occasion by the arrival of his master.

"Good afternoon, Morton." The earl smiled, nonchalantly tossing Morton his beaver hat. "Is her ladyship in the drawing room, or has she already gone up to the nursery?"

"Neither, my lord," and then, not knowing the why of it, Morton caused a great deal of trouble by only describing what had occurred. "Lady Juliet and the Bridings have gone for a drive in the park," he conscientiously informed his master.

For a half-second the earl halted in mid-stride, then recovering smoothly, required that Morton bring brandy to his study at once.

"Yes, my lord," Morton said, and realizing that for some reason the earl's mood had changed abruptly, he hurried to see to the task himself.

When the brandy was safely delivered, Morton remembered the portrait Lady Juliet wished taken to her room, but before he could see to the task, a street urchin was at the door asking to leave a note for "my lady." Morton debated the issue, but only briefly. His experience with Lady Juliet was such that he accepted the grimy note.

And then he was summoned to the kitchen to settle a crisis involving a leg of lamb which Mrs. Manning, the cook, decried in a frenzied voice as "only fit for a beggar."

Finally, having sent out for another leg of lamb, Morton, with a footman in tow, went to the drawing room to see to the removal of the covered painting. The young man had just carried it into the hall when the earl, apparently on his way out again, saw them.

"Did Mr. Briding bring this when he came?" the earl asked, and Morton, his nose quivering downward, thought there was an ominously still quality to his master's tone.

"Yes, my lord," he replied at once.

"Take it to my study."

Morton, to his credit, hesitated and even said faintly, "Her ladyship did ask that it be taken to her room."

"And I am saying it is to be taken to my study."

Morton and the footman changed direction with alacrity.

Several minutes later, Morton, in pursuit of a recalcitrant maid, happened to pass the closed doors of the study. From within he heard a crash. It was a sound which his ears, trained by long years of service, identified correctly as glass shattering violently upon the hearth.

"Morton!"

The butler jumped at the bawled shout.

"Have Ajax saddled at once!" the earl commanded upon finding his butler standing in the hallway.

Morton, his nose quivering with alarm, for he had

never seen his master so white-faced before, turned instantly to do as he was bidden.

"And, Morton . . ."

"Yes, my lord," Morton inquired with a sinking feeling.

"Do not remove Mr. Briding's picture from my study."

"Very good, my lord." Morton nodded, relieved by so simple, if puzzling, an order.

27

In the park Juliet instructed her coachman to drive toward the little lake where she knew Mrs. Adams often took Charlie for his stroll, and to her vast relief he yelled down to say that the smaller coach Mrs. Adams used was just up ahead. Leaning out the window to look, Juliet was further relieved to see its driver lounging at his ease upon the grass in deep discussion with several of his cronies.

"Ay, lad!" Juliet heard her coachman yell to the other. "Where be the little master and 'is nurse?"

The younger coachman leapt to his feet, obviously chagrinned to be caught by his mistress disporting himself in such a careless fashion. Juliet took notice of nothing but his answer that Mrs. Adams had gone with another nurse down to the lake.

Immediately Juliet called to the young man to let down the steps so she could go and look for them herself. She knew she was being foolish; nothing untoward could have occurred on such a beautiful day in such a civilized place as Hyde Park, but with Ferdie's words still ringing loudly in her mind she wanted to be quite certain.

By the lake there was still no sign of Mrs. Adams or of Charlie, though there was another nanny pushing a stroller. Without hesitation Juliet went to inquire whether she had been with Mrs. Adams.

"Why, yes, ma'am, she was here with me." The woman nodded. "She left some time ago, though. A man came to get her."

"A man?" Juliet asked sharply.

"Yes, ma'am," replied the nurse. "He were a footman, or so he was dressed. Came and told Mrs. Adams he'd been sent to fetch her home."

"But what did he look like? How was he dressed?"

The nurse screwed up her face, trying to recall what she could of a man to whom she had paid scant attention.

"He was a big 'un and not so young, either. Dark-lookin', and his livery was blue."

"You are certain it was blue?" Juliet asked in a tense voice.

"Yes, ma'am, right sure. It had gold on it too."

"But, Juliet, your servants' livery is green and gold!" cried Becky.

Panic welled up in Juliet at the news that Mrs. Adams had left the park with a strange man, and she could make no answer. Instead she walked quickly back to her carriage.

"Charlie will be home when we get there," Harriet tried to reassure her as they walked.

"Of course he will," agreed Jonathan. "This is all some absurd mistake. You'll see when we return to Hartford House."

Juliet nodded and smiled bravely in response to the young Bridings' attempts to soothe her, but in her heart she did not believe Charlie would be there. And he was not.

Morton said Mrs. Adams had not returned.

At once Juliet asked where Christoper was, certain he had come while she was away. He had told her that morning he would be home to have tea with her and Charlie.

But Morton surprised her greatly. "No, my lady." He shook his head, then added, his nose twitching oddly, "His lordship was here, but he left again."

Juliet's brow furrowed. "I see. Did he say where he would be?"

"No, my lady. There is a message for you, however. It was left by an urchin lad who came to the door."

"Now, you needn't worry, Juliet. Charlie will be here at any minute, brought by this other fellow, whoever he may be."

Juliet pocketed the note Morton had handed her without looking at it and turned a wan smile upon Jonathan. She supposed he must be right but wished it were Christopher and not Jonathan she had to consult.

"No doubt you are right, Jonathan. I shall feel quite foolish tomorrow when I look back on all my worrying. I hope I am not turning into a Mrs. Stokes."

All three Bridings rushed at once to tell her that she was no such thing, that any mother would worry in the circumstances, and that everything would be all right in only a little while.

It was a refrain Juliet had heard once too often, and with a determination which was no less powerful for being expressed politely, she saw all three of her visitors to the door. When they had gone, she sighed with relief. It was really a great deal easier to think what to do when there were not three people telling you there was really no need to do anything.

The first thing she decided to do was send for Christopher. To that end she had Morton take word to his clubs, Tony Halsey's, and, she added with a significant pause, anywhere else his lordship might be.

Morton, coughing delicately, said the matter would be attended to immediately. Secure in the knowledge that Christopher would be sought everywhere, even if it meant going to whoever currently held his interest, Juliet went into the drawing room to wait.

She untied the strings of her bonnet, absently noting that Morton had carried out her order to have her portrait removed, and felt in her pocket for the note Morton had given her. The staid old butler's description of its bearer had led her to believe it had been sent from the orphanage of which she and Lutetia were sponsors. There had been other notes brought by other young boys dressed in clean but extremely modest garments, and each time Morton had referred to them as urchin lads.

"Be ye lookin' for this, my lady?"

Whirling about, Juliet saw that Ferdie, who had been speaking with Morton when she had come in, had followed her into the room and was holding out the piece of tattered paper Morton had given her earlier.

"Why, yes, Ferdie, it is. I must have dropped it," Juliet said, taking it.

Without realizing that Ferdie remained in the room watching her, Juliet opened the missive.

"Be it fearful, then, my lady?"

Though Ferdie was only a street urchin turned servant, there was an unusual bond between the boy and his mistress. It stemmed of course from her rescue of him. She had taken responsibility for him that day, and he, with unswerving devotion, had, she knew, done the same in relation to her. It was why he had come back to London with her, and why he, and he alone, had journeyed all the way to Lincolnshire in the first place.

Consequently, when the boy asked if the note was fearful, Juliet did not hesitate to answer him.

"Charlie has been taken for ransom, Ferdie!" she cried, sinking down upon the nearest couch.

"Ah," said Ferdie in a voice which showed no surprise. "Where are you to take the blunt, then?"

Juliet frowned at the scrawling hand in which the note had been penned. "It says that I must bring five thousand pounds to the . . . let's see, I believe it says the Boar's Head Tavern at seven o'clock. Alone."

A long, low whistle escaped Ferdie. "Five thousand pounds!" he gasped.

Juliet turned wild eyes upon the boy. "I would gladly pay anything, Ferdie, if I could have Charlie back safe and sound."

"Now, m'lady. You can't be goin' to the Boar's 'Ead. They'd make mincemeat out o' you there. Wait'll the master comes 'ome. 'E'll know 'ow to make it right and tight."

"Do you know the place, Ferdie?"

The lad nodded his ginger head. "It be in Tothill

196

Fields, my lady. A rogues' den, if there ever was one."

Juliet became almost physically ill with fear when she heard Ferdie's description. Her little boy was in a rogues' den!

Pushing her hand through her hair and completely disarranging the coiffure Prym had spent half an hour on, Juliet sagged back on the couch. There seemed nothing to do but wait for Christopher.

An hour later, she was still there, though she had risen from the couch and was now pacing the floor before the window. A knock at the door sent her spinning about, but she saw at once that Morton did not bear good news.

In response to her breathless question, he said his lordship had not been found. "But . . ." he added slowly, clearly at a loss how to put his next words.

"Come, come, Morton," Juliet said impatiently. "There is nothing you can say that would shock me."

"It seems his lordship is at a cottage he . . . ah, owns in Hampstead."

"Hampstead!" Juliet cried, aghast to learn Christopher was so far away. "But it will take hours to get there and back."

"A footman is waiting to go straightaway, if you wish, my lady." When Juliet nodded, he left immediately.

Juliet pushed away all thoughts of what Christopher was doing in Hampstead. She knew, anyway; Morton's discomfort had made it too obvious. The only question was with whom, but that did not seem important at the moment. Later it would be, but now she had Charlie to think of.

Her first action was to dismiss Prym for the evening, and her second was to call for Sally. What she was considering doing was so unthinkable that only Sally, who was too young not to obey her mistress in all things, could be trusted to assist her. Even so, Sally's broad face puckered with concern when she heard what Juliet planned. Only after a considerable bit of arguing and, at last, a firm order, did Juliet prevail

197

upon her maid to lend her the oldest of her dresses and the plainest of her two cloaks.

It was half-past six when Juliet, her hair wrapped in a tattered shawl and a bag clutched under Sally's cloak, slipped out the servants' entrance unseen. Just down the street from Hartford House, she hailed a hackney, and though the man snorted that she had no business going there, she insisted he take her to the Boar's Head Tavern.

Juliet had never been out alone in London before, much less gone to a slum like Tothill Fields. The sun had set and the flickering beams of the infrequent streetlights cast eerie shadows on the tenement buildings, sagging on their rotten supports. Noxious smells filled the air, as did raucous, unintelligible cries. Even the gaits of those people on the street were strange—some furtive, some reeling, some obviously giving chase. Juliet shivered and made herself think of Charlie.

"Can you wait for me?" she asked the hackney driver anxiously when he had pulled up at last.

The driver took a long look at her, then shrugged. "If you're not overlong," he said gruffly.

Quickly, before she could lose heart, Juliet crossed the street to the door of the tavern over which hung a sign with a boar's head painted blue. Drawing her cloak about her tightly, she summoned all the courage she had, and opening the door a fraction, slipped in.

Her heart pounding heavily, Juliet was assailed first by a confusingly loud din. The room was much larger than she had expected, and filled, particularly on the main floor, with men and women who were all drinking and talking in shouts. Smoke like a pall hung thickly enough to make her eyes water, and though she was not aware of it, her nose wrinkled at the fetid air. A combination of unwashed bodies, gin, and smoke, it was nearly unbreathable.

"So y'came, Countess!"

Juliet's head whipped about as a coarse hand clamped onto her arm. "You!" she gasped, recognizing with sudden real dread the cruel countenance of the man who had been Ferdie's master.

"Aye, it's me. I see you've not forgotten." He laughed evilly, seemingly pleased to learn he was so remarkable. "I've bided my time real patient-like to make you pay for stealing my lad Ferdie from me. You never shoulda done it. You 'adn't the right. 'E was the best lad I 'ad, and I ain't found no one else does so well. I fed 'im, kept 'im, and then, just when 'e was startin' to pay off like, you stuck your nose in it."

"Where is my son?" Juliet demanded. Though her insides were quaking, she was determined she would not show the villain her fear.

Eyeing her lifted chin and angry eyes a moment, the man snorted. "Got spirit, don't you, Countess? Well, I'll show you just what that brings you."

So saying, the man roughly pushed her around the back of the crowd, up some steps to a slightly raised area where the crowd, though thick, was thinner than on the main floor of the tavern. Juliet's assailant shoved her into a chair along the railing across from a large muscled man. "This 'ere's Jim. 'E used to be a fighter, so don't go thinking you can pull any trick on us. Jim'll lay you out cold."

Jim grunted, but otherwise said nothing. He did not need to; it was obvious he could have strangled Juliet using only one hand.

"Where is Charlie?" repeated Juliet, turning away from the sight of Jim's massive hands. "You said that if I came alone, I could have him."

"And if you brought us the pitch and pay." The man's beady eyes narrowed to slits. "Where is it?" he demanded, once more grasping Juliet's arm.

"You don't think I would walk into a perfectly strange tavern with five thousand pounds and simply trust you to give me my son." Juliet jerked her arm from the man's hold. "The money is where it can easily be reached, but before I get it, I want Charlie and Mrs. Adams here."

The noise and the stench of the tavern receded as Juliet's eyes locked with her antagonist's. If he should decide to feel under her cloak, he would find the bag which held the St. Charles diamonds. There had been nothing Juliet could do but bring them into the tavern with her. He did not know that, however, and she had to convince him she had done otherwise, or he might well take her diamonds and demand still more ransom for Charlie.

When the man, swearing rudely, whispered something to Jim, the huge man rose from the table, and Juliet watched as he made his way to a set of stairs on the opposite side of the room, which led to a second-floor balcony. He rapped on a door just at the top of the stairs. It opened, and in response to a motion he made with his hand, a large blowsy woman appeared. Behind her came Mrs. Adams with a bundle which had to be Charlie in her arms.

"See?" the man beside her grunted.

"Bring them here," Juliet commanded in a low voice, her eyes not leaving her son.

"Now, wait a minute. It's me that's givin' the orders," he growled.

"Not if you want your money." Juliet turned her full attention to him. "I want them here." She jabbed at the space beside her. "Then I'll get your money."

He gave her another look, but what he read in her gray eyes must have convinced him, for, though he spit angrily, he motioned to the little group standing on the balcony.

Time seemed to move forward at a snail's pace as they made their way down the stairs, then elbowed through the crowd. No one, to Juliet's amazement, paid them the least mind other than to utter a rude noise for the elbow in their backs.

"Mrs. Adams, how are you? Is Charlie hurt?" Juliet kept her voice down, but her desperate worry was evident.

"Oh, my lady!" the older woman, tears in her eyes, cried softly. "We are as well as can be. Not hurt, at least. They've given Master Charles wine to keep him quiet."

Juliet mastered a nearly overwhelming desire to lash out at the man who had dared to take her son and subject him to his filthy wine. Beneath her cloak she fingered the bag which held not only her diamonds but also a small pistol of the earl's.

"It's yer turn, Countess."

At the man's hiss, Juliet reached into the bag and took a pistol into her right hand. Holding it inside her cloak, she tossed the bag of diamonds onto the table with the other hand.

The slatternly woman let out a jubilant laugh, but the man said nothing. He took the bag, and after looking around to see if anyone else was watching, reached inside. Even in the tavern's dingy light, the necklace glittered brilliantly.

"Cor!" exclaimed the woman, reaching out for the prize.

"Hold, there!" The man jerked around to Juliet. "This ain't no pounds!" he snarled angrily.

Juliet took a steadying breath, while her hand closed on the pistol. "No, it is not. It is a set of diamonds worth more than you asked. I could not in the three hours' time you gave me lay my hands on so much ready money."

"Well, this won't do. No, it won't do at all." The man's face contorted with rage. "We have to sell these before they're worth a ha'penny to us, and we're not likely to get 'alf what we should, only a ticket to Newgate."

Juliet's heart began to beat frantically as her hand tightened on the pistol. To her utter dismay, the man laughed wickedly.

"But now we've got you, the boy, and these. I reckon the Earl of Hartford'll be able to come up with the blunt we want. Now, don't go bawlin', Meg," he spit angrily at the woman who had made a protesting noise when she heard his plans. "We'll keep these, and we'll just get some more besides."

While the man's attention was turned to the woman, Juliet brought the pistol out from the folds of Sally's cloak. "I cannot allow that. If you value your life, sir, you will allow us to leave."

The man jerked around to find a small pistol trained unwaveringly on him. His initial astonishment vanished quickly, replaced by a deadly smirk.

"All I've to do is shout, and this crowd'll tear you apart. They'll not care for a gentry mort threatening one o' their own."

"And if I yelled there was a king's ransom in diamonds?" Juliet retorted. "What would they do for one of their own then?"

The man's beady eyes shifted toward Jim, obviously assessing what to do. Juliet's hand was sweating so she was afraid she'd drop the pistol, but she kept it steady just above the table.

"Indecision never pays, man. You really ought to have listened to the lady. Now I am afraid you'll lose everything except Newgate."

All five heads which had been intent on the drama being enacted at the table turned as one to gape at the owner of the silky voice. He had, proving he was lithe as well as quiet, vaulted over the railing dividing their section from the floor below. His cloak bulged slightly, and the glint of another, much larger pistol was plain to all.

"Christopher!" Juliet cried, thinking he was the most wonderful sight she had ever seen.

Her husband did not look at her. His narrowed gaze never wavered from the man, the ringleader as Juliet thought of him. He had grasped the bag with the diamonds tightly in his beefy hand and now made as if to rise.

"I wouldn't if I were you," Christopher said softly. "Not that I don't wish you would, it would give me the excuse to put a neat, deadly hole in you. However, if you will look over there, you'll see a pair of Runners come to fetch you to the place you belong."

Even as Christopher spoke, the two Runners, their pistols pointing at the man and his accomplices, came forward.

"I'll not be hanged!" the man cried, leaping around the woman and making for the stairs.

A shot sounded and the man dropped like a stone to the floor. Several shrill cries were heard, though an astonishing number in the crowd paid no attention at all. To those who looked up at the group on the platform, Christopher, aping the accents of the area, said, "Tried to cheat me, 'e did! Can't 'ave that."

It was all the explanation they needed, apparently, for to Juliet's horror, they shrugged and went about their business, stepping over the dead man on the floor as they needed to.

28

His arm draped about Juliet's shoulder, Christopher got them out then, quickly and quietly, while the two Bow Street Runners took charge of the woman and Jim.

Outside, Juliet saw no sign of the hackney she'd hired, but she did see the earl's light chaise with Ferdie holding the horses and Wickam in the box.

Before Juliet had found her seat, she took Charlie from Mrs. Adams.

"Is he all right, my lady?" the good woman wailed anxiously.

Because his breathing seemed steady, Juliet answered, "Yes, I think so."

As if the assurance released the tension within her, Mrs. Adams began to sob loudly.

At once Christopher took both the old woman's hands in his and soothed her with unexpected gentleness. "Now, now, Mrs. Adams, it is over, and has ended happily, thank God."

"They were rough people, my lord," she said, sniffing the last of her tears. "And smart. At least they fooled an old biddy like me. When that big one came to say you'd sent him to fetch me, I never thought everything wasn't right.

"It was only when I saw the old hackney they had waitin' that I stopped, but he had me and Master Charles in the carriage before I knew what was what."

Mrs. Adams began to cry again, and once more

Christopher consoled her. With tears still in her eyes, she looked to Juliet.

"I did the best I could to protect the little master, my lady, but he was crying so that woman forced some wine down him. It was likely for the best, for had he kept on crying it's possible that man would have done something awful to quiet him."

"You mustn't blame yourself, Mrs. Adams," Juliet assured her. "There was no reason you should have suspected anyone meant harm to you or Charlie. I know you did all that you could. I am only thankful neither of you has been badly hurt."

"Oh, Lady Juliet, I was never so glad in all my life as I was when I came out of that dirty little room and saw you down below. I knew then you and his lordship had come for us."

At last Juliet was able to turn her attention to her husband. "Which brings us to you, Christopher. How on earth did you happen to arrive to opportunely?"

"You weren't together?" Mrs. Adams gasped. "Never say you came alone, my lady!"

It was the earl who answered, his eyes narrowed upon his wife. "Indeed she did, Mrs. Adams," he affirmed. "And a more outrageous, outlandish, unreasonable, foolhardy, foolish thing to do, I have never heard of."

Juliet winced. In the darkness it was impossible to make out Christopher's expression, but she had little need to do so. His tone of voice told her all she needed to know.

"But to answer your question, my dear," Christopher continued, his tension making his voice curt. "I happened to arrive in time to save your imprudent neck, because young Ferdie persuaded Wickam to drive him at a breakneck pace to find me. He had no idea you would go alone to the Boar's Head, but he did believe Charlie might be harmed if someone did not appear at the appointed hour. I apologize for being late; it took the lad some time to persuade me it was not all a great prank. I wonder, Juliet, if you can imagine my surprise upon seeing you sitting in that foul place with my pistol in your hands?"

His voice was too dry not to spark a spirited retort. "I did send for you, but when it seemed you were . . . how shall I put it—otherwise disposed, perhaps?—at any rate too far away to come in time, I didn't know what else to do. I thought they would hurt Charlie if no one came with a ransom."

"And so you took the St. Charles diamonds."

"Oh, heavens above! My lord, I forgot the diamonds. They were on the table and—"

"No need to worry, my love. I was less distracted."

Juliet winced again. She'd never been called "my love" by him before, and if that were the way it would always sound, she hoped she never would be again.

Charlie stretched mightily then, drawing all her attention. Making the usual sorts of noises he made when he slept, he curled himself into a new position.

Juliet kissed his smooth cheek, holding him tightly to her. He was so small and vulnerable, and yet, of them all, he seemed the least affected.

When they reached Hartford House, Morton's amazement at the sight of Juliet in worn, inferior clothing was obvious, but he did manage a real smile when he saw Master Charles and Mrs. Adams.

The corner of Juliet's mouth lifted slightly, but she paid the butler little mind. She and Mrs. Adams continued up the stairs, leaving Christopher to tell Morton an abbreviated version of what had happened. "And, Morton," he added when he had finished, "I do not want this story to get about."

"Of course, my lord." Morton nodded, indicating that he understood very well that the servants were to be told what had happened and then told not to gossip about it. It said a great deal about the wages the earl paid his staff that he could expect them to forgo repeating such a story.

"He really is well?" Christopher asked Juliet when he strode into Charlie's room.

"Yes. He is breathing easily and is not the last feverish."

A knock at the door announced Sally. "My lady, you are safe!" she exclaimed in a rush; then, making out Christopher's tall figure in the darkened room, she gasped.

"It's all right, Sally," Juliet assured her.

"Ah, so it is Sally's attire you are wearing." Christopher's eyes fastened on the maid, who shrank back slightly.

Juliet nodded absently; then, her nose wrinkling, she said, "I shall have to buy you some new ones, my dear. These have the stench of that awful gin shop on them."

"It was a gin shop!" gasped Sally, thoroughly appalled, though a little intrigued too.

"I suppose so. It was a very nasty place, whatever it was," Juliet told her, not in the least satisfying the country girl's interest about the particulars of such an evil place.

"Well, I for one find, after a night spent rescuing my wife and son from the clutches of one of London's nastier gentlemen, that I am hungry," Christopher announced. "You cannot have eaten, Juliet. Surely you were too busy for that. I shall have Morton serve us a cold collation in your room. I think Sally can stay with Charlie. We'll be close by if he awakens."

"Oh yes, my lord," Sally rushed to agree. She did not think he was overpleased that she had helped her mistress go after Master Charlie, and though she would have done almost anything for her lady, she had no wish to be in his lordship's bad graces.

It was not until Christopher entered her room followed by Morton and a footman carrying their dinner that Juliet actually realized she would be entertaining her husband in her bedroom. What had once seemed a rather large, airy room suddenly seemed small with Christopher's tall, lean form in it.

"Some wine, my dear?" Christopher asked, pouring her a glass before she had answered. "You have earned it, I think."

Juliet took it and turned her attention to her meal,

finding that her appetite, if not immense, was nevertheless surprisingly good. When she had finished she looked up to find Christopher watching her, his wineglass in his hand. Her eyes darkened to see the stony way she regarded her. "You are angry with me, are you not, Christopher?" she asked.

Her husband's expression did not change. "I confess that I hardly know, Juliet. I am surprised . . ." He frowned. Then, evidently collecting himself, he finished in a more clipped voice, "I am surprised you did not ask anyone for help."

"But Serena is in Richmond, and you must know Lutetia and Ronald are attending a gala in Chiswick. I might have sent for them, but by the time I realized where you were, it was too late. I'm not certain I'd have called on them anyway, for the note did say I was to come alone." As an afterthought Juliet added, "Of course, I had no idea what sort of place I was going to."

"Of course," her husband agreed in the driest tones. "Please satisfy my curiosity on one point, if you would."

When Juliet nodded, he asked, "Did you have the least idea now to use my pistol?"

"Not really, no," Juliet admitted, her gaze flicking away. "I had seen Robbie shoot a friend's once. I only knew you kept a pistol in the drawer by your bed because Sally knew it from Harkins, and I thought I should take it just in case. I'm not certain, really, what I'd have done if I'd had to use it."

Christopher, seeing the grave expression on her face, relented. "I'm glad the Runners saved you the decision," he told her quietly. When Juliet looked at him, her eyes dark, Christopher read her thoughts aright. "He had to die, Juliet. He'd have tried again, else. He was Ferdie's former master, was he not?"

Juliet nodded and then explained as much as she knew of the man and his motives.

"We owe Ferdie a great deal," Christopher said when she had finished. "If he had not acted so wisely, you'd have come to harm."

Juliet looked down at her half-empty plate. Her husband was angry with her again, and like the other times, it was because she'd acted hastily. She couldn't undo her actions, indeed in this case she would most likely do the same thing again in the same circumstances. Perhaps she could make it up to him, though. She did have the means to please him.

Glancing at him through her lashes, she saw he was regarding her with a grim expression. It was that expression which decided her.

"Christopher?" she said, looking up. He only arched his brow, and she continued, "I want to go home to Lincolnshire."

"Ah!" The stem of Christopher's glass had broken in his hand, cutting him.

"Good heavens!" Juliet exclaimed at once, jumping up to fetch a napkin from the table. "How on earth did you do that?"

Christopher jerked the napkin from her hand. "It is nothing," he informed her so coldly she stared openmouthed.

"But . . ." Juliet began.

"Nothing," he insisted, and with the same edge to his voice. "As for Lincolnshire, you may do as you wish. But Charlie will stay here."

"What?" Juliet gasped. What he had said was so unreasonable, she looked at the bottle to see how much wine he'd had. "But he is the reason I wish to go."

"There's no need to lie," snapped Christopher angrily. "I know perfectly well what attracts you to the Hall."

"Whatever do you mean?"

"Still playing the innocent? Well, you won't for long."

Reaching across the table, Christopher grabbed Juliet by the arm and pulled her after him from the room. Running to keep up with his long strides, Juliet attempted to twist free, but he tightened his hold so it hurt her.

Flinging open the door to his study, he jerked her unceremoniously inside, and without stopping dragged her across the room.

"Christopher!" she protested, frightened enough by the violence of his actions to cry out.

Saying nothing, Christopher drew up before his desk, and it was then that Juliet saw, propped against it, the covered portrait. She had completely forgotten it until now.

"This is what I mean," Christopher ground out, flicking off the covering to reveal Juliet's likeness smiling enticingly back at them. Juliet had not realized before how very enchanting the smile in the portrait was, and how damning.

"Perchance Briding plans to paint another portrait, Juliet? Is that the reason you wish to leave London so abruptly? I thought you were enjoying yourself here, or was that fiction as well, like the pose of wronged wife you played so convincingly?"

It had been a very long day for Christopher, in some ways the longest of his life. There had been his deep anxiety on account of Charlie, of course. But in addition, Christopher had had to experience all the unpleasant sensations associated with acquiring a bit of self-knowledge he had, until now, held out against.

Much of the evidence had been there for some time. He had enjoyed his stay in Lincolnshire as he never had before. His removal to town had been sadly flat. Corinne, his newest mistress, had seemed both dull and, God forbid, insipid. Their tryst in Hampstead today, only the second time he had seen her since coming to London, had been a complete failure. Whereas once he'd have been able to distract himself with her lush charms, today he had been able to see nothing but a pair of luminous gray eyes and a diaphanous scarf covering firm rose-tipped breasts.

He had not allowed himself to consider these changes, for fear he'd have to consider the cause. To do so would have meant admitting to feelings he had never experienced before.

It was only when he'd entered the tavern and seen

210

Juliet that the sheer enormity of his fear for her had forced him to admit the truth. He loved her.

He loved her sweet face, her expressive eyes, her boundless compassion. He had come to cherish her intelligence, her courage, even the innocence he had so mocked.

A wave of anger nearly snapped the exceedingly tenuous control over his emotions which his exhausting day had left him, and hitting his desk so hard the inkwell overturned, he roared, "It sickens me that you should be so deceitful! You are like so many of your sex—good at maintaining a pose while it suits you!

"Well, I will not have Charlie growing up with that! He'll never be left alone to wonder where you are while you dally with your lover!"

Juliet's cheeks had become very white. She knew at least a part of Christopher's fury originated with Lady Eunice, not herself. Serena's confidences had helped her understand that.

But he hurt her deeply nonetheless. That he could, whatever the reason, misjudge her so that he intended to take her son from her . . .

"Christopher—" she began.

But her husband was in a rage and did not heed her. "Go away!" he stormed at her. "I will not listen to your lies."

Something broke in Juliet then. "You *will* listen!" she retorted, her eyes, which he had seen flash with anger, blazing now. "How dare you to condemn me without a hearing! Where were you, Christopher St. Charles, when your son was being born?"

Christopher's eyes gleamed back at her, his mouth tight. "Do not try to play the high hand with me. There"—he pointed to the portrait— "is all the argument I need."

"Where were you?" Juliet stamped her foot. "You will not say? Then I shall. While we both lay near death, you were probably in your mistress's bed, just as you were again tonight when we needed you!"

Standing almost toe to toe with her, Christopher

211

yelled back, "You cannot tarnish me with your brush. I've never deceived you!"

"No, only abandoned me."

Christopher's lip curled scornfully. "And so you turned to Briding out of loneliness. Is that what you are saying? Well, it makes no difference why you did what you did, the fact remains that you did it and then tried to deceive me and everyone who knows you."

"You fool!" It was the closest Juliet could come to a roar, and it served rather well. She had up a fine head of steam, and, her eyes sparkling with anger, she told her husband exactly what she thought of him and of his suspicions. "That is not at all what I am saying! I am saying you see me through eyes which are compromised. You think everyone is like you, capable of putting pleasure before everything!

"Do you really have so little idea who I am that you can believe I would so quickly violate my marriage vows? That I would violate them carrying your child? That I would violate them for Jonathan Briding, a silly boy who has not one unselfish bone in his thin body? That I would put my soul in such jeopardy when I have you for—"

Her hand flying to her mouth, Juliet stopped too late.

A resounding silence filled the room, while Christopher stared at her, a new expression forming on his face. Juliet did not see it; her eyes had clouded with angry tears.

"Oh, now look at what you have made me say," she said, biting her lip. Without waiting for any response from Christopher, she whirled and ran to the door.

Christopher, quick as a cat, was there before her.

"My God, Juliet," he murmured softly, lifting her chin.

Tears streamed down her cheeks. "Don't!" Juliet tried to lift her chin away.

"You don't love him?" Christopher asked, his other hand coming up to hold her firmly in place.

"Of course not." It was the merest whisper.

"You were only lonely, then," he remarked almost to himself, pulling her into his arms.

"No, no! You don't understand at all!" Juliet sobbed loudly, though her voice was muffled by Christopher's comforting chest. It seemed the last straw that, though she had admitted she had eyes for no one but him, he should still believe her capable of a liaison with Jonathan. Struggling mightily, she broke loose from his hold.

"I only sat for Jonathan. I did nothing else. I wore that green dress with the high collar, and my hair was up as it always is in company. I don't know how he was able to paint me so . . . so accurately. Nor even why! I suppose he thought it was the artistic thing to do."

Silence fell once more, only now Juliet was not crying, and she could see the very instant Christopher's grave expression gave way to laughter.

Laughter! It incensed her. "You are laughing at me!" she fairly shouted.

Christopher tried to stop. When she whirled from him this second time, he did stop. Pulling her close, but not so close he could not see her face, he addressed her as earnestly as possible, though he only succeeded in looking as if he might smile again at any moment.

"I am sorry," he tried. A grin could not be suppressed. "No, don't be angry. Please."

Juliet blinked hard. He had never said "please" before.

"I didn't mean to anger you, little goose. It's just that only an innocent like you would think Jonathan painted you with only a flimsy covering because he felt it was the artistic thing to do. Don't you see he painted you that way because he wanted you? And a damn good imagination he has, too. Good enough to make me furiously jealous."

"You?" Juliet's voice conveyed astonishment.

"Me," Christopher affirmed.

Juliet gazed at him with great wonder. He had been

jealous. He had been jealous! A smile began to curve her mouth.

"Ah, you like that, do you?" Christopher teased softly, entranced by the lift of her lips. But he could stand merely looking no longer. His hands cradled her head as his lips lowered to claim hers.

Slowly, hesitantly, as if she could scarcely believe what was happening, Juliet's mouth opened to her husband's touch. Her blood quickened, and with a moan, when she knew without a doubt what was happening was really happening, her arms encircled his neck.

After a very long while, Christopher drew back to look at his wife's face. Her eyes were the color of smoke. He kissed her nose, her cheeks, her chin, nuzzled her neck, and then addressed himself to her ear.

"My sweet, sweet, brave darling," he murmured. "I've so much to ask forgiveness for. I've been an arrogant brute. I love you. I may have loved you from the first moment I saw that silvery mane of yours hanging down to your waist. I don't know. I couldn't admit to anything so un-*ton*-ish as love, and for my own wife too! I was afraid, I suppose. You must know my parents weren't the best examples of wedded bliss. I've been waiting for you to turn into Lady Eunice, but you haven't of course. It was when I saw you in that blasted place tonight, holding that tiny pistol on those rogues, that I knew. I was so afraid that for a moment I couldn't breathe. Say you'll forgive me?"

An arrogant brute he might have been, but Christopher St. Charles, when he tried, was also nothing if not utterly charming. His entreating smile was enough to take Juliet's breath away.

But she did not answer him immediately. A little imp of mischief told her he deserved a little uncertainty before she capitulated. "A thing earned is dearer still," as her father had said often enough.

The effect was immediate. "You do forgive me?" Christopher demanded, his hands unconsciously tightening on her arms.

Juliet could hold out no longer. Her face lit with an enormous smile. "Does this mean you would come to Lincolnshire with me if I went?" she tested him.

"To Hades, if need be," he swore promptly with a smile to match hers.

"Ah, such loyalty cancels all debts, then, my lord."

"And you love me too?"

He sounded for all the world like a little boy.

Juliet's expression lost its playfulness. "And I love you too," she whispered. It was the last thing either of them said for a very, very long while.

COMING IN MARCH 1988

Sandra Heath
A Matter of Duty

Marion Chesney
The Savage Marquess

Gayle Buck
Lord John's Lady

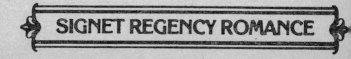
SIGNET REGENCY ROMANCE